"That's not   at me.

The White Wyrm and Grain Brain suddenly looked in my direction. Gorgon Son clearly was about to charge, and Diabolist Mage pointed his staff at me.

I threw a grenade towards the White Wyrm and Grain Brain; they both dove for cover, scrambling to get behind some computer equipment. I phased myself and the box containing Rune as Gorgon Son dove at me. He passed through without making contact with anything and smacked his head on a worktable that was behind me.

The Diabolist shot a beam of purple light my way, but it passed right through me. This time, however, I felt something — like the beam had tickled me a little. It occurred to me then that maybe Diabolist Mage had gotten enough power to somehow affect me in my insubstantial form. It was not a prospect I relished.

At that moment, the grenade went off, blasting a hole in the floor and sending shrapnel and shards of stone everywhere. Something grazed the Diabolist just below the eye, making him jerk his head to the side in pain. When he looked my way again, I saw a jagged red line near his cheekbone that was starting to weep blood.

The Diabolist gingerly put a finger to his cheek, flinching when he touched the wound. He gave me an absolutely murderous look. Near the computer equipment they had hidden behind, the White Wyrm and Grain Brain were just getting to their feet, as was Gorgon Son. They, too, all looked as though they'd like to bite my eyeballs out. Obviously, I had overstayed my welcome.

"Toodles," I said, holding up a hand and giving a little finger wave. I wrapped Rune, box and all, in my power and tried to teleport us to safety.

Nothing happened.

INFILTRATION

Kid Sensation Novels
Sensation: A Superhero Novel
Mutation (A Kid Sensation Novel)
Infiltration (A Kid Sensation Novel)

The Warden Series
Warden (Book 1: Wendigo Fever)
Warden (Book 2: Lure of the Lamia)

Short Stories
Extraction: A Kid Sensation Story

INFILTRATION
A Kid Sensation Novel

By

Kevin Hardman

INFILTRATION

Copyright © 2013 by Kevin Hardman.

Cover Design by Isikol

This book is published by I&H Recherche Publishing.

ISBN: 978-1-937666-16-3

Printed in the U.S.A.

INFILTRATION

ACKNOWLEDGMENTS

I would like to thank the following for their help with this book: GOD, first and foremost (as always) who has continually provided me with strength and guidance; and my family, which has always offered immeasurable encouragement and support.

INFILTRATION

Chapter 1

I was actually having a good day until I heard the words no guy ever wants his girlfriend to say:
"We need to talk."
Even worse, my girlfriend Electra hadn't said it to me directly. Instead, she had left it as a message on my cell phone, along with a time and place to meet after school.
Her call had come in while I was in class. In accordance with school policy, I had left my phone in my locker. Thus, I didn't get her message until my lunch break.
Needless to say, I was in something of a funk for the rest of the day. Not that anyone really noticed; I had always been a bit of a loner, and now that I was back at my old high school, I had fallen back into my regular pattern of keeping to myself.
In a perfect world, I wouldn't have been here at all. Instead, I would have been attending school at the Academy — the prestigious high school that served as a training ground for teens with super powers. Unfortunately, the Academy was gone now — completely destroyed — and as a result, super teens the world over found themselves attending traditional high schools. (At least for now. Word on the street was that various superhero teams were coming up with options to help teens with powers attend "alternative" schools that would pick up our educations where the Academy left off.)
For me, the change was barely worth noting. I only got to attend the Academy for a few weeks before the place was obliterated, so coming back to my old

school for my junior year wasn't a big deal. For Electra, though, the change was a seismic shift.

As an orphan raised by the Alpha League — the world's greatest superhero team — she had never spent much time in the company of "normal" kids (not to mention that her last two years of formal schooling had taken place at the Academy). Thus, there was a bit of a culture shock when she started attending a regular high school: how they talked, how they dressed, etc.

That said, it didn't take her long to fit in. Within a week, she was one of the most popular girls in school and accepted by the most prominent cliques on campus. Thankfully, we didn't attend the same school, which might have made things awkward.

Of course, I dreaded what the end of the day would bring, mostly because I already had an idea of what Electra wanted to talk about. Thus, after the last bell of the day rang, I slowly dragged myself to my car and headed to our rendezvous point — a diner called Jackman's, which was owned by a couple of former superhero sidekicks.

My car was a boxy little number given to me as a gift by my mother and grandfather, a kind of thanks-for-not-getting-killed present after the Academy went belly-up. It was good for getting from place to place, but — at ten years old and with almost 200,000 miles on the odometer — it was far from anyone's idea of a dream ride. Moreover, with my power set, a car was really a superfluous expense. Frankly speaking, it would probably have been years before I even thought about getting a vehicle, had it not been for a singularly embarrassing incident over the course of the previous summer: in essence, after arranging my first date with Electra and agreeing to pick her up, it came to light that I didn't know how to drive.

Since then, I'd been on a tear in terms of getting comfortable behind the wheel of a car. Aside from my brief sojourn at the Academy, my grandfather had given me driving lessons almost daily until I was able to get a permit two weeks ago. That same day, I'd returned home from the DMV to find that Mom and Gramps had gotten me a new car ("new" being a relative term). Again, it wasn't the trendy sports car that most guys my age dream of, but it was getting the job done.

****

I arrived at Jackman's about ten minutes after our designated meeting time. Electra was already sitting at a booth, head down as she apparently typed out a text message on her cell phone. She was wearing jeans, sandals, and a light blue blouse. Her hair, naturally straight and dark, was pulled back into a ponytail, except for a couple of recently-added blond streaks that hung down in front and gently framed her face. As usual, she wasn't wearing any makeup, but she was blessed with an inherent beauty that didn't require any kind of artificial enhancement. On the table in front of her sat a quartet of stacked saucers, a basket of tortilla chips, and a dipping bowl full of warm, melted cheese.

"You're late," she said without looking up from her phone as I slid into the seat across from her.

"Traffic," I countered as I grabbed a saucer and helped myself to some chips. "Thanks for ordering the chips and queso."

She placed the phone on the tabletop and gave me an appraising stare. "You can teleport and you have super speed. You've got no business being late for anything."

"I also have a jalopy now that I use regularly so I can get used to driving."

Electra groaned slightly, then gave me an odd look as she took a few moments to mentally prepare herself for what she needed to say. Sensing her emotions, I already knew what was coming.

"Look," she said after taking a deep breath, "there's no easy way to say this, so I'm just going to put it out there. I think we've been trying, but things just aren't working out."

"I know," I said, lowering my eyes.

"I think you're just too used to being by yourself, Jim. You've been doing things on your own for so long that you don't know how to incorporate others and include them."

I shrugged. "I can't completely deny that, but I have been trying."

She reached across the table and squeezed my hand. "I know you have, babe, but I just don't think you're ready to be with other people yet."

"But I really want this. I mean, I really do."

She sighed. "Look, let's not make it official until after the exhibition tomorrow."

I simply nodded, eyes staring down at the table. This was exactly what I knew was going to happen.

"Geez, man," said an unexpected voice, but one that I recognized. It was my best friend, Smokescreen. "Did somebody run over your dog or something?"

"Huh?" I asked. I was still absorbing what Electra had said, so lost in thought that I hadn't even noticed him approaching us.

Smokey slid into the booth next to me. "You've got this look on your face like somebody just died. Or did the light of your life here just break up with you?" He nodded in Electra's direction.

"I almost wish she had," I said, which made Electra's mouth drop open. I ignored her foot connecting with my shin under the table as I went on. "She's kicking me out of the band."

"What?" Smokey asked, slightly confused. "You mean off the team?"

"Yeah," I said. "Apparently I don't play well with others."

"He's a lone wolf," Electra said defensively. "Every time we have a training exercise where we're supposed to be acting as a team, trying to take down a supervillain, he goes off and does his own thing."

Smokey appeared thoughtful for a second. "She's got a point, Jim. You do tend to act like it's the Kid Sensation Show sometimes."

"I'm not trying to," I said. "I'm just doing what comes naturally when it comes to taking down bad guys."

"But when we're working as a team, you can't treat it like a solo act," Electra countered. "You've got to know what your role is and be willing to play it."

"I understand that," I said, "but if I can end a confrontation without anyone else getting in harm's way, why shouldn't I?"

"Because if we're operating as a team and hitting on all cylinders," Electra answered, "*nobody* has to be in harm's way."

I sighed in resignation. Although I hated to admit it, she definitely had a point — several of them, in fact. I'd been trained extensively in how to use my powers by my grandfather (a former superhero) and Braintrust, a family friend who was actually a huge cluster of clones sharing a single hive mind. However, most of that training was centered on me operating solo; I hadn't been groomed in how to function in a team environment. (And apparently that's a necessary skill when you're a member of a superhero team's teen affiliate — even more so when the superhero team in question is the best in the world: the Alpha League.)

"Look," said Smokey, ending a silence that wasn't so much awkward as it was prolonged, "it's not like it's forever." He turned to Electra. "When does your rotation as team leader end?"

"Next week," she answered.

"Next week," Smokey repeated, then turned to me. "So it's like you're being benched for one game — assuming we have another training exercise before Electra passes the torch to someone else. You've still got the rest of the season to showcase your moves."

Electra's phone rang before I had a chance to respond.

"Sorry guys," she said, glancing at her phone screen. "I need to take this."

She slid out of the booth, putting the phone up to her ear and giving a perfunctory "Hello" as she headed towards the exit. Smokey slid out of the seat next to me and into the opposite side of the booth.

"I told them," I said, watching as Electra stepped outside in order to speak with some degree of privacy. "I told them not to put us on the same team. We both did. But they did it anyway."

"What did you expect?" Smokey asked. "You two are teammates *and* you're dating. They need to know that one aspect of your relationship isn't going to interfere with the other."

"So it's better to put us in this awkward situation — not just on the same team, but with one the team leader and the other a subordinate?"

"Like I said, it's one of the ways they're testing you. Remember Paramount?"

I nodded, even though it was obviously a rhetorical question. Paramount had generally been regarded as the most powerful teen super on the planet and presumed to one day become the world's greatest superhero — until, just a few months earlier, he became completely deranged, killed a bunch of people, and tried to destroy the Alpha League (including his own father). He was also my half-brother, but almost no one knew that — not even Paramount himself, as far as I knew.

"Well," Smokey continued, "a year or so ago, before he became unhinged, Paramount started dating this flyer named Skye Blue."

"Let me guess: the League put them on the same team."

"Ding! Ding! Ding!" Smokey intoned, like a bell announcing that I'd won a prize. "Got it in one. Now, to advance to the next round of our tournament, can you guess what happened to them?"

"They broke up?"

"Within three days."

"I'm guessing Paramount wasn't very good at taking orders." Not that that was a surprise of any sort. He was a pompous, egotistical jerk.

"Yes, a lot like some people at this table, who shall remain nameless."

I knew Smokey was exaggerating to make a point, but the comparison with Paramount was quite the wake-up call. "Am I really that bad?" I asked sheepishly.

"Yes and no," Smokey answered. "You know that bomb simulation we just ran?"

I nodded. We'd recently participated in a training exercise that required us to deal with a chemical bomb. One member of our team, Actinic, had the ability to render the chemicals in the bomb inert and harmless, and as team leader, Electra had ordered him to deal with the explosive. However, when it seemed like he wasn't moving fast enough — and we were partly evaluated on the speed with which we resolved the problem — I took it upon myself to teleport the bomb to a remote location where it could detonate without harming anyone.

"That stunt you pulled is the kind of thing we're talking about," Smokey continued. "Electra was team leader, and she had her reasons for wanting to disarm the bomb."

"I know that *now*," I said despondently.

For the bomb scenario, most of the team had been briefed only on the fact that a bomb was set to go off in a populated area. As team leader, however, Electra was given additional, need-to-know info: in our exercise, this was the third such bomb discovered, and it was vitally important that the experts get to examine it in order to try to figure out who was planting these devices. Needless to say, my impertinent actions prevented us from achieving the desired result. Even though it was only a training exercise, just thinking about it made me feel awful.

"Look, man," Smokey said, clearly aware of my dejected mood, "it's not the end of the world, and it's easy enough to fix. Just quit flying solo and learn to stay in formation."

Before I could respond, Electra — apparently finished with her phone call — stepped back over to our booth.

"Guess who I found wandering around outside?" she asked. That's when I noticed the girl standing next to her: a complete knockout with exquisite Asian features. It was Sarah, Smokey's girlfriend, and she slid into the booth next to him while Electra sat down next to me.

Sarah was normal, with no special abilities to speak of, so with her arrival the dialogue shifted to more typical teen fare: movies, music, etc. Even though Sarah knew that we were supers and loved hearing about our exploits, talking about that stuff would have excluded her from much of the conversation. Thus, as always, we tried to avoid talking "shop" in her presence.

We ordered another batch of chips and queso, as well as some sodas, and hung out for another thirty minutes or so, at which point Smokey announced that he and Sarah had to get going. (Apparently they had a date.) Electra and I used their departure as our own impetus for leaving. I settled the tab, and then we saw them off in the parking lot.

"So," said Electra, as we walked towards my car so I could give her a ride home, "why aren't *we* going out tonight?"

"Are you kidding?" I asked. "After you just booted me off the team?"

I felt a slight bit of confusion coming from her; then, realizing I was joking, she reached over and took my hand.

"Actually," I said, "I'm going to a game with Alpha Prime."

"Oh yeah," she said in recollection as we reached my car. "You did mention that a few days back."

"It's just a preseason game, but a big rivalry," I said as I opened the passenger door for her.

"This is what — the third game in two weeks? You two sure have been spending a lot of time together. I'm starting to get jealous."

I closed the door without responding and headed to the driver's side of the car. There was kind of an unwritten rule between us regarding discussions of family: Her being an orphan, we never discussed her biological parents (although I knew that she actually had some information about who they were). Likewise, we never mentioned my father, who had never really been part of my life. Avoiding those topics of conversation wasn't something we'd deliberated and decided on; we both just instinctively knew that those were sensitive areas and avoided them. (I suppose a psychiatrist would probably say that we both had abandonment issues.)

Needless to say, she didn't know that Alpha Prime was my father, or that these outings we were engaging in were attempts to try to get to know each other. Thus, there wasn't any reason for her to feel like she was stepping on some sort of landmine.

"Just for the record," I said as I opened the driver's door and climbed in, "the other two were baseball and football games. This is basketball."

"Still," she said, "it doesn't take a genius to figure out what's going on between you two."

"Oh?" I said, raising an eyebrow as I pulled out of the lot and into the street. There was no way she actually knew the truth...was there?

"Yes," she said. "And I think it's wonderful. Alpha Prime never talks about it, but I know he misses Paramount. Going to football games and stuff is the kind of thing they used to do together. I think AP is maybe subconsciously looking for someone else to have that same kind of father-son bond with, so it's nice of you to step in and fill that role."

I looked at her in surprise. She might not have known the truth, but she certainly hit a lot closer to home than I was prepared for. I found myself forming a new respect for her insights.

"That's nice of you to say," I replied. "But being a replacement for Paramount isn't very high on my to-do list."

"Regardless, I'm sure AP appreciates it. But please tell him to stop hogging my date nights."

"It's not like he's holding me the entire weekend. I'll still see you tomorrow night — we'll be together then."

"That's not a date!" she exclaimed. "That's an exhibition. A date would be me and you, alone. This is a showcase in front of forty million people."

"Fine," I said. "I'll make you a deal: for every outing that I have with Alpha Prime, I'll owe you two."

She gave me a sly smile. "Buddy, you got yourself a deal."

The rest of the drive consisted mostly of Electra bringing me up to speed on how things were going at her new school. As I had already noted, she was truly enjoying the so-called "normal" environment of a regular high school. A short time later, we arrived at her house.

"Home" for Electra at this time consisted of a modest two-story brick house in a quiet suburban neighborhood. Until recently, Electra had lived her entire life at Alpha League headquarters. However, following the destruction of HQ by Paramount a few months back and the subsequent obliteration of the Academy (where Electra usually lived in-residence during the school year), a new abode had to be found for her. She had lived for a while at an Alpha League safe house, but that had only been a short-term solution. Thus, she now lived here with Esper, the League's resident psychic (a generic term for anyone with mental powers) and the reigning queen of all telepaths on the planet.

I pulled into the driveway next to a trendy red sports car and shifted my vehicle into park.

"Okay," Electra said, grabbing her purse and book bag from the floor. "I have to go." She leaned over to give me a quick kiss. At least that was the intention; five minutes later, we'd done an excellent job of fogging up my windows.

Suddenly a voice boomed in my head like a bullhorn.

<Enough, you two! Electra — inside *now!*>

It was Esper, speaking to us telepathically. I glanced towards the house and saw her staring at us from a huge bay window. Hands on her hips and her brow

12

severely creased, you didn't need to be an empath to know that Esper was in full mother bear mode and being fiercely protective of her cub — Electra. This really didn't come as a great surprise to me; the Alpha League had raised Electra since she was an infant. Thus, they were all wildly vigilant with respect to her safety and well-being — even when it came to someone they trusted, like me.

Mentally, I said hello to Esper. In response, I got the telepathic equivalent of a curt nod — and then a door being slammed in my face.

"You better go," I said to Electra. "Before Esper comes out here and flash-fries my brain, or worse."

"Even if she did," she said with a smirk, "it's not like anyone would be able to tell the difference."

"Get out," I said in mock anger. She laughingly exited my car. I shifted into reverse and was preparing to back out of the driveway when Electra politely knocked on my window. I rolled the window down (manually, of course — no automatic doors or locks on this clunker).

"One more thing," she said, leaning down to look me in the eye. "That crack about preferring to break up with me than be kicked off the team? You'd better have been joking." And with that, she sashayed towards the door and into the house.

Chapter 2

I arrived home about a half hour after dropping Electra off, electing to park on the street in front of the house rather than the driveway. "Home" was, of course, a relative term. The house we'd actually lived in had been burned to the ground a few months back by a supervillain. Since then, we'd been staying in a loaner (courtesy of a family friend) while our new place was being built.

Telepathically, I could sense my mother and grandfather inside, and I knew they could feel me as well. Thus, it was no surprise when I came walking through the door.

"Just in time for dinner," my mother shouted from the kitchen. "I was afraid you'd leave for the game with your father without eating anything."

I bristled slightly at her casual use of the phrase "your father" as I followed her voice into the kitchen. Alpha Prime and I were still in the getting-to-know-you phase of things, so I still had trouble thinking of him as my father in any way other than a biological sense.

"I was going to grab something at the game," I said in response to her comment. "Plus, I already had some chips and queso at Jackman's."

Mom had just pulled a baking tray full of scones from the oven. She tossed it onto the stove and then turned to me with her hands on her hips. "So your plan was to binge on a buffet of unhealthy snacks after school, then come home, skip dinner, go to the game, and fill up on a bunch of junk food there?"

I shrugged. "More or less."

"Not going to happen," said a voice coming from behind me. I looked around to find my grandfather walking into the room. "You need to eat something healthy, boy, before you leave this house."

"Fine," I said in resignation. "I'll get some fruit."

I went to the refrigerator and got some grapes from the fruit bin. After rinsing them off, I placed them in a bowl before flopping down at the breakfast table. Mom and Gramps joined me, ironically plucking and devouring some of my grapes — the healthy snack that they had encouraged *me* to eat.

"So," said Mom, "how's Electra?" Surprisingly, my mother and girlfriend had developed a strong bond — so strong, in fact, that I had come to realize that any breakup between me and Electra would almost affect those two more seriously than myself.

"I guess she's fine," I answered noncommittally. "Probably thinks I'm spending a little too much time with Alpha Prime, but fine beyond that."

"Well, don't be too hard on her about that," said Mom. "She doesn't really know what's going on there, just that you aren't taking advantage of opportunities to spend time with her."

"You should probably do something to make it up to her," said Gramps.

"Like what?" I asked almost sardonically, then immediately regretted it.

For the next twenty minutes, we had a somewhat embarrassing conversation that consisted of my mother and grandfather giving me advice about my love life and asking intrusive questions about the same. Suddenly I couldn't wait to get to that game with my father.

After making me promise that I would attempt to effectuate at least some of the advice she'd given me, my mother excused herself. This was typical for her; my grandfather being the primary male role model for most of my life, Mom frequently gave us the opportunity to have one-on-one conversations.

"So," Gramps said, "did we embarrass you with the advice we offered?"

"Frankly speaking, yes," I said. "I'm just glad there was no one else around to hear it."

"Also, I couldn't help but notice that your response was a little ambivalent when we first mentioned Electra. Are you sure everything's okay?"

"Yeah, everything is going fine between us. She may be taking the team leader bit a little too seriously, but we're good."

"What do you mean?" asked Gramps.

I gave a quick explanation of how Coach Electra was sending me back to the minors.

"Well," Gramps said when I'd finished, "the team leader position is rotated every couple of weeks, right? Everyone will get a chance to be top dog — even you, so quit bellyaching."

"Easy for you to say. You didn't just get booted from the team."

"You're not booted from the team. You're just sidelined for the rest of her tenure. Plus, think about it from her point of view."

"What do you mean?" I asked, frowning.

"You're her boyfriend, and all the teen supers know it. If she takes it easy on you when you make a misstep, nobody will respect her."

I contemplated that for a moment. "So you're saying that she's coming down hard on me because she has to. Because otherwise…"

"Otherwise, no one will take her seriously."

"Still, I bet Grandma never kicked you off the team."

"You're right; she never did. But I did it to her once."

"Really? What happened?" This was something I'd never heard before. As far as I'd ever known (or been led to believe), my grandparents never even had so much as an argument. They were yin and yang — inseparable, melded together forever as a seamless whole.

"She didn't take it well," Gramps said, reminiscing. "When I got home that night, she'd already packed up and left to go back to her home planet."

My mouth practically fell open. Again, everything I was hearing was all news to me. My understanding had always been that my grandmother Indigo, an alien princess, had been compelled to return to her home world because of some type of crisis. It turns out it was just a marital spat, resulting in her pulling an interstellar version of "going home to Mother." Innumerable questions started bubbling up in my mind, so fast that I didn't know which to ask first. Then I saw my grandfather snickering.

Of course; it was a joke. I couldn't help but smile as well.

"Sorry, I couldn't help myself," Gramps said between chuckles. "Seriously though, Indigo took it just fine. She understood why I had to make that call and accepted it. Of course, it helped that we were both telepaths and able to be completely open and honest with each other."

I nodded in understanding. Gramps was a retired cape, but at one time he was the most formidable telepath on the planet. Although no longer in his prime, he still possessed one of the most powerful psychic minds in the world. Mom was also a telepath (and a world-class one at that), but had never really gone down the superhero path. These days, she was a mid-list author of superhero romances.

On my part, I had apparently inherited the telepathic gene, but in a diluted form. I could project my own thoughts, and pick up the surface thoughts of others, as well as any other information they wanted to willingly share. However, that was about as far as I typically went in terms of mindreading.

In essence, I find other people's minds to be cluttered with unsanitary mental detritus and offal, and going too far inside makes me physically ill. Thus, doing a deep dive into someone else's cranium (for example, trying to pry out nuclear launch codes) is off the table as far as I'm concerned.

"Anyway," my grandfather went on, "you and Electra seem to have a special connection. I think it'll take a lot more than team politics to break you guys up."

"I hope so."

"Well, that's enough of this hearts and flowers stuff. Let's talk about tomorrow night."

"What? The exhibition?"

"Yeah. Are you ready for it?"

I shrugged. "I suppose."

At some point during the past few months, someone in charge of public relations for capes had decided that superheroes weren't getting enough positive press. (And, in light of what had happened with Alpha League HQ and the Academy, maybe they were right.) The end result was that an exhibition had been arranged — with all proceeds to go to charity — in which supers would get to showcase their powers while engaging in some friendly competition with one another. It was scheduled to be broadcast live, coast-to-coast the next night.

Ordinarily, it wouldn't have been a big deal. This kind of dog-and-pony show happened every couple of years, and for a while there you could count on seeing all of the big-name supers participating (even a few from foreign countries). Needless to say, the exhibitions traditionally raised tons of cash and scored incredible ratings. However, they also led indirectly to another, more ignominious statistic: during the broadcast of the exhibition, criminal activity would skyrocket.

Of course, that's something that should have been expected. If the capes are otherwise occupied, it's the perfect time to commit a felony. To combat this uptick in crime, fewer and fewer of the A-List superheroes volunteered to be in the exhibition, with the result being a noticeable decrease in donations and viewership over the years. Now, however, all of that was purportedly about to change.

With respect to participants in this year's exhibition, someone had gotten the bright idea to jettison the old guard and focus on the up-and-comers. Basically, they decided to showcase the future of crimefighting: teen supers. That being the case, I and quite a number of my colleagues had "volunteered" to be on the show. (In my case, the process had involved what can only be described as a direct order from the Alpha League consisting of four words: "You are doing this.")

"You don't seem particularly excited," Gramps said, interrupting my thoughts.

"I don't know about all this," I said. "I mean, for two years now, I've been pretty much a mystery — ever since that wretched induction ceremony."

My grandfather nodded but remained silent, knowing that this was one of the topics I really hated discussing. Two years earlier, I had aced the Super Teen Trials and had been looking forward to being part of a superhero team (or rather, the teen affiliate of one). During the induction ceremony to officially commence my stint as part of the Alpha League, a quarrel with another teen (Paramount, to be specific) had erupted into a full-blown battle royal between me and a bunch of supers (the Alpha League, to be precise). Captured on tape, the entire episode had been shameful and embarrassing for everyone involved, and afterwards I had gone into a sort of self-imposed exile with respect to the superhero community. It was only recently that everyone had decided to kiss and make up.

"Plus," I said, going on, "I kind of like the fact that no one knows very much about me — that I fly below the typical superhero radar."

"I see," Gramps said, thoughtfully rubbing his chin. "You like the mystique that's been built up around you as Kid Sensation, and if you let the general public get too up close and personal then their fascination with you will go away."

"I wouldn't put it exactly like that," I said, frowning. "You make me sound like some sort of conceited, self-centered diva" — my grandfather laughed at that — "when all I'm really trying to say is that there's a certain level of privacy that I want to maintain."

"That's easy enough to do. You're a shapeshifter, and there's no law that says you have to go to the exhibition with *that* face." He pointed a finger squarely at my nose.

I blinked in surprise. My grandfather had subtly reminded me of something that I had practically forgotten: when I'd initially gone through the Super Teen Trials, it had been in a different persona — I'd altered my appearance. Rather than my own countenance and racially ambiguous complexion, I had chosen an appearance based on a high school picture of my grandfather: a handsome-but-gangly teen with a rich, brown skin tone. It was *that* face that the world had come to associate with Kid Sensation, not my own. Hmmm…maybe it *would* be possible to preserve a certain level of anonymity.

Of course, I felt like an idiot for having to be prompted on how to use my own power set, and I admitted as much. (In my defense, however, I also had another related issue weighing heavily on my mind, but I didn't feel like bothering Gramps with that.) My grandfather just laughed.

"Sometimes you're too close to a problem to see the obvious solution," he said. "Can't see the forest for the trees."

I conceded his point, and then — glancing at my watch — mentioned that it was getting close to time for me to go meet Alpha Prime.

"Of course," my grandfather said. "You don't want to be late." Telepathically, he sent a humorous image of me forgetting to use my power of teleportation and super speed. We both snickered at that. At the same time, however, I detected an odd twinge from him emotionally — an ever-so-slight pinch of bitterness and loss — as well as what it related to.

"Gramps," I said, after taking a second to carefully frame my question, "are you okay with me hanging out with Alpha Prime?"

The look of surprise on my grandfather's face made it clear that I'd caught him slightly off-guard. Apparently he thought he'd had his emotions tightly boxed up.

He drummed his fingers on the table for a moment before answering. "I don't have a problem with it, per se. It's just that…"

He trailed off, sighing deeply, but I knew what he wanted to say. "It cuts into the time we used to spend together," I said, finishing his thought.

He nodded absentmindedly, and again I felt a pinprick of emotion coming from him. Before Smokey, Gramps had been my best friend, and he still was in a way. We played video games together, hung out, went to movies, you name it. He'd also been the centerpiece with respect to my training, the person most responsible for teaching me how to use my powers. Finally — and most important — he'd been the only male role model in my life; he was the person I'd essentially patterned myself after.

"Look," I said, after a few moments of silence. "Why don't I just stay here and kick it with you tonight? I'll tell Alpha Prime we can catch ano—"

"No," he said, adamantly shaking his head as he cut me off. "Don't do that."

"It's no problem," I said.

"Look," he said, giving me an appraising stare, "I was on the Alpha League with AP for a long time. He's not perfect, despite the way they portray him in the media. He has his flaws. But deep at heart, he's a good man, and I don't doubt that he loves you. You giving him a chance — it's the right thing to do.

"As for me and you, I've seen you almost every day of your life. Most grandparents would kill just for a tenth of that. Moreover, we've always had a great relationship. Long story short, if I keel over tomorrow, you and I will be good. There's nothing left unsaid between us. The same's not true about you and Alpha Prime. You need this time together. *Both* of you."

There was a time in the not-too-distant past when I would have hotly disputed that last statement; a father-son relationship with Alpha Prime had been the last thing I'd wanted. Since then, however, I'd come to accept that it was important to reach some type of common ground with him.

"We're working on it," I said to Gramps, before adding, "*Both* of us." (Just to make it clear that I was doing my part.)

"Good," he noted with approval. "Now get out of here before you're late."

With that, I teleported to Alpha Prime's house.

Chapter 3

I popped up in the foyer of my father's house —
one of his homes, anyway. This one was a regal mansion
set on a palatial estate in one of the most exclusive parts
of town — a big pimpin' pad with a zillion bedrooms,
twice as many bathrooms, and closets the size of aircraft
hangars.

The foyer where I had appeared opened up into a
great room that seemed as big as a concert hall. The floor
was tiled wall-to-wall with opulent marble, and majestic
columns were geometrically spaced throughout the room.
Two lavish, winding staircases on opposite walls twisted
up to the second floor, and a grandiose chandelier hung
down from a stained-glass ceiling that was several stories
in height. Million-dollar paintings, sculptures, and the like
hung on the walls and in art niches, while posh furniture
— most of it hand-carved and more aesthetic than
functional — littered the room.

Ordinarily, I wouldn't simply teleport inside
someone else's home — even if they were expecting me.
It just seems rude. Alpha Prime had practically insisted on
it, however.

"How are we going to develop a real father-son
relationship if we keep everything formal between us?"
he'd asked a few weeks back. "You need to treat my
house like it's your house. That means coming directly
inside when you're here, not standing on the front stoop
and ringing the doorbell."

In other words, I could come and go as I pleased.
Alpha Prime had even inputted my biometrics into his
security system, so that his automated defense systems

wouldn't view me as an intruder or a threat if I showed up when he wasn't around.

"I'm here," I said, speaking aloud although there was no one nearby. Not that it mattered; regardless of where he was inside, I had no doubt that Alpha Prime had heard me. Like his other senses, his hearing extended well beyond the normal range.

A few seconds later, there was an audible click that seemed to come from all around me, followed by a short droning and then my father's voice boomed out over the mansion's intercom.

"I'll be there in a second," he said in his trademark, deep baritone. "Make yourself at home."

"No rush," I said to the empty air. "We've got time."

With that, I began to mosey through the house at a leisurely pace, intending to explore the place a little more (which was something I did almost every time I came here). Naturally, I could have zipped through the place at super speed, but — in a lot of instances — that's like trying to wolf down a delicious T-bone steak in thirty seconds. It's a lot more enjoyable if you take your time and savor the experience.

In all honesty, I both loved and loathed my father's house. On the one hand, I was fascinated with the scale and scope of the mansion, as well as getting a bird's-eye view of how the other half lived. On the other hand, I couldn't help seething to a certain extent when I thought about Alpha Prime living here like a fat cat while I, his son, lived like a...what? It would be disingenuous to act as if I'd been wallowing in squalor my entire life. Truth be told, I hadn't really wanted for anything growing up, thanks to Mom and Gramps. Still, I'd certainly never had an opportunity to partake of *this* lifestyle, nor had my father made any overt efforts to include me.

As to how Alpha Prime could afford all this, supers on top-notch teams like the Alpha League actually operated under lucrative contracts (of the multi-million dollar variety) and often had agents, publicists, etc. Thus, along with being the world's greatest superhero, my father was also its highest-paid. However, salary was a verboten topic among most supers; they were certainly worth every penny, but the fact that they made millions clashed with the public images they presented of individuals serving a higher calling.

All of this flitted through my mind as I headed down a spacious nearby hallway towards a room I'd only gotten to peek in last time: the library. Purportedly, my father had some of the rarest books about supers in existence, and I was eager to take a look at them. After a few minutes, I came to an elegant set of wooden double doors that marked the entrance to my destination. I opened the doors with a theatrical flair and stepped inside, at which point the lights in the room automatically switched on.

Like the rest of the house, the library was massive — at least several thousand square feet in size. It covered two stories, and had its own colossal, dome-shaped glass ceiling. Moreover, it was meticulously designed, with all the wood present — from the bookshelves to the balustrade to the hardwood floor — made from a rare, exotic species of tree. All in all, it looked like something you'd find designed for a billionaire in the pages of an architectural magazine.

As with all libraries, I felt a compulsion to be silent as I walked through, passing a monstrous fireplace that was big enough for a bear to hibernate in. I wasn't exactly sure where I was going, but figuring out what was in here was going to be half the fun.

With that thought in mind and a grin on my face, I floated up to the center of the room and looked around. As with much of the mansion, there was a geometric design here, with bookshelves and other permanent fixtures all evenly spaced. However, a darkened recessed area between two bookcases along one wall caught my eye. Curious, I flew over to it and came back down to the floor.

The area in question turned out to be a narrow hallway, not exactly hidden but definitely obscured unless you were standing in the right part of the library. My interest piqued, I took a step into the dim corridor, and — as I suspected — automatic lights immediately came on. My path brightly illuminated, I walked slowly down the hall, noting that the walls on both sides were lined with various framed press clippings:

Alpha Prime Diverts Meteor, Saves City!
Terrorist Threat Exposed by Alpha League!
Brazil Declares "Alpha Prime Day"!

There were at least a dozen of them, all noting either the heroics of the Alpha League in general or Alpha Prime in particular.

After about fifteen feet, the passageway terminated in a spacious study with a large window overlooking the mansion's well-manicured and well-maintained grounds. Like the hallway I'd just left, the walls in the study contained framed newspaper articles. As to furnishings, there was a large desk that had obviously seen more use than most of the furniture in this place, as well as a high-back, executive chair. A computer monitor and keyboard sat on top of the desk.

The most dominating feature of the room, however, were several high-end display cases that resided in each corner of the study. Within them were pictures of my father in his black-and-gold costume with various heads of state, as well as the many awards and medals he had received over the years from numerous nations: a Medal of Valor from this country, a Star of Merit from that one, a Distinguished Service Award from another. There seemed to be an endless parade of them.

After noting the umpteenth award received, I turned my attention back to the rest of the room, and for the first time took note of two additional items on my father's desk: on either side of his computer monitor was a photo in a rectangular picture frame.

I walked over to the desk and picked up the frame closest to me. I was surprised to note that it was made of sterling silver, with an intricate design on the front that ended in a pair of tortuously detailed baby shoes in the bottom right corner of the frame. The picture inside was, of course, that of a baby — an impossibly cute kid in a striped blue-and-white T-shirt and a pair of blue shorts. He was sitting up on some sort of artificial turf with a forest in the background. Finally, the youngster was bright and cheery, with one of those adorable, infectious baby grins on his face — the kind you can't see without smiling back.

In essence, it was a near-perfect photo, the kind that parents and grandparents would cherish for decades. The only defect visible was the fact that the kid seemed to have red-eye in the picture, a subtle flash of color across his pupils. However, that's the kind of thing that's pretty easy to fix with today's technology, which made me wonder why it hadn't been done. The picture seemed a little dated, maybe fifteen or twenty years old, so maybe they didn't have the capability—

My train of thought suddenly derailed as a more obvious answer suddenly occurred to me. But it couldn't be...

My alien grandmother's appearance had been very close to that of ordinary humans, but she had a few physiological traits that were unique. For instance, she had pointed, elfin ears — a feature that my mother inherited but I did not.

One of her more distinguishing characteristics, however, was the fact that her eyes flashed various colors when she experienced strong emotions. This particular legacy both my mother and I had inherited. However, while Mom usually wore contacts to hide this idiosyncrasy (she also tended to wear her hair over her ears), I had developed the ability to control it. Thus, for as long as I could remember, my eyes had rarely ever displayed this part of my alien heritage.

All of this flew through my mind as I fumbled with the frame, almost dropping it twice. Finally, I got the back of it off, took a last look at the baby as I removed the picture, then turned it over. There, in handwriting I recognized as my mother's, was the following inscription:

John Indigo Morrison Carrow — *9 mos. old*

Me. This was a picture of me.

I flopped down into the office chair, somewhat stunned. My father frequently mentioned how often he thought about me over the years, wondered how I was doing. It never occurred to me that he might have actually kept me close, figuratively, via this photo. I pondered this for a second before placing the picture back in the frame. I took one last look at myself as an infant (something I'd rarely seen before, as we aren't a picture-taking family), then put it back on the desk.

Since my own photo was on one side of the computer, I had little doubt what image the second frame would hold. I reached for it anyway, and got confirmation of what I'd been thinking. The other frame held a picture of Paramount.

He was older in this photo than I was in mine, but still a toddler — maybe three years old. Big for his age, he bore a striking resemblance to Alpha Prime even way back then, making it easy for me to recognize him. Another giveaway was the fact that the image showed him grinning while lifting up the back end of a car.

With any other kid, you would be safe in assuming that this was trick photography of some sort, an illusion created to give the impression of a toddler with super strength. There was no doubt in my mind, however, that this was the real deal; Paramount had been known to display super powers from almost the moment he was born.

"There you are," said an unexpected voice, snapping me out of my reverie. Alpha Prime stood there in front of me. I had been so engrossed in my own thoughts that I hadn't even noticed him come in.

He was wearing a dark blue T-shirt and jeans, and I had to admit that it still sometimes seemed odd to me to see him out of his black-and-gold Alpha League costume. That said, at six-foot-seven and looking like a Greek god come to life, he still had a commanding presence.

"Wow," he continued, looking around the study. "This place must make me seem a little vain."

"Just a smidgen," I said, putting the thumb and forefinger of my left hand close together.

"It's not how it looks. This is all overflow." He made a sweeping gesture encompassing the display cases.

"What do you mean?"

He sighed, almost in exhaustion. "I've been receiving medals and awards for decades now. If you melted them all down, you'd have enough hardware to build a skyscraper. I ran out of room in my hideaway, so I brought the excess here."

In addition to multiple homes, Alpha Prime also had a secret base that only he knew about — his "hideaway." Although few knew it, my father seemed to be growing increasingly weary of his role as a superhero. His hideaway served as a retreat for him, a sanctuary — a place for him to recharge his batteries.

I had no doubt that, if I asked him, he'd show it to me, but I understood and respected his need for privacy. In truth, I'd had a similar place myself, a condo that I owned. However, someone had been murdered there several months back in an attempt to frame me, and I'd essentially shunned the place since then.

"So," I said, turning my mind back to the conversation at hand, "everything in these cases is extra?"

"Yeah. Even though I don't have many people over, it seemed disrespectful to leave them in boxes — like I didn't value them or what they represented — so I got the display cases."

"And at what point did you realize that the place looked like a shrine to the great and powerful Alpha Prime?"

"Not until some of the League members came over and started razzing me about it. They haven't been invited back," he said with a wink.

"That's too bad. It's a nice crib. You should have people over more often."

My father snorted sharply. "I'm barely here. Usually, I keep this place shuttered. I only opened it up because…"

He kind of trailed off, looking at me in an odd way. Emotionally, I felt a surge of hope and a small measure of anxiety from him, all directed at me. It took me a second to interpret it and meld it into what my father had just been saying, but then I understood: he'd opened the mansion up for me.

Not for me in the sense of having me live there, but more so in the sense of a father wanting a son to know that he was successful. He wanted me to be proud of him and his accomplishments.

I was somewhat at a loss for words, and I found myself absentmindedly tightening my grip on the framed photo of Paramount, which was still in my hand. It was at that moment that Alpha Prime seemed to notice that I was holding something, as well as what it was. I followed his gaze to the photo, abruptly remembering that it was still in my possession.

"Sorry," I said, placing the picture back on the desk.

Alpha Prime picked the photo up. He stared at it in silence for what seemed like ages, but was probably no more than fifteen seconds. During that time, his expression never changed, but I felt a huge wave of sadness, disappointment, and similar emotions swelling within him.

"I've always kept this photo close — yours, too — regardless of where I was living," he finally said. "My boys."

"Did he, uh, did he know about me?" I asked.

"Paramount? He's seen the picture before, but didn't think or care enough to ask any questions about it. Of course, I get pictures of babies all the time — thousands of them every month, and most come in their own frame. Kids I've saved, the kids of people I've saved, fans who named their kids after me, and so on. Paramount probably saw your picture hundreds of times without it ever registering that it was the same one or that he'd seen it before."

"In other words, there was nothing about my photo to make him wonder about you having it. Nothing to make him ask questions about it."

"Looking back, though, I wish he had. Maybe some curiosity on his part would have prompted me to…to do things differently."

"Don't beat yourself up about it," I said, attempting to offer support but probably sounding indifferent.

"Anyway, I should probably put this away somewhere," he said, placing the frame facedown on the desk, with a faraway look in his eyes.

I could sense his emotional pain; it was almost palpable. Paramount had undoubtedly been the favored son while I had basically been neglected — supposedly for my benefit — and if I dwelled on those thoughts for too long, I knew I'd become angry. Nevertheless, there was no way I could ignore my father's grief.

"No," I finally said, sitting Paramount's photo upright. "Don't do that. He was your son, too, and you can love what he was in the beginning without condoning what he was in the end."

Alpha Prime nodded, then reached out and put a grateful hand on my shoulder. "Thank you, son."

Oddly enough, for the first time, his use of the term "son" didn't immediately get my ire up on some level, and I found myself giving him a supportive smile. That was surprising enough, but what was even more bizarre was that we seemed to be bonding over something related to Paramount. You'd have thought the guy was dead, the way we usually tiptoed around talking about him, but in truth my half-brother was being held in some high-end, super-secret security facility. Alpha Prime knew where it was, but on this topic I was the one who hadn't cared enough to ever ask.

"It's too bad you two never really got to know each other," he said, glancing at the photo of Paramount again. "Maybe knowing you, or even just knowing *about* you — that you were out there — would have made some kind of difference. Kept him...balanced."

I kept my thoughts to myself, but I didn't think there was anything short of a lobotomy that would have changed Paramount's warped view of the world and his own existence. I wondered for a brief second if Alpha Prime was also thinking of his own brother (from whom he was estranged), and I was tempted to mention that I'd actually had an opportunity to meet my uncle.

Of course, I didn't know he was my uncle at the time, and I was actually in the process of breaking into a government facility when our paths crossed. (In all honesty, it was more of a skirmish than a meeting, since my uncle was one of the supers guarding the installation that I broke into.) Bearing that in mind, as well as the fact that I committed about a dozen or more felonies when my uncle and I had our run-in, it didn't seem prudent to mention the recent family reunion. (There was a silver lining however: I had been successful in rescuing my friend Rudi — a young psychic — and her little brother from the facility in question, which had been the whole reason for breaking in there in the first place.)

"Anyway, we should probably get going," my father said, glancing at his watch. He turned to leave the room, and I rose to follow him. As he reached the hallway that led back to the library, he turned his head to the side and said casually over his shoulder, "Race you to the car."

There was a sudden whooshing sound of displaced air and he was gone, leaving a powerful wind in his wake that buffeted me slightly as it whipped through the confined space of the passageway. I grinned and teleported to the garage.

The main garage, that is. There were apparently something like three of them. One housed classic cars that were essentially museum pieces — primarily just for show and rarely ever driven. Another held autos that were in need of some work (awaiting a rare part or the like).

The last garage, the one that I had popped into, was a cavernous chamber that echoed if you spoke too loudly and also housed about two dozen "drivable" cars — those that my father would occasionally take out for a spin. I was standing there, arms crossed, tapping my foot in mock impatience when Alpha Prime showed up a few seconds after I appeared.

"Took you long enough," I said.

"Hmmm. I'll have to check the dictionary to see when the definition of 'race' was altered to include teleportation," he said.

"It'll be right there next to the definition that says one guy can just shout out 'Race you!' and get a head start before his opponent is even ready."

"Touché," he said, then looked around, taking stock of the various vehicles. "Well, which one do you want to take?"

His question caught me a little by surprise, but I recovered quickly enough. Previously, Alpha Prime had selected the vehicles we'd taken to the games we attended. (While he drove, I usually spent my time oohing and ahhing over the car's features.) Still, I was happy to take on this particular chore.

I spun around in a slow circle, looking over the garage's inventory. There wasn't a car in sight that cost less than half a million dollars. They were all posh, luxury vehicles, so it was difficult to pick one over the other. However, after a few minutes (and some ardent urging from Alpha Prime) I narrowed my options down to two: a sporty little silver import with butterfly doors and a monstrous, black SUV that looked like it had been built to withstand a missile attack. In the end, I settled on the SUV.

"Good choice," my father said when I finally announced my decision, "even if it did take you forever. Now you're going to have to step on it to get us there by tip-off."

"What?" I asked incredulously.

"Didn't I tell you? You're driving," he said with a wink.

INFILTRATION

Chapter 4

As massive as the SUV was, it was extraordinarily easily to handle and provided an amazingly smooth ride. Thus, I was able to get us to the game on time and without incident. Even parking wasn't a problem; although the SUV had a wider-than-normal wheel base, my father — along with a bunch of other bluebloods — had paid out a hefty fee to have an oversized parking spot at all the sporting venues. (Apparently this was intended to keep other cars from getting too close to his own luxury vehicles, but it worked out well when he drove large autos like the SUV.)

The game itself was fantastic. My father had gotten courtside seats, and even though it was preseason, it's just a different game when you're that close to the action. You get sucked into everything that's going on.

As my mother predicted, I gorged myself on junk food: hot dogs, popcorn, pretzels, soda, etc. A normal kid probably would have gotten sick eating the same volume, but I have a high metabolism.

During the game, I couldn't help expressing amazement at my father's uncanny ability to blend in. Despite his height, he stood and moved in such a way that he never drew unwarranted attention to himself.

"It's the costume," he said when I asked him about it later as we were driving home. "Just like a police officer automatically gets a certain amount of respect and deference when he's in uniform as opposed to out of it, people automatically switch to a certain mode when there are capes around in costume. It's actually less about me and more about the general public's perception and reaction when I'm not in the black-and-gold."

"So it's not really you they love and respect," I said. "It's the outfit."

"More like what the outfit represents," he said, laughing. "People act in certain ways in response to specific stimuli. For instance, if I told you that the car immediately behind us was a police car, you'd immediately slow down and stop going twenty miles over the posted speed limit."

"What?" I asked, totally caught off-guard. And he was right, of course; I had turned into a lead-foot without even noticing, going far faster than the law allowed.

"Sorry," I said as I immediately began braking.

"Not a problem. Besides, it's not really you; it's the SUV. It's such a smooth ride that it's easy to lose track of how fast you're going. However, speaking of cars, it's odd that your choice of which one to take tonight came down to the SUV here and the sports car with the butterfly doors."

"Why's that?"

"Because that's the car I'd planned to give you. I had — Whoa!!!"

The exclamatory part of Alpha Prime's statement came as the SUV began drifting across lanes, accompanied by a cacophony of blaring horns. Needless to say, his remarks had caught me a little unprepared; I'd snapped to attention, staring at him in shock rather than watching the road. Fortunately, my lapse only lasted a second or two as I quickly regained control of the vehicle. Then I sat there stone-faced as a car that I'd cut off roared by me, the driver leaning on the horn, screaming obscenities, and making a number of rude gestures. My father thought it was hilarious.

"As I was saying," he began after he stopped laughing, "I had wanted to give you the sports car after you got your driver's permit. However, John and Geneva put the kibosh on that plan. I think they were afraid of it being viewed as me trying to buy your affection."

"For a car like that, my affection is for sale and will even come gift-wrapped."

"Ha ha," my father said mockingly. "But I happen to agree with your mother and grandfather."

At that juncture, my father began pontificating on the importance of family and how he wanted our relationship to be based on the right kind of connections (which apparently didn't include half-million-dollar sports cars as gifts). Mentally, I rolled my eyes. It wasn't that I didn't care about what he was saying; it was the fact that this was a sermon that I received — in one form or another — almost every time Alpha Prime and I got together.

That said, I understood that this was important to him — that maybe he was saying to me all the things he wished he'd said to Paramount. Still, I was grateful when an odd beeping noise started sounding from somewhere in the SUV's interior, effectively cutting off my father's speech.

"What the heck is that?" I asked. I scanned the instrument panel, expecting to see a "Door Open" light or something similar flashing, but there was no indication that anything was wrong with the vehicle.

"It's a call-in beacon," Alpha Prime said.

"What's it mean?"

"It's a request for me to call in," he said, shaking his head at my ignorance.

INFILTRATION

Alpha Prime popped open the glove compartment and reached inside. I assume he pressed a button of some sort because the irritating beeping immediately stopped. When he withdrew his hand and closed the glove compartment, I saw that he was holding a wireless headset device, which he slipped over his ear.

"Alpha Prime," he said. "Where?...Are you sure?...How's that?...What do you mean you don't know?...Alright, give me five minutes."

He took off the headset and tossed it back into the glove compartment almost disgustedly. After a few moments of silence, I glanced in his direction and saw him giving me an odd, appraising stare. I'd kept my eyes on the road while he had the headset on, but I'd been listening intently. Finally, he spoke.

"Hey," he said. "How'd you like to see your old man in action?"

INFILTRATION

Chapter 5

Alpha Prime slipped out of the car while I was still driving — just opened up the passenger-side door and zipped up into the air, slamming the door behind him. However, he'd given me some basic instructions before he left.

"Just take a right at the next intersection, then drive straight," he'd said. "I'll find you. This will only take a minute."

Of course, I knew where he was going: back home to get "dressed" for work. True to his word, he was back just a minute or so later — this time fully decked out in his black-and-gold uniform.

He had come in low and was flying right next to the driver-side window. Seeing him now in his full Alpha League regalia, I had to admit that he'd been right earlier: in costume, he seemed like an entirely different person, radiating confidence and competence, as well as inspiring trust.

He looked in my direction and gave me a snappy salute, exaggerating the motion so wildly that I couldn't help but smile.

"You got your seatbelt on?" he shouted.

I nodded, then watched as he rose up and drifted over towards the roof of the SUV. I couldn't see him, but — since I had a feeling regarding what he was about to do — I knew that he was taking up a position above the vehicle. A second later, I was proven right when the SUV's tires left the road as it became airborne. Alpha Prime had picked the SUV up and was flying with it.

****

Alpha Prime brought the SUV down in a deserted, unkempt parking lot that had riotous weeds sprouting up through numerous cracks in its surface. Looking around, it became obvious almost at once that we were in a deserted area of town: boarded-up buildings, streets in a state of utter disrepair, huge swaths of vacant land littered with rubble where structures had been torn down.

All in all, it looked like a bombed-out war zone. Urban blight at its finest.

Alpha Prime actually held the vehicle aloft just a few inches from the parking lot surface, making me think that perhaps he felt actual contact with the ground here would soil his tires or something.

"Hey, Einstein," he shouted from above me. "You want to turn the engine off?"

For a second I didn't know what he was talking about, and then it struck me that, even though I hadn't been driving, the SUV was still cranked up. I switched it into park and then turned the engine off. A moment later, my father set the vehicle gently on the ground before floating down beside my door.

I stepped out of the car, not even trying to hide my excitement. I didn't even know what was going on here, but just getting to tag along on a real mission had my blood pumping.

"So," I said, practically rubbing my hands in anticipation, "what are we doing here?"

"You see that highway over there?" Alpha Prime asked, pointing.

I looked in the direction indicated. About half a mile away, I could see what appeared to be a deserted stretch of highway, including an overpass, although the area — like much of the neighborhood we were in — was dimly lit. In fact, the primary source of light in closest proximity to us was the SUV's automatic headlights, and even those winked off after a few seconds, as if afraid to draw attention in our current surroundings.

"I see it," I said, telescoping my vision and switching over to the infrared at the same time. "I also see some construction equipment — a bulldozer, a backhoe and some others."

"They're working on the highway, extending a portion of it to this part of the city. The hope is that ease of transit — among other things — will make the area attractive again to businesses and residents."

"Good luck with that," I scoffed. "You'll have better luck teaching a fish to ride a bike."

Alpha Prime ignored my comment. "There was supposed to be a construction crew out here tonight working on the highway, but the police received an anonymous call saying there was a bomb on that overpass. They checked it out, confirmed there was a device, set up a perimeter, and then sent for me."

"Perimeter?" I asked. I looked around and noticed about a half-dozen sets of flashing red-and-blue lights, all spaced equidistant from the overpass. (Thankfully, their sirens weren't on.)

"Yes, a three-mile radius," my father said, pointing out the squad cars. "That puts them a little farther out than us. I'm surprised you didn't notice them before."

I didn't say anything. In truth, however, I had actually seen the flashing lights when my father was transporting the SUV here, but didn't assign any special significance to them at the time. Since the mayor had recently threatened to fix the city's budget problems by furloughing government employees (including cops and firemen), I had just assumed that they were all doing their part to raise revenue by issuing traffic tickets.

"If it's just a bomb," I finally said, "why do they need you? Why can't the bomb squad take care of it?"

"Well, it was identified as a bomb by whoever initially called the police, and they think that's what it is. But it doesn't look like a conventional device, so no one knew what to do with it."

"And that's why they called you."

"Correct."

"Okay, so what do we do now?"

"Actually, 'we' don't do anything. You're going to wait in the car — where it's safe — while I check things out."

"But—"

"No 'buts,'" he said adamantly. "Look, I know that you've got an awesome power set and that you've been holding your own against formidable supers for years now, but I'm only just getting a chance to be a parent to you. A father. That means I'm probably more protective than I need to be, but I can't help it. Even with you being part of the Alpha League's teen affiliate, it's going to take time for me to adjust to the thought of you willingly putting yourself in harm's way."

My natural inclination was to continue protesting, but I could sense the sincerity of his emotions, which included a healthy dollop of anxiety with respect to me.

"Alright," I said. "I'll just hang out here and watch the show from the cheap seats."

"Thank you," he said in obvious relief. Then he flew towards the overpass while I climbed back into the SUV.

Of course, I wasn't happy with this turn of events. Being in danger was almost the last thing anyone had to worry about with me — especially with my abilities. But it wasn't worth getting into an argument about, particularly when we'd been getting along so well thus far. Besides, with my vision telescoped, it would be like I was in the middle of everything anyway.

I watched as Alpha Prime approached the highway. When he got close, he went from flying horizontally to a vertical position. Even then, however, his feet didn't touch the ground, but that was normal for him. Rather than stride anywhere, my father had a tendency to float from place to place when he wasn't in a rush — just another sign of his preeminence. More than one late-night talk show host had joked about his legs being stuck together, or atrophying from lack of use.

Cape rippling slightly in the nighttime breeze, Alpha Prime drifted beneath the overpass. Head up, he scanned the underside of the roadway, apparently looking for the bomb. Presumably he found it, because after a few seconds he stopped gliding parallel to the ground and floated up, hand reaching for something. Unfortunately, whatever it was he was trying to grab, he never got a chance to touch it, because all of a sudden — with a thunderous roar — the overpass collapsed on top of him.

My first thought was that he had inadvertently set off the bomb. However, although it was indeed loud (a normal person in close proximity would have certainly had their eardrums shattered), it hadn't sounded quite like an explosion. Rather than the short, dull flat sound I would have expected based on my own experience, this was more like a giant hammer striking an equally gigantic nail, leaving a sharp pinging sound reverberating through the atmosphere.

Beyond that, though, it bore just about all the earmarks of a traditional bomb. A monstrous cloud of dust billowed out from where the overpass had been, enveloping everything within five hundred feet. The ground shook maddeningly for a moment, like Mother Earth was a wild bronco trying to throw off a determined rider, and the SUV was actually tossed two feet into the air before slamming back down with a massive jolt as debris rained down around it.

Two nearby buildings collapsed under the force of the tremors, and I could only imagine their owners thinking that Christmas had come early this year with what they'd save in demolition costs. A third building, a deserted tenement with excessive fire damage, began leaning dangerously to the side with an ominous creak of metal and stone, but somehow remained standing, looking like the Tower of Pisa's crackhead brother.

Still in the SUV, I scanned the area where the device had gone off, desperate for any sign of my father, my infrared vision allowing me to see through the dust. The overpass was gone, smashed down like a gargantuan foot stomping a bug. Shattered chunks of concrete in all shapes and sizes lay around, many with jagged pieces of rebar sticking out of them

Although Alpha Prime was considered to be invulnerable and had been to known to survive much worse than this, I still couldn't help feeling apprehensive for his well-being. I was just about to go into action when I saw some of the rubble on the ground shift, and a moment later my father stood up, concrete and debris rolling off him. Smiling in relief, I let out a breath I didn't know I'd been holding.

Alpha Prime floated about a foot up into the air, then spun madly for a few seconds, like a ballerina doing a pirouette. I initially thought this was just to shake the debris from his costume, but his motion also had the effect of dissipating the dust cloud that had formed. In a few moments, it was gone, blown away by my father's actions.

Alpha Prime looked around, seeming to assess the damage and taking stock of the situation. However, with the bomb having detonated, there really wasn't much more for him to do. Needless to say, it was a rather anticlimactic end to this adventure, and I was saying as much to myself when I saw something out of the corner of my eye.

Behind my father's back, the darkness seemed to shimmer and come alive with a soft, barely noticeable incandescence. It was an obscure, shapeless blob at first, big enough to wrap around a hippo and with edges that undulated almost rhythmically. I was so fascinated that it didn't immediately register that what I was seeing might constitute a danger. That all changed when the blob suddenly coalesced into forms I recognized.

<Behind you!> I telepathically shouted to my father. <Look out!>

My father's head jerked in my direction — evidence that he had heard me. Heeding my warning, he was in the process of turning around when something like a laser bolt struck him, sending him flying face-first into a circular pillar of concrete that supported the highway.

INFILTRATION

There were three of them, three figures that had appeared out of the shimmering darkness I had previously noted. They were all male, and dressed in dark bodysuits. With one look at their heavily-muscled frames, I knew that each of them had to have super strength. (Not to mention the fact that they were purposely engaging Alpha Prime in a fight — a bad move for anyone unable to lift a supertanker.)

I recognized one of them — a seven-foot brute with blond hair that had been buzz-cut military-style. Built like a block of granite and with a head that seemed too small for his body (and brains to match), he went by the name Imo. It was supposed to be short for "Immovable Object," so one would think that he'd have chosen the name "Io," but the last person who brought that to his attention won a free trip to the emergency room, along with shattered ribs and a broken jaw.

The second guy had an odd appearance. Although nearly as tall as my father, he was extremely rotund, almost round, in fact. His face and the other exposed areas of his skin had grooves, ribs, and dimples like a tire — as if he'd been run over by a tractor-trailer, with the wheels leaving impressions on his skin. He wasn't anyone I'd ever run across before (no pun intended), but I knew him by reputation. He went by the name Retread Fred, and as a result of a hi-tech lab accident, his body was formed of some kind of futuristic, vulcanized rubber and steel. His skin was purportedly impenetrable.

The last member of the landing party was someone I hadn't seen before and couldn't pin a name to. He was about my height, but so heavily muscled you would have thought he started lifting weights in the womb. He also had long, dark hair that came to the middle of his back, so luxurious that most women would have envied it.

Each of the three carried the same type of weapon: a two-foot length of metal with a heavy, rounded ended — like a mace or a morningstar, except that the end of their weapons glowed with a red light. They also radiated a certain menace that I couldn't help picking up on, but you didn't need any special powers to figure out that these guys were dangerous.

The three fanned out, totally focused on Alpha Prime as he stepped back from the now-cracked pillar. I doubted that he was seriously injured. (There wasn't much that could hurt the world's greatest superhero.) He turned around to get a look at who had attacked him.

By now his three assailants had taken up triangular positions around Alpha Prime — Retread Fred in front, and the other two on either side. Retread Fred held up his mace and pointed it in my father's direction; another short beam of light lanced out, striking Alpha Prime in the mid-section. Obviously, these weren't ordinary weapons.

My father frowned slightly, but didn't otherwise react. Retread Fred pointed his mace again, and this time, instead of just a short laser bolt, a continuous ray of light blasted out. Alpha Prime braced himself as the laser beam struck him. Like before, I didn't think this was likely to hurt him, so I was surprised to see him grimace slightly in pain. Still, when I reached for him empathically, I didn't get the sense that he was in any real danger so I stayed put.

While my father's attention was focused on Retread Fred, Imo rushed in from the side. He didn't have super speed, but was far faster than a normal human being. As he approached Alpha Prime, Imo shifted his mace into a two-handed grip above his shoulder, like a baseball player getting ready to knock one out of the park.

When he got close, Imo swung for the fences, with Alpha Prime's face poised to connect with the glowing head of his weapon. The mace whistled through the air, swung with a speed, power, and ferocity that almost defied belief, its glowing head tracing an arc of ruby light through the air. Even as strong as he was, I couldn't help but think that my father's head would be taken off if the blow connected.

At the last second, his hand moving impossibly fast, Alpha Prime reached up and grabbed the head of the mace, halting its momentum less than an inch from his nose. Still frowning from the assault being waged upon him by Retread Fred, my father snapped his head in Imo's direction. On his part, Imo didn't just seem surprised that his attack had failed; he looked almost catatonic.

The red glow of Imo's mace intensified, and wisps of smoke began rising up where Alpha Prime gripped it. However, if it was harming him to any degree, my father did a great job of masking it. Imo, seeming to come to his senses, tugged frantically at his weapon, trying to release it from Alpha Prime's grip. It was almost comical, like watching a toddler engaging in a tug-of-war with an adult.

Unfortunately for Imo, Alpha Prime seemed to tire of the game after a few seconds. He yanked on the mace, jerking Imo off his feet. At the same time, the guy with the long mane of hair rushed into the fray.

As Imo flew towards him, Alpha Prime headbutted him, sending the big man soaring backwards. Surprisingly, Imo actually cleared the rubble from the collapse of the overpass before hitting the ground like a block of granite; he then skidded for another twenty feet, plowing up pavement along the way.

Without hesitating, my father casually flipped Imo's mace — which he still held — in the air so that he now gripped it by the proper end. Ignoring whatever discomfort he felt from the laser beam that was still focused on him, he flung the weapon towards Retread Fred. It struck the tire-faced fiend square on the nose, snapping his head back slightly (and apparently breaking his concentration, since the ray of light that had been trained on my father winked out).

Retread Fred's face seemed to collapse inward, folding under the force of the mace as it hit. Like a balloon being squeezed between someone's hands, his cheeks and jaws spread out symmetrically to an almost impossible degree, as if under enormous pressure. In truth, seeing how his face seemed to expand after being hit, I half-expected his head to burst. To my great surprise, however, the mace's forward progress appeared to get checked, and its assault on poor Fred's visage ground to a halt. Moreover, Retread Fred's face began to resume its natural (for him) shape and appearance, pushing the mace back out.

Almost immediately, I realized what had happened. What I had assumed was Retread Fred's face getting mangled by the mace was actually his head absorbing the force of the weapon's impact. It wasn't exactly proof of the rumor that his body was impenetrable, but it was obvious that his rubberized frame could take a lot of punishment.

As I was reaching this conclusion, Fred's features resumed their original positions of repose when his nose finally popped back out, sending the mace sailing through the air in a lazy arc. Retread Fred shook his head groggily for a second but looked none the worse for wear, the only evidence of what he'd just experienced being a few wobbly steps backwards that he took.

To the extent that my father felt any satisfaction in the way he'd handled Imo and Retread Fred, he had no opportunity to gloat. The longhaired guy was on him the next second, attacking from a direction that put his back to me and swinging his mace with the expertise of a medieval knight. Unlike Imo, however, his blow actually connected — a mighty swing to Alpha Prime's abdomen that made my father double over. This was enough to make me sit up and take notice.

I'd seen dozens of clips of Alpha Prime being struck by metal — projectiles, clubs (much like the maces in our current encounter), etc. The result was invariably the same: the metal always proved to be the less durable material, with bullets bouncing away deformed, clubs bending, and so on. Thus, I had anticipated something similar here, but the mace that had hit Alpha Prime appeared undamaged. The fact that these weapons actually seemed capable of inflicting pain on my father meant that they were even more unusual than I had suspected.

The guy with the mane swung again, this time bringing the mace down from overhead while Alpha Prime was still bent over. The weapon struck my father between the shoulder blades, knocking him to his hands and knees. Before his longhaired attacker could swing again, Alpha Prime's fist shot out like a cannon, striking the inside of his assailant's right knee and wrenching it painfully to the side. His attacker went down to one knee, grunting in agony, as the leg collapsed.

Alpha Prime rose up and cocked his fist back, preparing to hit the longhaired man before he could recover. Before he could swing, however, his attacker's head seemed to come alive, sprouting a dozen boneless limbs that squirmed and writhed madly, like an octopus touching the third rail of a subway station.

The man's back was still to me, and it took me a second to realize that the wildly wriggling mass on his head was actually his hair, moving as if it were a living thing. And in front of the man, arm still drawn back to throw a punch, Alpha Prime stood as if frozen — like someone had turned him into a statue.

He was still in that position when, a moment later, Imo and Retread Fred, maces in hand, rushed in and started pummeling him with their weapons. While his comrades attacked my father, the third man slowly came to his feet, his gaze never seeming to waver from Alpha Prime's face.

I wasn't sure exactly what was happening, but empathically I was picking up two distinct sets of emotions. The first was an overall sense of smug satisfaction that emanated in triplicate and which I recognized as coming from Alpha Prime's attackers. The other emotion obviously came from my father, and while there was a slight underpinning of pain from the maces, it was by and large an overwhelming sense of agonizing frustration.

<Hang on!> I telepathically shouted. <I'm com—>

<No!> Alpha Prime mentally shouted. <Stay in the car!>

<But—>

<I can handle this! Just stay in the car like we agreed!>

Resentfully, I broke off contact, but I had already made my decision; there was no way I was just going to idly sit by and watch them bludgeon my father — even if it wasn't really hurting him. At the same time, though, I'd promised to stay in the car — out of harm's way, as Alpha Prime had put it. Of course, there was a way to kill two birds with one stone here...

I teleported myself and the SUV en masse to the heart of the action, appearing maybe five feet behind the man with the long hair. The moment we arrived, I switched on the vehicle's high beams and leaned on the horn for all I was worth.

Startled at having someone crash the party, the guy with the long hair spun around so that he was facing me, his free hand raised to shield his eyes from the bright lights of the SUV. He barely hesitated before taking a quick step forward and swatting at the front of the SUV in an upward manner with the mace, like a pitcher throwing a baseball underhanded.

Just before the weapon hit, I phased, becoming insubstantial. Under the force of the impact, the SUV crumpled like an old tomato can (although it passed harmlessly through my ghost-like form) and went flying end-over-end, spewing fluid and debris along its trajectory. It hit the ground about fifty feet away, turning a few cartwheels and throwing off fragments before coming to rest on its side.

With the SUV gone, the guy with the mane of hair lowered the hand that had been shielding his eyes from the vehicle's high beams. His hair was still wiggling ferociously, as if it had a mind of its own, but that turned out to be his second most-distinguishing feature; the real show pony was his eyes. They glowed with a pulsing, amber light that was almost mesmerizing.

I was entranced. I tried leaning in to get a better look – and then came to the horrifying realization that I couldn't move. I was paralyzed! I wasn't even able to break eye contact with him, and was only able to stop staring at those amber orbs when *he* averted *his* eyes to peek behind him and check on his colleagues. Even then I still couldn't move and found myself stuck staring straight ahead to where the other two thugs were still pummeling Alpha Prime. In short, eye contact may have induced the paralytic state that I found myself in, but wasn't required to maintain it.

I concentrated ferociously, mentally straining so hard to move that I'm surprised I didn't burst a blood vessel. Nothing worked. I couldn't even blink.

Now I understood not only why Alpha Prime had stood still while being attacked, but also why he felt so tremendously frustrated. The third attacker had some kind of ability to induce paralysis.

The guy in question passed in front of my line of sight, smiling evilly and tapping the head of his mace into his open palm several times with a satisfying smack on each occasion. (His companions only spared a quick glance in my direction to see what was going on before turning their attention back to Alpha Prime.) Then he swung the weapon at me…and went sprawling off-balance as it passed right through my body.

I was still phased. That being the case — despite the inability to move — I was essentially safe from harm. My assailant didn't seem to grasp that fact, however. He stood up, dusted himself off, and went back to swinging at me repeatedly, somehow confident that at some juncture he'd make contact with something solid.

Now it was his turn to be frustrated; no matter how hard he tried, it simply didn't seem possible to inflict any damage on me. That was one piece of good news, and mentally I was tempted to laugh at him.

In addition, my assailant's preoccupation with me seemingly caused a critical lapse in judgment on his part. While I had no clue exactly how my attacker's power of paralysis worked (*Was it permanent? Did it require continuous effort? What?*), he either overestimated its effect on my father, wholly forgot about him, or something along those lines. Regardless, it would prove to be a fatal error.

Alpha Prime was still directly across from me, and a few seconds after my attacker began his relentless assault on my phased form, I saw my father blink. Then he blinked again.

Apparently Retread Fred and Imo didn't notice, because they never let up with their maces, despite the fact that the weapons were clearly ineffective for the task at hand. The first indication they had that my father had come out of his stupor was when he suddenly reached out, gripped their heads in his hands, and then slammed them against each other like a couple of stooges in a vaudeville show. The sound of their two skulls clacking together was like one coconut being used to crack another one open, and they slumped to the ground, unconscious.

The remaining villain must have either heard the noises to his rear or sensed that something was amiss, because he suddenly stopped trying to hit me and turned to look behind him — or at least tried to. His body had barely moved before Alpha Prime's hand clamped down on the back of his skull.

Staying behind Mr. Longhair, Alpha Prime spun in a semi-circle and flung the man face-first towards the concrete embankment that sloped down from where the overpass used to be. He hit with bone-breaking force, creating a body-shaped impression in the hardened slab.

As soon as Mr. Longhair hit the concrete, the paralysis vanished. I was able to move again. I stretched, flexed my fingers, and wiggled my toes, taking immense joy in simply being in control of my body again.

"You alright?" my father asked.

"Peachy," I replied. I glanced around at the three villains, all of whom were still unconscious.

"Good to hear. Now, I thought we agreed—"

Alpha Prime was cut off as a high-pitched beeping suddenly began sounding. My father and I looked at each other, frowning.

"What's that sound?" I asked, glancing around. It seemed to be coming not from any particular direction, but around us.

"Sounds, you mean," my father said, as he floated over to where Retread Fred and Imo were lying on the ground, heads nestled together like a pair of lovebirds napping after a picnic.

"Huh?" I was confused, but followed in my father's wake, floating behind him. The beeping noise began sounding faster, as well as increasing in pitch and volume.

"They're sounding simultaneously, but there's actually three sets of beeps," he answered. "One coming from each of these guys."

INFILTRATION

He settled down on the ground next to Imo, then squatted down beside him. A second later, he lifted the big man's arm. There, on Imo's wrist, was something that looked like a black watchband. However, in the spot where the actual timepiece should be, there was instead a dark circular crystal that flashed crimson in sync with the beeps we were hearing. In fact, all three of our attackers were wearing the odd wristbands. The beeping increased in tempo again.

Suddenly, Alpha Prime dropped Imo's arm and stood up. "Jim, get out of here."

"What?"

"Something's about to happen here — I don't know what. You need to get to a safe distance."

"What about you?"

"I'll be fine."

"So will I. I can phase, remember?"

Alpha Prime shook his head in the negative, not apparently caring that, in my own way, I was as impervious to harm as he was. Empathically, I could feel his parental instincts overriding what should have been clearly obvious facts and simple logic. Before he could give voice to any argument, however, the beeping stepped up its pace once more, this time becoming a single, annoying, high-pitched tone. Whatever was happening, it was happening *right now*.

"Fine," my father said anxiously. "Phase. Right this second."

I did as he instructed, but he clearly wasn't satisfied. Arms outstretched in a protective manner, my father placed himself between me and the three villains. Then he began floating backwards, away from the scene of the battle we'd just had.

It was obvious that he intended for me to stay behind him so I did, but floated high enough to be able to see over his shoulder.

As had occurred when the three had appeared, there was a shimmering in the darkness around our erstwhile attackers. It spread over them, seemed to swallow them up. Then, as quickly as it had come, it faded — apparently taking the three unconscious men (and their weapons) with it.

My father didn't display any outward emotion, but I felt undeniable relief flooding through him. He was obviously grateful, for my sake, that the beeping hadn't turned out to be a weapon of any sort.

"Well," he said a few moments later, "how'd you like getting paralyzed and having supervillains try to bash your brains out?"

"Meh," I said noncommittally, as I held up a hand and let it waver from side to side. "It's got its pros and cons."

"Now you know why I told you to wait in the car."

"The car!" I exclaimed, suddenly remembering. I turned and looked at where it had landed. Alpha Prime followed my gaze to what remained of his half-million dollar SUV, then stared at me like I'd used a stack of hundred dollar bills to start a campfire.

"Well," he finally muttered, "got anything to say for yourself?"

"Yeah," I replied, staring at the wreckage. "I think your 'Check Engine' light is flashing."

INFILTRATION

Chapter 6

I woke up late the next morning. Shortly after showing my father the mangled remains of his SUV, I had teleported home while he stayed at the site of the fight to deal with the official wrap-up of the incident. I was so pumped up, though, that I was barely able to sleep, and when I did finally doze off, it was several hours later, which resulted in me sleeping in.

I raced through my morning routine, getting dressed and washing up at super speed. According to a phone text that had come through while I was sleeping, I was going to be officially debriefed at Alpha League headquarters in about half an hour, and I was eager to get it out of the way. (In all honesty, it should have taken place asap following our fight with the supervillains, but my father had simply told me to go home and worry about it the next day.) I also wanted to talk to Mouse, the *de facto* head of the Alpha League, before the exhibition later that evening.

Wearing a T-shirt and jeans, I went downstairs to find something to eat. When I entered the kitchen, my grandfather was sitting at the breakfast table reading the morning paper. My mother, per her usual routine, was probably in her office, hard at work on her next novel. I poured myself a bowl of cereal and milk, then sat down at the table across from my grandfather, munching loudly on cornflakes. After a few seconds, my grandfather laid down the paper and mentally pinged me.

<So, how was the game?> he asked.

I kept eating, but telepathically responded. <It was fun. We're going to struggle defensively this year, but

we'll probably be able to shoot our way out of most games.>

    <Sounds good.> He went back to reading his newspaper.

    Of course, that wasn't everything and my grandfather knew it; he could always discern when there was more to the story where I was concerned. However, he liked to occasionally display disinterest, even though I knew he was as eager to hear the rest of my tale as I was to tell it. It was kind of a game between us, to see who would break down first.

    <Fine,> he said about a minute later. <What else?>

    I smiled, happy to have won this round, and then told him about the fight at the overpass. When I was done, he simply nodded, brow furrowed in thought. It wasn't an official debrief like I was going to get later, but I always enjoyed getting my grandfather's insight into a battle.

    <Sounds like your father hasn't changed much since I was his teammate,> he said after a few seconds. <Thinks nobody is capable of handling a problem except him. I told him years ago that, even with *his* powers, he'd burn himself out trying to take the lead on everything. I'm surprised it hasn't happened yet.>

    I didn't respond. I wondered if Gramps knew exactly how close he was to being accurate with that prediction.

    <Anyway,> he continued, <I think you did fine.>

    <Sure didn't feel like it,> I said.

    <Why, because of the paralysis thing?>

    <Yeah. I was practically helpless at that point.>

My grandfather laughed. <I can't count the number of times I've been frozen still, tied up, paralyzed, and so on. Trust me, you're rarely ever completely helpless — especially with your power set.>

<Well, I was.>

<Are you sure?>

<Yes! I couldn't so much as blink. It was like I was hypnotized. And I still don't know how he did it!>

<Well, let's think about that for a second. You say you were fine until you made eye contact with him?>

<Yeah.> Finishing the last of my cereal and pushing the bowl away, I switched to speaking verbally. "Is that important or something?"

"It might be," Gramps said, answering out loud and drumming his fingers on the table. "You do know that the eye connects directly to the brain through the optic nerve, right?"

"Yeah, so?"

"Well, the brain controls body movement. That's why, when telepaths like me get inside someone's head, we can make them do what we want — shoot a gun, eat dirt, do the Watusi—"

"The what?"

"Never mind," my grandfather said, waving off my question. "The point is that this guy's powers sound similar to what a lot of psychics can do."

"So you think this was some kind of telepathy?"

"Possibly."

"But if it was telepathy, I should have felt it. I didn't sense anything like that."

My grandfather shrugged. "Maybe it was outside your range."

"Huh? What do you mean?"

My grandfather sat silent for a second, obviously deep in thought, before responding. "Think about your vision powers. Normal people can only see across certain wavelengths of light."

"The visible light spectrum," I said.

"Yes. You, however, can see across various other wavelengths — infrared, ultraviolet, and more. Wavelengths outside the range of most humans. Most supers, too, for that matter. This guy's powers may work in a similar fashion."

I pondered that for a second. "So, you're saying that this guy's power may be some form of telepathy that's outside the range of most telepaths to detect?"

"Exactly."

"But even if you're right, how'd he get past my safeguards? Mentally, my brain is full of booby traps — snares, trapdoors, tiger pits. Stuff *you* taught me to help ward off psychic attacks. How'd he slip past those?"

"If I'm right about him using a form of telepathy you can't detect, I'd assume that whatever he's doing just doesn't trigger your defenses. It's like you've got a spring-gun aimed at the front door but he's slipping in through the back."

"That's just great — a mental cat burglar running around in my brain," I said disgustedly.

"It could have been worse," Gramps said.

"How's that?"

"It could have happened to *me*," he said with a grin.

INFILTRATION

Chapter 7

I spent about another ten minutes hanging out with my grandfather, then teleported to Alpha League headquarters. I popped up in an area that was still undergoing construction, as evidenced by the unpainted walls and lack of carpeting on the floor, among other things. After walking around for a few moments to investigate further, I sighed despondently at the fact that the work was nowhere near completion.

In truth, I was in a suite of rooms that were designated as my future domicile. Alpha League HQ had several floors that served as on-site residences, and every League member had their own living quarters here (although few of them were habitable, or even finished, at the moment) — including those of us who were part of the teen affiliate. Historically, however, the teen quarters were seldom used; they were really only here for the few times each year that teen supers were required to stay at HQ for extended training — usually during summer. Still, they were *our* rooms, and — since I'd been allowed to select a few custom features — I was anxious to see the finished product.

Obviously, finishing the teen apartments wasn't very high on the list of priorities. I briefly pondered if it would be worth asking Mouse, leader of the Alpha League, to move up the timetable for completion. However, it was a subject I'd have to broach with care, since Mouse had made it clear that he was making some changes to the rooms. In fact, I wasn't even supposed to be here.

"What do you think you're doing?" said a disembodied voice that seemed to come from all around me. It was Mouse, of course. Still, having come from nowhere, his voice had startled me slightly and I looked around anxiously for the person speaking.

"Over by the door, genius," Mouse's voice said, almost impatiently.

I walked over to where the entrance to my quarters was located. Next to the door, at roughly chest level, a circular plate was set into the wall. The plate contained a numbered pad like you'd find on a phone, and beneath that a flashing green button marked "Intercom/Phone." I pushed the button and the green light ceased flashing and became steady.

"Now," said Mouse, with a slight hint of aggravation, "I'll ask you again: what do you think you're doing?"

"I just wanted to see if my place was ready yet," I responded.

"And asking somebody never works, right?"

I ignored his question. Now that I was paying attention, I noticed that his voice was coming from speakers mounted in the ceiling. There must also be a couple of mikes in order for him to hear me.

"How'd you even know I was up here?" I asked.

"Motion-activated cameras," he said. "They're in all the rooms at the moment."

"All the...?" I frowned, not liking this at all. "So, wait a minute. You'll be able to see exactly where everyone is? Whether we're in our own rooms or someone else's?"

"Yes. We'll also know whether you've been naughty or nice."

"Isn't that a flagrant invasion of privacy?"

"What are you going to do, file a complaint with the co-op board?"

"Maybe."

"Well, since I am, ostensibly, the co-op board, when it comes across my desk, you may rest assured that I will give due attention and deliberation to your concerns. Then I'll shred it."

I couldn't help laughing at that. Mouse really had an awesome sense of humor.

"Okay," I said, still grinning, "what's the real reason for the cameras?"

"The real reason? So I'll know when boneheads aren't listening when I tell them to stay out of certain areas of the building."

I laughed again, and this time I even heard Mouse chuckling on his end.

"Alright," he finally said. "You're going to find out soon enough anyway. When they're finished, all of the living quarters will have a secret exit. While we're in the process of constructing them, I want to make sure that no unauthorized individuals are roaming around on the floors in question. Hence the cameras, which will come out when everything is complete. Satisfied?"

I nodded. "Seems to make sense."

"I'm glad you approve, milord. Now, are you ready for your debriefing?"

"Sure."

"Great, how fast can you get to my" — I teleported and popped up behind him — "lab?"

"Pretty fast, I'd say," said an attractive blonde standing next to him. Mouse turned around, already knowing what he would see.

"One day I'll learn," he said, seemingly to himself, "never to ask him that."

I grinned, as this was something Mouse said almost every time I popped into his presence, as if he couldn't get used to the immediacy of my teleportation power. Dressed in the trademark black-and-gold uniform of the Alpha League, he often feigned irritation at the way I popped in, but we both knew that he wasn't bothered by it in the least.

At six-foot-three and with the physique of someone who lifted weights regularly, you would have assumed that the nickname Mouse was an intentional misnomer — like calling a bald guy "Curly" or a big brute "Tiny." However, I always felt there was something more to it than that, although I hadn't been able to find out what it was yet.

Mouse, who was standing at a worktable, leaned over and pressed a button on a small, palm-sized device on the tabletop. It looked like some kind of mobile speaker, obviously his connection to the intercom. Next to the speaker sat an open laptop, with an image of the room I'd just left on the screen.

The blonde, who was wearing a black tank top and a pair of chinos, came over and gave me a hug.

"Nice to see you, Jim," she said.

"You, too," I replied, returning the hug a little stiffly.

The woman was actually a clone, part of the hive mind known as Braintrust. I'd known Braintrust almost my entire life and considered "BT" one of my closest friends and allies. Along with my grandfather, BT had played a significant role in my training and development as it relates to my powers. However, the clone I'd normally dealt with had been male; when he was killed during the previous summer, his replacement had turned out to be this stunning blonde. ("Killed," of course, meant something entirely different to Braintrust. To BT, replacing a clone was probably not much different than swapping out dead batteries in a remote for new ones.)

On the whole, I still hadn't fully adjusted to thinking of BT as female — despite the fact that I didn't really know if the original Braintrust was male or female. (In fact, having only dealt with its clones, I didn't even know if the "real" BT was even human.)

I glanced around Mouse's lab, an exceedingly large room with several oversized worktables covered with hi-tech contraptions. A large array of complex computers and machinery were lined along one wall. A steady stream of information flowed across no less than a dozen large, flat screen monitors placed strategically around the room. This was, in general, the way Mouse's lab appeared at almost any given time, but it suddenly occurred to me that something was missing.

"Hey," I said, turning to Mouse. "Where's Li?"

Li was an AI (artificial intelligence) previously housed in an android body. He had been indispensable during the crisis at the Academy, but had sustained irreparable damage during the conflict. Mouse was in the process of building him a new body, which he usually kept on one of the nearby worktables.

"We moved Li's construction to a more private area," BT responded.

"'We'?" I repeated.

"Yes," Mouse said. "Braintrust is helping out with Li's new body."

INFILTRATION

I nodded, as this shouldn't have come as a surprise to me. Mouse was undoubtedly one of the smartest people on the planet, and BT was a living repository of knowledge and information. It made sense that they would collaborate on something like this. I had introduced them a short time ago, essentially in response to a request from Mouse's girlfriend Vixen, another member of the Alpha League.

"What's this about privacy, though?" I asked, perplexed. I would be the first to admit that Li had a lot of life-like qualities, and — despite the fact that I hadn't detected any emotion from him — even I had initially assumed he was human. However, I was pretty sure that, while Li understood concepts like privacy, it wasn't anything that bothered him. Thus, I was a little confused as to why privacy would play a role in anything concerning him, and I said as much.

"Look," Mouse said, "when I first started dealing with Li, I just assumed that he was a typical AI, albeit one whose mainframe — for lack of a better term — was shaped like a human being. But in working on a new body for him and dealing with him every day, I've come to realize that he's more than just some computer program. He has thoughts, intellect…even desires, although he may not express them in the same way you and I would.

"Bearing all that in mind, building his body out here in the open, where anybody who stops by could see it, felt a lot like performing oral surgery on someone on a busy street corner. No one would want to be exposed like that. Even though Li may not emotionally care about that kind of thing, if I'm his friend *I* should care and take steps to protect him."

As usual, Mouse was right. If I were truly Li's friend, then there were certain efforts I should be undertaking on his behalf, even if he himself did not realize they were necessary.

"Point taken," I said.

"Good," Mouse said. "Now, let's get the 4-1-1 on this cage match you and AP had last night."

"You sure you want to do this now?" I asked, with a short nod towards BT. She wasn't a League member (she had no official standing, really), so I didn't know if it was appropriate to officially report on what had happened in her presence.

"Why not?" Mouse asked, after following my gaze to BT and then looking back at me. "You'll just tell her anyway if she asks, so let's just save you the trouble of doing it twice."

He was right, of course. I had full faith and confidence in BT, having put my life in her hands on numerous occasions in the past. In fact, she and Mouse were the two people I trusted most outside of my immediate family, and both were among the select few who had full knowledge of my pedigree. In short, regardless of how the debriefing went, I was bound to talk to her about it sooner or later.

"Okay," I said. "What did you learn from Alpha Prime?"

"Never to loan you a car, for starters," Mouse said.

"I'm just trying to avoid reinventing the wheel," I replied, ignoring his attempt at humor. "Repeating things he's already told you."

"Don't worry about that," Mouse said. "The entire point of debriefing the two of you is to get both your insights into what happened. You may have noticed something he didn't, and vice versa. So just tell us how things played out as you remember them."

****

It didn't take particularly long to tell my version of what happened. During my soliloquy, I noticed that neither Mouse nor BT took any notes. Mouse, I knew from experience, would remember all the pertinent details. (I suspect he actually has total recall.) BT, to the extent it was necessary, probably had a dozen clones out there somewhere writing down my every word like it was soul-saving gospel.

When I was finished, Mouse merely nodded.

"That's essentially the same report Alpha Prime gave," he said.

"So, what do you guys think?" I asked.

"About which part?" Mouse asked.

"What do you mean?" I asked.

"Well, there are a lot of moving pieces here," BT said. "First of all, what's the significance of an explosive on *that* overpass? It's typical construction, although in a deserted — practically uninhabitable — part of town."

"In other words," I said, "it's not anything someone could have demanded a ransom for, like threatening to set off a dirty bomb in a densely populated urban area unless they got paid."

"Exactly," chimed in Mouse. "And then there's the matter of the explosive itself."

"What about it?" I asked.

"It caused a lot of destruction like you'd typically expect with such a device," Mouse said, "but, aside from that, I can't seem to find much evidence that it acted like a bomb. There's no blast epicenter, no explosive residue, no device fragments."

"But there was actually a bomb, right?" I asked. "Alpha Prime saw it."

"AP saw what looked like a timer attached to something," Mouse said, "but never got a chance to look it over closely. It may have had some kind of proximity trigger."

"Any chance that all the bomb remains were destroyed in the explosion itself?" I asked.

BT shook her head. "That rarely ever happens. I suppose an incendiary device could have destroyed *some* of the bomb material, but there's nothing indicating that any type of combustion took place. No char, no fire damage, nothing."

I frowned in concentration, trying to remember. The sound I'd heard, the unheralded destruction of the overpass...

"I think you're right," I said. "Thinking back, I don't recall there being any smoke or fire. There was just the overpass suddenly being razed."

"Sounds like we might be dealing with a new type of weapons technology," Mouse commented.

"What about those three goons who showed up?" I asked. "Maybe whatever allowed them to appear and disappear also affected the detonation of the bomb in some way."

Mouse seemed to contemplate this for a second. "Possible, but not probable. Are you sure they weren't teleporting?"

INFILTRATION

"No way," I answered. "This wasn't teleportation. It was more like…" I paused, searching for the right words. "Like matter transference."

Mouse and BT shared an odd glance, and I assumed that they were both thinking how unlikely my last comment was. Matter transference was the technological equivalent of my teleportation ability. However, whereas teleporters move objects en masse from one place to another, matter transference actually operates by deconstructing an item — breaking it down into its constituent elements — then transferring those basic components to another location where they are reconstructed (hopefully in their proper order).

Moreover, just like brakes failing on a car and engines shutting down on a plane, there was always a chance that something could go wrong in matter transference, and nobody wanted to come out the other end looking like something Picasso had painted while drunk. Thus, even though the technology had purportedly been perfected by a select few, matter transference had a long way to go before it overtook something even as basic as a unicycle in terms of being a preferred mode of travel.

Bearing all that in mind, I half-expected Mouse to make light of my comment. Instead, he seemed to mull it over, saying, "Hmmm… That's actually pretty much what your dad said, and he's not really prone to exaggeration."

I raised an eyebrow, surprised at having gotten an unexpected assist from my father. Even more, I didn't feel any type of irritation at having Alpha Prime referred to as my "dad," although I still couldn't see myself ever calling him that.

"Great," I said. "Speaking of our attackers, I don't suppose you've got an ID on the third guy?"

"Of course," said BT, which should have come as almost no surprise. There was very little info BT didn't have or couldn't get her hands on. "His name is Saul Gorgon, but he's known as the Gorgon Son."

"Gorgon?" I repeated, frowning. "You mean like Medusa?"

"Yes, except with him you don't actually turn into stone," BT replied. "You just become paralyzed, as you experienced firsthand, although he does have augmented strength as well."

"Unfortunately," Mouse interjected, "we don't have a firm idea of how his power works, so we don't have effective countermeasures for it yet."

"I may have some info on that," I said, and then told them about my grandfather's theory.

"That actually makes a lot of sense," Mouse said after I finished. "It would certainly explain why almost no one has a defense against Gorgon Son's power."

"But it seems to be limited," BT added. "I mean, he only seems to be able to paralyze people. He's not like a true telepath, who could get in there and take control."

Mouse contemplated that for a second, then turned to me. "Well, how about it? Were you able to use any of your other powers?"

"Huh?" I was caught a little off-guard by the current line of questioning.

"Your other abilities," Mouse said. "Physically you may have been petrified, but if Braintrust is right, you should have been able to use your other powers — telekinesis, for example. Could you?"

"Point A," I said, mustering up a bit of indignation, "I resent the term 'petrified.' It makes it seem like I was cowering in a corner."

"Fine," Mouse said. "You weren't petrified. You were dazed, stunned, frozen, what have you. What's Point B?"

"Point B, with respect to my other powers…" I trailed off, not quite able to say the words.

"Yes?" BT queried anxiously, after a few seconds of silence.

I looked sheepishly from BT to Mouse, who suddenly threw up his hands, grunting in exasperation. Obviously he knew what my silence was saying, but BT appeared a bit befuddled.

"Don't you get it?" Mouse said in response to her look of confusion. "He didn't even *try* to use his other powers! It's like he forgot about them!"

"Hey, man," I said defensively, "when you wake up blind, your first thought isn't 'I wonder if I still have my sense of smell?' It's 'Oh, snap! I'm blind! How do I get my sight back?'"

"So," BT said, "your concern over fixing what was broken overrode your thoughts of finding out what else still worked. That's understandable."

"It was boneheaded, is what it was," Mouse chimed in, brow creased. I knew, however, that the frown on his face, as well as his irritable tone, was more indicative of worry than anger.

Every teen member of a superhero team gets assigned a mentor — someone you can approach with any questions you have, any issues you're dealing with, etc. Mouse was mine. In general, we got along exceptionally well, and part of that derived from the fact that we spoke frankly with each other — especially Mouse. In that sense, he was probably more like the older brother that I never had, as he was seldom shy about telling me when he thought I'd screwed up. Obviously this was one such occasion, but I had no doubt that any harsh words spoken were rooted in concern for my welfare.

"Boneheadedness aside," I said, "any idea how I should deal with him if our paths cross again?

"Yeah," Mouse said. "Don't look him in the eye."

BT smacked him lightly on the shoulder, to which Mouse simply raised his arms in a what-did-I-do gesture.

"On the more practical side," BT said, "all indications are that Gorgon Son's power is only temporary. When exactly did you get free of his control?"

I thought for a moment. "After Alpha Prime knocked him out."

"And when did Alpha Prime break free of his paralysis?" she asked.

"After Gorgon Son became preoccupied with me," I said. "He seemed obsessed with hitting me with that weird mace."

"Well, based on those last few statements, I'd venture to guess two things," Mouse said. "First, Gorgon Son's paralysis doesn't affect your other powers. After all, you stayed phased when he tried to hit you, so the odds are favorable that you'll still have your other abilities if it happens again."

"Hmmm." I rubbed my chin in thought. "And what do the unfavorable odds say?"

Mouse hesitated a moment before answering. "That the paralysis affects your other powers by locking them into place the moment you become frozen."

I blinked, processing what I'd just heard. "So in other words, I may have stayed phased while paralyzed last night because that's the ability I was using when Gorgon Son used his power on me. Whatever power is in the 'On' position when he freezes me will stay on, while the others stay off."

"In a nutshell," Mouse said.

"Okay," I said a little numbly, still mentally chewing on the info I'd just been fed. "What's your other observation?"

"I think Gorgon Son's ability requires him to focus on his victim," Mouse said. "The minute he got caught up in trying to beat you down, Alpha Prime was able to move again. As soon as AP coldcocked him, you got control of your body back."

"In essence," BT said, "assuming it actually *is* a form of telepathy, you fight it the way you would with any other telepath. Based on what we know, I'd suggest trying to break his concentration."

"Easier said than done," I replied, reflecting on how this guy had mentally slipped past all my defenses. Any future encounters with him had a real risk of serious harm.

Chapter 8

Our discussion of Gorgon Son essentially brought my debriefing to a close. We still had more questions than answers — Who was behind this? What did they want? — but we weren't likely to get any more information in the near term. That being the case, BT excused herself and stepped over to the other side of the room, where she became absorbed in the data streaming across one of the monitors. I decided to take the opportunity to have a discussion with Mouse about something else that had been on my mind: the exhibition. Mouse, however, beat me to the punch.

"So," he began, "you ready for tonight?"

I shrugged. "More or less."

"You don't sound particularly excited. Most kids would be thrilled to be on national TV."

"I'm just ready for it to be over with."

Mouse stared at me for a second before responding. "Listen, I know you're not one of those guys who's all wrapped up in the trappings of fame that often come with being a super. You just want to do your job."

"Exactly."

"But doing that job — like being a cop, soldier, or the like — is a lot easier when the public is behind you. When the people you're serving support you. And it's a lot easier to win that support when the public feels like they know you. Tonight is a great way to make that happen."

"I don't recall seeing the broadcast of your coming-out party when you joined the League."

"I'm a special case. A couple of years ago, you couldn't have paid me to be part of the Alpha League.

They'd already rejected me three times, so it was clear that they didn't value my talents."

I already knew this part of Mouse's story. He had participated in the Super Teen Trials three years in a row and had been rebuffed each time.

"And yet, here you are," I said.

Mouse snorted in mock contempt. "I was coerced into joining. Oddly enough, although they made some other concessions to me, I only had one real requirement when I finally agreed to put on the uniform."

"What was that?"

"I told them that I'd do my job, but I wanted absolutely no involvement with office politics. You know, League leadership and all that."

I laughed. "How's that working out for you?"

"It'll be great as soon as I can get some dumb schmoe to take the job from me," he said, grinning.

"How exactly did you end up as the boss man here? You've never said."

Mouse sighed. "It's not a position I set out for, and I was actually serious about telling them that I didn't want to be involved in office politics. I just wanted to do my job."

"So what happened?"

"I got here and almost immediately started asking questions about the way the League did things. Based on the answers I got, I started making suggestions for improvements, and the other members tended to adopt ninety-nine percent of what I proposed. From there, it was just a short hop to go from offering suggestions to giving unsolicited opinions, and then I moved on up to simply making decisions about what I felt was important. Before I knew it, I was running the joint. Go figure."

"Anyway, we've gone off on a tangent here," he said. "The point I was trying to make is that you've got to open up a little and let the general public get a glimpse of who you are."

"They'll get a glimpse," I countered, "but probably not much more than that. I'm shooting to get through this thing as fast as I can."

"Wait a minute...aren't you part of the last act in the exhibition?"

"Yeah, me and Dynamo. They've got us pitted against each other in some kind of competition."

"If you're last, that means you're the main event. You're the reason everyone will stay tuned until the bitter end. Knowing that, are you really planning to just zip through whatever they have set up for you at the speed of sound?"

"Only if I can't get up to the speed of light."

Mouse shook his head in exasperation. "That's a bit of a juvenile attitude, don't you think? This isn't like you, Jim. What's *really* bothering you?"

I was silent for a moment, and then — without actually intending to do it so bluntly — found myself blurting out what was really weighing on my mind. "The whole thing's kind of stupid. I mean, me and Dynamo? What kind of competition is that? Our powers don't even match up! He's the super-strong, impossible-to-hurt type, while I've got super speed, teleportation—"

"And too many other abilities to list in a reasonable time," Mouse chimed in. "I'd just assume that the event organizers thought that it would be a good match-up. His strength against your versatility."

"It's about as good a match-up as a basketball team playing a football team in ice hockey. Whatever they have planned, neither of us is likely to be in our element."

"So exactly what are your respective elements, if I may ask?"

"Dynamo should be in some strongman competition — lifting sedans and the like. For me, maybe something with another speedster, or another teleporter like Vestibule or—"

"Vestibule's already signed up for another event."

"My point is, Dynamo and I shouldn't be battling head-to-head. The last thing I need is some silly face-off that's going to perpetuate the myth that there's some type of competition between him and me. Or worse, erupt into some sort of blood feud between us."

"Hold on," Mouse said, frowning. "There's supposedly some sort of rivalry between you and Dynamo?"

"Not as far as I'm concerned, but that's the rumor."

"Since when? And what are you supposedly fighting him for?"

I threw up my hands in exasperation. "Where've you been, man? There's all kinds of constant chatter about who is going to lead the next generation of supers. With Paramount and that mindless Gestapo who were following him locked away, the title is up for grabs."

"And the smart money is on either you or Dynamo," Mouse said, finally catching on.

"Apparently we're the top two contenders."

"Okay," Mouse said. "I get the rumor. In fact, I think I've actually heard it before but simply didn't pay much attention to it, so it didn't even register that that's what you were referring to when you mentioned a rivalry with Dynamo."

"*Alleged* rivalry."

"But if that's all it is, what's the big deal? Even if the event organizers paired you guys for that reason and the exhibition thing doesn't perfectly mesh with either your powers or his, it's just a little friendly competition. There's no reason that it has to escalate into more than that."

I let out a deep breath. "You don't understand, Mouse. That whole thing with me and Paramount...it started with a little 'friendly competition.' A paintball game."

"Huh?" Mouse was, of course, a bit confused. Not many people knew this part of the story, and even those who did probably hadn't considered the information as a whole and connected the dots.

"Everyone knows that my on-air fight with the Alpha League started off as an altercation between me and Paramount. What they don't know is that, prior to the theatrics that were caught on film, Paramount and I had been on opposite sides of a 'friendly' paintball game."

"Let me guess: you beat him. That kid never learned how to be a graceful loser."

"No, my team actually lost; they clobbered us. But I did something worse than beat him. I embarrassed him during the game, made him a laughingstock."

I half-expected Mouse to ask for more detail, but he didn't. Instead, he just pursed his lips and let out a long, low whistle. "Yeah, that would do it with Paramount. He always took himself way too seriously, especially for a kid. A lot of other things make sense now,

82

but of course, hindsight is always twenty-twenty. Regardless, you should have told me all this before."

I shrugged. "It didn't seem important."

"Well, at least now I understand your issue with the exhibition: the last time Kid Sensation was on TV it was a disaster, and you're worried about inadvertently putting on an encore performance."

I nodded. "To be honest, part of it, initially, was the thought of losing my privacy, but there's a workaround for that, of course. I'll just change my appearance — make myself look like the Kid Sensation that everyone's grown accustomed to. But yes, the main thing is the fisticuffs. I just don't want anything like that happening again. I mean, I'm only just coming back out of the woodwork after two years."

"First of all, those two years were a self-imposed exile; no one banished you, and you were always welcome here. I will admit, however, that we probably didn't do a great job of conveying that.

"Second, I don't think you have to worry about history repeating itself. You're older — and hopefully more mature — so that any incident that occurs can probably be resolved without a battle royal. Plus, I'm going to go out on a limb here and assume that you don't have any vendettas going with any of the current teen supers."

"Not that I'm aware of," I said, "although I'm still in favor of getting the entire thing over as soon as possible."

Mouse rubbed his eyes and let out a frustrated sigh, then gave me an appraising glance. "Look, you went to the game last night with Alpha Prime, right?"

"Yeah."

"Did you enjoy it?"

I nodded. "It was a lot of fun."

"What did you like about it?"

I frowned, thinking. "The display of skill, the competitiveness, the rivalry. The clash of equals. Guys giving it their all — digging down deep and trying to come up with a way to win. The go-for-broke attitude when your team is on the ropes and everybody fights with the heart of a warrior to get back in the game."

"And do you feel like you got all that last night? Like you got your money's worth?"

"Sure."

"Now, what if — instead of a typical basketball game — the two teams just line up in front of the basket at opposite ends of the court, and the players get, say, ten shots each. Then, at the end, the team that had made the most baskets wins. What would you think about a game like that?"

"Wait, you're saying that each player just gets ten free shots at the basket?"

"Yes."

"And there'd be no defense, nobody trying to block the shot?"

"Correct. No interaction between the teams whatsoever."

"And then you just count the number of baskets made, and the team with the most wins?"

"That's right. What do you think about that?"

"I think it's the worst idea for a sport ever conceived."

"So I take it you don't like golf," Mouse said, grinning.

"What?" I asked, confused.

"Forget it," Mouse said with a dismissive wave of his hand. "As for the sport I described, you wouldn't pay money to see something like that?"

"Nobody would! First of all, there's no competition between the teams, which is the whole essence of sports. It's just a bunch of guys shooting free throws — lackluster and boring! On top of that, the whole thing would be over in a flash! It probably wouldn't last more than fifteen min—"

I froze, suddenly catching on to what Mouse was trying to get me to realize. Mouse himself just smiled, obviously pleased at having fulfilled his role as mentor by teaching me something.

"Okay," I said. "I get it. Nobody wants to tune in just to see me race through an event at Mach speed."

"Exactly. There's very little entertainment value in it."

"And if viewers aren't entertained, they may not donate to the sponsored charities."

"Or they may not tune in next time because we'll have a reputation for being boring," Mouse added. "Look, we both know that you've got game-changing abilities and you could probably get through whatever this event is tonight in a flash. The thing about game changers, though, is that they're often most effective not by their actual use, but rather by the threat or potential of their use.

"Take the atomic bomb, for instance. Our country developed it, but we didn't have to use it every time we came into conflict with another nation. Its mere existence was a game changer."

I saw where Mouse was going. "So what you're saying is, I should go slow tonight and give the audience a good show — regardless of how fast I could conceivably get through the exhibition — and not necessarily put everything I have on display because it's not necessary."

"More or less," Mouse said, shrugging.

I just nodded, essentially agreeing to behave as suggested. I still wasn't wild about participating in this thing, but I could certainly take one for the team in that regard.

INFILTRATION

Chapter 9

After getting everything off my chest, I had to admit that I felt better about participating in the exhibition. I still didn't feel *great* about it, but definitely better. Mouse, however, was adamant that it could be a lot of fun if I just relaxed and tried to enjoy it.

Following our chat, Mouse got ready to go back to whatever he and BT had been working on when I showed up. Of course, I was free to hang around, but Mouse seemingly believed that idle hands were the devil's workshop, and if I stuck around in his lab too long without a specific task to do, he'd eventually put me to work.

Normally, Mouse has one or two interesting things going on, so hanging out in his lab is usually a good time — even if he does make you get your hands dirty. However, there were a few errands I still needed to run, so I would be making my way to the exit soon. But before I left there was one thing I needed to do.

"Hey," I said. "Where exactly did you guys move Li to?"

Mouse, who had turned his attention back to something on his worktable, looked up and then inclined his chin towards a set of floor-to-ceiling bookcases along a portion of one wall. I gave a brief nod of acknowledgment and then teleported.

****

The bookcases in question actually covered the entrance to a secret chamber, which is where I popped up. The place was cavernous, and while there were some

87

tables and chairs, it primarily appeared to serve as storage. There was an endless array of boxes, crates, and bins, as well as an extensive amount of shelving that housed a voluminous amount of miscellany, salmagundi, and curios.

Glancing around, it only took me a second to pinpoint Li's location: a body-shaped mass covered with a white sheet, lying on top of a worktable. I walked over and reached out to pull the sheet away from what I assumed was Li's head, then remembered Mouse's comments about giving Li a certain degree of privacy.

"It is okay, Jim," said Li's voice, emanating from above me. "You can look."

Previously, Mouse had integrated Li with the computer system in his main lab, allowing Li to speak through the lab's audio system. Apparently he had done the same thing in here.

"Thanks," I said, pulling down the sheet just enough to uncover Li's face. "How'd you know I was even in here?"

"I still lack visual perception, but Mouse has given me access to motion detectors, thermal imagery, and other devices located in this alcove that allow me to recognize when others are present. He said that I should know when someone was 'sneaking up on me.'"

"How'd you know it was me, specifically?"

"You have a distinctive physiology — unique even among supers — and you visit me regularly. Thus, using the instruments I now have access to, I have learned to recognize your biological telemetry."

I nodded, only half listening as I found myself staring in fascination at what would eventually be Li's new face. (Actually it was his old face — Asian features, bald head, etc. — but Mouse and BT had done an excellent job in recreating the visage of someone they had never met in the flesh.) He looked exactly as he had the last time I'd seen him whole, which meant that he resembled nothing more than an ordinary teenager. Only his eyes, open and staring blankly at the ceiling, gave any present indication that there was anything unnatural about him.

I smiled, happy and thankful that my friend would, hopefully, be up and about soon.

"So, what's the estimate on when you'll be able to move into your new home here?" I asked, patting the android body on the shoulder.

"Mouse wishes to increase the inherent defenses of my body, so he is making some improvements to the synthetic epidermis, among other things."

"What, the skin?"

"Yes. In human beings, it is the largest organ in the body and also serves as the first line of defense against such hazards as disease and the elements. The skin on my original body did much the same for me, but Mouse is of the opinion that he can enhance the abilities of my new epidermis without sacrificing its natural look and feel. He estimates three to four weeks before it will be ready."

"So you could be on your feet in a month? That's great! I can't wait to show you around."

"Unfortunately, while I may be able to 'move in,' as you put it, in a month, I will probably need an additional month before I am ready to go out in public."

"Why's that?" I asked, curious.

"Because of my new body. Although it resembles my old one, it is not an exact replica by any means, and I will need time to orient myself to it and perhaps make adjustments in terms of balance, internal processes, and the like."

"In other words, you're going to need time to break in your new body, like a new pair of shoes."

"Exactly."

"Then I look forward to showing you around in *two* months' time," I said.

INFILTRATION

Chapter 10

Li and I spent another thirty minutes or so chatting, which primarily consisted of me talking about the things going on in my life — training with the other super teens, the upcoming exhibition, etc. For the millionth time, I felt bad for him being constantly cooped up in Mouse's lab. Thus, as always, when I got ready to leave, I promised to come visit him again soon.

I teleported back out into the main lab, wanting to say goodbye to Mouse and BT before I left. This time when I appeared, however, there was another Alpha League member in the room: Vixen. I immediately and automatically raised my mental and empathic defenses.

Vixen was a Siren, a stunningly beautiful empath with the power to manipulate the opposite sex. She'd never really given me cause for alarm, but I had a natural tendency to keep my guard up around her.

She was actually standing off to one side of the lab when I appeared, talking to Mouse. Whether she sensed my entrance empathically or not I didn't know, but almost the second I popped in, Vixen turned towards me. She seemingly excused herself from the conversation with Mouse, then made a beeline for me. Face resolute and luxurious red hair bouncing, she walked with a determined and tenacious stride that told me that she had something very serious on her mind.

"You," she said as she got close to me, almost hissing. "We need to talk."

Gripping my arm at the elbow, she practically frogmarched me to a far corner of the room. Once there, she let go and crossed her arms in front of her.

"Do you recall a little chat we had before you left for the Academy?" she asked in a hushed tone.

"Yeah," I whispered in reply. "You asked me to do well so that I could basically come back here and be Mouse's assistant."

That wasn't exactly true. Some tests I'd taken to determine my academic placement level had shown me to have a high IQ. That being the case, Vixen had wanted me to come back from the Academy a scholastic genius capable of working with Mouse on some of his projects. Long story short, Vixen had been concerned that Mouse wasn't having enough intellectually stimulating conversations, which might result in him becoming bored and leaving the Alpha League (and her).

"Yes, so why is *she* here?" Vixen asked, nodding in the direction of BT.

"Because you asked me to become the intellectual peer of a guy whose IQ has more digits than my zip code! I couldn't fill that order, so I found someone who could."

"No, you didn't just find 'someone.' 'Someone' would have been a wizened little man with a beard down to his belly — maybe brilliant and just a little bit absentminded, but charming nevertheless. 'Someone' would have been some nervous nelly with freckles, unkempt hair, beer-bottle glasses, and a massive overbite. 'Someone' would have been a nerdy klutz with ten degrees who wore pocket protectors and had never been on a date. 'Someone' would have—"

"Okay, I get it," I said, cutting her off.

"Well, you didn't get any of those types of people. What you showed up with was a bikini model in a lab coat."

"Why are you getting all bent out of shape about this *now*? I made the intros way back around the time I left for the Academy, and BT's been coming around here for weeks at this point. What's changed to put you on the warpath?"

"That," she said, tilting her head towards Mouse and BT, both of whom had just burst out laughing at some joke between them. Still chuckling too intensely to speak, BT laid a hand upon Mouse's chest, as if needing his support to stay standing. There was a harsh intake of breath from Vixen, who curled her fists at her side. Empathically, I felt jealous anger rolling off her in waves.

"They're getting just a little too chummy in my opinion," Vixen continued, clearly vexed. On their part, Mouse and BT continued chortling, paying virtually no attention to us, which wasn't particularly surprising. Despite the intensity of our conversation, Vixen and I were still practically whispering.

"I think you're blowing this way out of proportion," I said. "First of all, BT's a clone. That's not a real person over there."

"She looks real enough to me."

"But she's not — not in the sense that you and I are. Mouse developing feelings for her would be like you falling in love with someone's pinkie toe."

"Does that look like a pinkie toe to you?" she asked, hooking a thumb in BT's direction. "There's an old saying: if it looks like a duck, and walks like a duck, and quacks like a duck, guess what? It's a duck!"

"Regardless, why are you telling *me* all this? You should just talk to Mouse about how you feel."

"I'm talking to you about it because this is your mess. They're only hanging out because *you* introduced them."

"I did that as a favor for *you*! You're talking like I'm this mad scientist, and their friendship is some monster I created in my lab."

"That's exactly what it is. *You* put this Frankenstein together," she said, poking me in the chest to emphasize her point. "I expect *you* to take it apart."

With that, she walked back towards Mouse and BT, but not before putting on a happy face that I found somewhat disconcerting because I could feel the sea of emotions roiling underneath.

Chapter 11

"She's insane," I said, speaking to Electra by cell phone from my bedroom.

After Vixen and I had finished talking, I'd said goodbye to Mouse and BT, and then teleported home. After a quick lunch, I'd gone to my room to rest for a minute. As is often the case, stretching out on your bed to rest is typically a bad idea (unless your plan is actually to take a nap). Before I knew it I was snoozing, and I didn't wake until Electra called me a couple of hours later. I had quickly filled her in on everything that had happened at HQ, including my conversation with Vixen.

"She's not insane," Electra replied. "Vixen's just in love."

"Well, you're in love, and you haven't gone into a jealous rage about anything."

"Says who?"

"You've gone into a jealous rage about something?"

"No, idiot. Who says I'm in love?"

"Huh? Well, uh...I kind of thought..." I stammered, caught flatfooted by her question.

"I think your empathic abilities are off," she said, laughing haughtily. "You've been picking up a false positive, buddy."

"So it would seem," I said, laughing as well as I caught on. This was kind of a game between us, with Electra occasionally acting as though she were still on the bubble in terms of how she felt about me. Basically, as someone had casually mentioned, it was a subtle reminder to me to not take her for granted.

"Anyway, you need to look at this from Vixen's point of view."

"Which is?"

"She's a Siren, with the ability to completely influence and beguile the opposite sex. She's never had to work to maintain a man's interest."

"But Mouse is different," I tacked on. "Yes, I know all that."

"And she's got that whole DNA thing going."

I didn't say anything, but I knew what she was talking about. Sirens, despite their reputations as incorrigible flirts, actually bond with a single man for life. When they meet the right individual, something in their genetic makeup is triggered so that the man in question becomes the only person they can be with romantically. Mouse was that man for Vixen.

That said, Mouse apparently had some level of immunity to Vixen's charms as a Siren. In essence, he was probably the only man she couldn't truly force to love her.

"So," I finally said, "Mouse isn't fully susceptible to her charms, she thinks she has a rival, and she's feeling jealous."

"All of which is undiscovered country for her. She's dealing with things — emotions — that probably no other Siren has ever had to face."

"No wonder she's going crazy."

"She's not going crazy!" Electra insisted. "She just doesn't know how to process any of this."

I sighed. "Okay, it's none of my business, but I'll say something to Mouse about it."

"Great!" she said, and I could imagine the smile she had on her face.

"But you've got to talk to Vixen and ask her to try to stay on an even keel."

"Will do."

I shook my head, thinking how twisted the concept of romance had to be when a couple of teenage lovebirds had to advise adults on relationship issues.

"Are you ready for tonight?" Electra asked, changing the subject.

"I suppose," I said. As previously noted, I felt better about the exhibition since my conversation with Mouse, but still wasn't particularly enthused about it.

"What time are you planning to show up?"

"The show kicks off at seven o'clock, so I guess I'll show up around then."

"That's just the live broadcast. You do know some events are going to be prerecorded, right?"

"I think I heard something along those lines, but I hadn't really thought about attending."

"Jim, some of our friends are going to be in the prerecorded segments. It would be nice if we showed up for moral support."

I opened my mouth to speak, but nothing would come out. She was right, of course. I had been so focused on the issues that I was having with being part of the exhibition that I hadn't really given much thought to anyone else. Aside from Electra, who was also going to be on during the live broadcast, I'd been walking around almost oblivious to what any of the other super teens would be doing.

"Jim?" Electra said. "Are you there?"

"Yeah, sorry. I'm here," I said. "Now that I think about it, do you think you could email me the schedule for the prerecorded events? I believe I'd like to attend after all."

****

It was around three o'clock when I finally got off the phone with Electra. Immediately after ending the call, I rolled off the bed. Even though I wasn't tired, I didn't want to run the risk of falling asleep again now that I was committed to attending some of the activities taking place before the live show. I went to the bathroom to freshen up, then went to get my attire for the evening.

A pair of bifold doors served as the entrance to my closet. I pulled them open, noting the seven-foot metal rod inside running from one side of the closet to the other, on which most of my clothes were hung. Above the rod was a shelf that was about the same length as the rod and with about two feet of depth. The shelf was packed from side-to-side with numerous boxes of various sizes. The contents of the boxes varied in the extreme, from winter clothes (sweaters, thermals, and the like) to favorite childhood toys to items earmarked for charity. However, there was one container in particular that I was looking for, and I knew exactly where it was.

Sitting at the far left of the closet shelf were a number of shoeboxes stacked all the way to the ceiling. Telekinetically, I pulled them down, balancing them so carefully that they didn't so much as move a hair's breadth in relation to each other, and then sat them on the floor next to the bed. Tucked on the shelf behind where the shoeboxes had been was a small metallic briefcase — the kind you always see cuffed to some guy's hand in the movies, with a combination lock and all that jazz. I teleported it into my hand.

I flopped down on the bed, placed the briefcase on my knees and just stared at it. Physically, I hadn't actually held it in a long time — two years. Being fireproof (as well as bulletproof, among other things), it was one of the few items that had survived the fire that had consumed our original home. However, even after I'd come across it in the charred remains of our house, I had simply teleported it to our new digs rather than actually touch it.

The front of the briefcase held two latches, each of which had a three-digit combination lock next to it. Moreover, in the center space between the two latches was a glowing red square with a similarly-sized ID plate next to it.

Deciding not to waste any more time, I spun the two combination locks to the proper sequence, and then pressed my right thumb to the ID plate. The red light on the front flashed twice, then turned green. At the same time, the two latches popped open of their own accord. I opened the briefcase and then stared at its contents, which I hadn't thought I'd ever lay eyes on again: my Kid Sensation costume.

Of course, the black-and-red outfit (and cape) that I was holding hadn't been known as that when I'd worn it to the Super Teen Trials two years earlier. In fact, I'd completely neglected to pick a superhero name in advance and had been forced to make one up on the spot.

I set the briefcase on the floor and stood up, holding the costume out in front of me by the shoulders. The briefcase was hermetically sealed, so the costume was as clean and fresh as the day I'd put it in. I had grown a few inches and filled out a little more since I'd last worn it, but that wouldn't matter since I would be shifting shape, taking on the appearance I'd had when I participated in the Super Teen Trials.

A short time later I slipped downstairs, fully decked out in my old costume and wearing the face that everyone knew as Kid Sensation. About the only thing different than the way I'd appeared two years earlier was that I chose to maintain my actual height, since some growth was to be expected. (Fortunately, my costume was of the one-size-fits-all variety so it stretched to accommodate the change.)

Mom and Gramps looked me over, with my mother pinching my cheek and making cutesy comments about my outfit that would make me die of embarrassment if anyone ever heard them. It was my grandfather, however, who I was focused on; basically, I wanted his approval that I was actually pulling off the look. Superhero costumes are sometimes very unflattering to the people wearing them, and there would be nothing worse than appearing on national TV looking like a doofus in an ill-advised wardrobe. Thankfully, Gramps gave me the thumbs-up via a subtle nod.

With that, I teleported to the exhibition.

Chapter 12

The exhibition, although referred to in the singular by almost everyone, was actually set up at multiple venues as opposed to one single location. It was just too difficult to try to have one staging area to accommodate everything the producers were trying to do. That said, there was a broadcast stage at a local television station serving as the central hub of all the action, and that's where I teleported to.

As luck would have it, the television station in question was actually the place where my induction ceremony (and subsequent fight) had taken place two years earlier. That being the case, appearing there again brought up a lot of unbidden memories, but it couldn't be helped. In essence, Electra hadn't had a complete schedule of events that were being prerecorded; she'd only noted the activities that she was interested in seeing. Thus, I had decided to come by the command post to see if a more extensive list was available.

I popped up in a hallway right outside the studio control room. Various members of the television crew were running to and fro at a frenzied pace, completely preoccupied with tasks such as looking at info on clipboards, chatting on walkie-talkies, or simply trying to get from Point A to Point B. So engrossed were they with what they were doing that my sudden appearance didn't really startle anyone the way it usually does when I teleport. Hopefully one of them would know where I could get a schedule of events.

"Excuse me," I said to a young guy with a goatee who was passing by, mumbling to himself as he looked over a sheet of paper. He held up a finger in a wait-just-a-second gesture, but kept on walking without pause.

"Pardon me," I said to a twenty-something young lady who was headed in the opposite direction and speaking into a two-way radio. She held up a palm in my direction and wagged it from side to side while shaking her head in a negative manner, as if to indicate "Not now," while she berated someone about the lighting on the broadcast stage.

This wasn't going well. Getting anything out of these people was like trying to hitch a ride at the Daytona 500. Apparently I needed to be a little more forceful.

With that in mind, I reached out and snagged the elbow of a pretty brunette who was walking past with a headset resting around her neck, her attention fully occupied by the computer tablet she was carrying. Apparently she didn't appreciate being waylaid in the hallway, because she had a knee-jerk reaction to being touched; her head snapped around, and then she stared at my hand like it was a tree frog secreting toxin on her.

"I'm sorry," I said, releasing her elbow, "but I'm trying to get my hands on the agenda for the exhibition."

"Try the producer," was her immediate response, and she turned to walk away.

I stepped into her path. "Uh, where can I find the producer?"

The brunette let out a grunt of frustration. "Check the control room," she said, and then stomped off like a movie monster trying to destroy Tokyo. (Honestly, these TV people were like sharks that had to keep moving in order to stay alive. If I'd held her up a second more, she probably would have developed a facial tic.)

INFILTRATION

I looked towards the control room, which actually had a glass wall allowing me to see in. Like the hallway, the room appeared to be full of people, although most seemed to be technicians sitting at workstations of some sort, fiddling with various types of equipment: a video switcher, audio console, character generator, and so on. The far side of the room consisted of a video wall, with numerous monitors displaying a multitude of images.

I walked over to the door, preparing to step inside. As it turns out, the room was locked. In fact, there was a little pad next to the door that was obviously the place for a key card (which I did not have) to be swiped.

No big deal.

I phased and stepped into the control room, then solidified. Just as it was when I initially teleported to the studio, no one in the control room was really paying attention to me. (It also probably helped that I was actually at the back of the room.) Everyone was listening to a bespectacled, middle-aged guy in a blue polo shirt who stood at an angle in front of the video wall, staring at the monitors. He seemed to be verbally going down some sort of checklist, to which the technicians in the room responded, with indecipherable gibberish in the background that originated from the monitors all being on simultaneously. Going on gut instinct, I assumed the man in blue was the producer.

"Excuse me," I said when he paused to draw breath. All eyes in the room turned towards me; the only chatter in the room now was from the monitors. "I was looking for the producer."

"That's me," the man in the blue polo said. "Who are you, and how'd you get in here?"

Rather than answer, I phased my hand and swiped it through a nearby tabletop.

"A super," the man said. "Figures."

"What, the costume didn't give it away?" I asked.

"Hey," the producer said defensively, "we've had capes coming in and out of this place for a week! Plus, half my techs showed up in costume today, like it's Halloween or something."

Glancing around, I noticed that he was right; several of the people in the room were dressed as superheroes.

"I didn't mean to interrupt," I said. "I was just trying to get my hands on a schedule of events."

The man grunted in annoyance and then reached for a stack of papers sitting on a desk near him. He flipped through them, then pulled loose a sheet that had info typed on both sides and held it out in my direction.

"Here, take it," he said. "We've got a million of them floating around here."

"Thanks," I said, as I stepped towards him and took the sheet.

"Hmmm," the producer muttered, giving me an intense look as I was about to turn and leave. "I know I've seen your costume before but I just can't place it. Who are you again?"

"Kid Sensation," said a voice behind me before I could even answer the question.

The monitors were still the only source of sound in the room, but at the mention of my *nom de guerre*, the entire vibe in the place changed tremendously and immediately. There were a few sharp intakes of breath and a number of bug-eyed stares (including the producer) as almost everyone in the room suddenly devolved into a jittery bundle of nerves, like they were afraid I was going to set off a bomb.

I ignored them as I turned to see who had spoken. Standing in the doorway with a smile on her face was world-famous talk show host Sylvia Gossett.

"Holy smoke," Sylvia murmured. "It really *is* you."

"Hey, Sylvia," I said. "How've you been?"

Looking svelte and captivating, she ignored my question and instead stepped forward and gave me a fierce but unexpected hug. Fortunately, I recovered from my surprise quickly enough to hug her back.

Sylvia had been a low-level TV news reporter when we had first met at the Super Teen Trials two years earlier. While all of the newsmen with name recognition had been focused on popular super teens like Paramount, I had talked Sylvia into interviewing me, an unknown (and therefore presumably unremarkable) participant in the trials.

Following my on-air fight (and subsequent disappearance), however, that footage proved to be the mother lode for Sylvia, and she mined it for all it was worth. As the only person to have interviewed Kid Sensation (as I later came to be called), she catapulted to fame and now had her own nationally syndicated talk show, her own production company, and more. Not bad for someone still under thirty.

After a few seconds, Sylvia stepped back from hugging me and looked me over.

"You've barely changed," she said. "Where have you been all this time?"

"On sabbatical," I answered. "Anything interesting happen while I was gone?"

INFILTRATION

She laughed at that, then took my arm in hers. "Come on. Let's go someplace where we can talk."

INFILTRATION

Chapter 13

We ended up going to Sylvia's dressing room, which was a small suite populated by, among other things, a luxurious couch, a couple of easy chairs, and a dresser with a lighted mirror. Sylvia's assistant and a makeup artist were actually waiting inside when we arrived, but she chased them out so we could speak privately. She plopped down on the couch, kicking off her shoes, while I sat down in one of the chairs facing her.

"I hope you aren't upset," she said.

"About what?" I asked.

"The producer. He didn't know who you were."

"Should that be a problem?"

"It is for some capes. They like being recognized, and feel insulted when they're not. Trust me, I've interviewed enough of them to know."

"Not me. I couldn't care less, although it did seem a little odd since almost everybody on the planet has seen my *Fight Club* audition."

She laughed. "You have to remember, the attention span of the average person is only about ten seconds. Your fight was like two years ago."

"So you're saying everyone's forgotten about me?"

"Not exactly, but think about it. There's a world-famous photo of some guys eating lunch atop a New York skyscraper with a whole cityscape below them. You know it?"

"I've seen it," I said.

"Assuming they still looked the same, do you think you'd recognize any of those guys if you saw them on the street?"

"Unlikely," I said with a frown.

"That's my point. Seeing them outside that photo removes their familiarity, even though most people have seen the picture before. Likewise, people will probably have a hard time placing you outside the context of that film clip."

"So basically, you're saying that I'm still in the public consciousness, just not in the public eye."

"That's an apt way to put it."

"And people aren't likely to recognize me — even in costume — unless I put myself in the proper context by getting into a fight."

"Maybe not even then," she said. "At the height of his popularity, comedic actor Charlie Chaplin purportedly entered a 'Charlie Chaplin Look-a-Like Contest' and didn't even place."

"Wow. That's got to be rough."

"Yeah. Just keep all this in mind if there's not a mad stampede to get your autograph today."

"I'll do that."

"Anyway," she said, changing the subject, "what have you been up to?"

I frowned a little, unsure of how to answer. Anyone listening in would have thought that we were old friends simply catching up, but the truth of the matter was that Sylvia and I didn't know each other at all. In fact, despite the extreme familiarity Sylvia had shown in hugging me, the entire time we'd previously spent in each other's company probably amounted to about ten minutes, max — including a roughly five-minute interview. Based on that, I'm not sure we could even call ourselves acquaintances. Thus, I felt obliged to give a somewhat impersonal response.

"Just the usual high school stuff," I said after a few seconds. "Homework, hanging out, etc."

"Ah, yes. I remember those days."

"The good old days?" I asked.

"Hey!" she exclaimed in mock indignation. "I'm not *that* old!"

"Really? There's an internet rumor that you're really in your eighties, but you've been keeping a lot of plastic surgeons busy by going under the knife regularly."

"Funny," she said sarcastically. "You should take that act on the road."

"Speaking of being on the road," I said, speaking sincerely, "it was nice of you to come here and host the exhibition. I was actually surprised when I heard that you were going to be the emcee. Normally they get some washed-up, B-list actor to be the front man, not someone of your stature."

"Actually, I volunteered."

I raised an eyebrow at that. "Really? Why?"

"Because of you! Once they told me Kid Sensation was going to be part of the show — the main event, in fact — it was a done deal for me."

I was a little perplexed (and it must have shown in my face), but she went on.

"I never got a chance to thank you before," she said.

"For what?"

"That interview you gave me. After your fight with the Alpha League, the whole world wanted to know about you, and I was the only one with any info. The networks played that clip so much that I became a household name. Next thing you know, I'm part of a national morning news show, then six months later I'm being courted to helm my own talk show. Flash forward another year, and I'm a media superstar — all in less than two years."

One would think that all of this was good news, but she spoke about it almost with sadness, and I could feel melancholy emanating from her.

"All that sounds great," I said. "But you talk about it like it's a problem."

She sighed, looking forlorn. "Part of the reason that the bigwigs at the media conglomerate I worked for started moving me up was because they thought I had some kind of nose for news after that interview — like I somehow sniffed you out, knew that you were special, and got you to talk to me. The truth, though, is the exact opposite; it was *you* who had to convince *me* to do the interview."

"No big deal," I said, shrugging. "Doesn't matter who convinced who. Six in one hand, half a dozen in the other. The main thing is that the interview happened and you experienced positive gains from it."

"Except I feel like a fraud. Everything I have in my life — all the success, all the adoration, all the fans — comes from that one moment, and I've been taking credit for it like it was something *I* did or set in motion. The truth of the matter is that I almost didn't do the interview."

"I know," I said, nodding, remembering how she had debated on whether to accept my offer to be interviewed.

"Long story short, I feel like my life since that moment has been one big lie, and I knew I'd never feel right about it until I talked to you, let you know how I feel. Thanked you."

"There's no need," I said. "You got where you are because you deserved it, and if it hadn't been the interview with me, it would have been something else."

She smiled. "That's nice of you to say, but I think we both know the truth. You're the reason I'm here, and I just wanted to express my gratitude."

"As I said, no thanks necessary."

"Well, be that as it may, you now have a friend for life. If there's anything I can ever do for you — any way I can ever help you — just let me know."

I simply nodded, acknowledging her offer.

INFILTRATION

Chapter 14

Sylvia and I chatted amiably for about another fifteen minutes, with me picking her brains about the various events on the schedule and their locations. Surprisingly, the more I heard, the more excited I actually became about everything that was going to take place. (There are few things that are quite as fun as watching supers put their powers on display — even powers that you yourself possess.) However, I pointedly avoided asking her or letting her tell me anything with respect to the competition that was scheduled to take place between me and Dynamo.

By the time I left, Sylvia's assistant, makeup artist, and a few other people were all dying to get into the room and had been banging on her door almost non-stop. Sylvia actually had a little time before she had to be in front of the cameras, but some of the events — which would be helmed by other reporters in the field — would actually be getting underway very soon. In fact, most of the exhibition broadcast was going to be prerecorded, with only a few events (like my own) actually being broadcast live.

I looked at the schedule I'd been given (which also included the names of many of the participants), trying to figure out which activities would be the most interesting. There were speed contests, strength competitions, and more — basically the super teen equivalent of a track meet. A number of them were slated to begin at the same time but at different sites — not really a problem for a teleporter, but I didn't like the idea of popping up all over the place like some hyperactive kid with too much sugar in his diet. Thus, I was trying to come up with my own itinerary regarding which events to attend. In the end, as suggested by Electra, I felt it was important to be supportive of my colleagues and made my decisions primarily based on which activities included teens from the Alpha League.

All in all, there were about five events that I felt I should attend. Not all of them were occurring at places I'd been to before (ergo, I couldn't teleport directly there), but I could get close enough and then zip over at super speed with no problem.

With that in mind, I teleported to the bottom of a mountainous area located in a state park about ten miles outside the city limits. This was to be the venue for a race between speedsters. The participants were to run along a scenic but twisting, curving hillside road all the way through the mountains — making certain to hit specific checkpoints along the way — and then back again. First one across the finish line, of course, would be the winner.

When I popped up, I got a bit of a surprise: there were hundreds of people present — most of them teens, and quite a few in superhero costumes. Several were even dressed as Kid Sensation, which shocked me until I remembered that a number of savvy clothing manufacturers had pounced on the popularity of my fight clip and profited enormously by marketing copies of my costume and likeness. I sighed; everything always seemed to come back to that stupid, on-air brawl.

There was a bright side, however. With so many other people in costume and several clones of me walking around, the real Kid Sensation didn't stand out. The companies that made the costumes had done an excellent job in terms of duplicating my outfit — especially when they didn't have the original to work with — and for the umpteenth time it occurred to me that I should be receiving royalties.

While the crowd of onlookers I found myself in seemed to be a shapeless mass, there actually was some level of order to its randomness. The spectators were formed up on both sides and the rear of the starting line, creating a huge *U* around those competing in the race. Many of those present, especially the teens, seemed to be rabid fans of one speedster or another, and they screamed the names of their favorites so loudly that I knew they'd be hoarse the next day. They also held up homemade posters and signs as encouragement for their personal picks.

There were about twenty supers competing in the race. Looking out over the runners, I saw Pronto, a fifteen-year-old speedster from the Alpha League teens. He looked nervous as he stepped to the starting line along with his fellow competitors, and maybe he was right to be. Although he had good speed, I had the distinct feeling that he was a bit out of his depth here. Unfortunately, I was proven right when the race started just a few moments later.

Immediately after the starting gun fired, the runners streaked away at speeds almost too fast for the human eye to follow. Wind from their passage buffeted the crowd, kicking up dust and blowing away several posters (much to the dismay of the fans who had made them). I shifted into super speed, and the world went into slow motion all around me — except those participating in the race, who now appeared to be running at something akin to normal speed from my perspective. I then telescoped my vision in an attempt to keep the runners in view.

INFILTRATION

The race itself was structured somewhat differently than what one would normally expect. Although the runners had begun their trek in the area where the crowd was assembled, the actual start/finish line was about a mile up the road. Once they reached that juncture, the race would begin in earnest and they could run flat-out at full speed.

The reason for this odd setup was simple: some, if not all, of the runners were capable of exceeding Mach speed. Letting them start off at that pace in close proximity to the spectators would have been a very poor decision. The sound of a score of sonic booms sounding almost simultaneously would have certainly been startling — if not outright terrifying; somebody probably would have had a heart attack. Thus, the runners were initially limited to subsonic speed.

From what I could see, a flag marked the spot where the runners could go supersonic. As they reached that point, they really stepped on the gas, and the air filled with a number of sharp cracks as speedsters began breaking the sound barrier.

As I mentioned, the road that the racers were on had lots of twists and turns through the mountains, and — even with my vision enhanced — I soon lost sight of the runners. Fortunately, each of the speedsters was wearing a tracker, and as they passed various checkpoints their names appeared in the appropriate spot on a giant leaderboard located near the assembled fans.

The race itself covered a distance of approximately one hundred miles — fifty through the mountains and fifty back to the finish line. Sounds like a lot, unless you have an idea of exactly how fast some speedsters can run.

The winner of the race ended up being a guy known as Sol, which apparently stood for "speed of light." He was with a British team of supers known as the Golden Circle, and he finished the race — to much cheering and applause — in just under three minutes. He wasn't even breathing hard when he crossed the finish line.

Pronto finished in ninth place, and looked crestfallen at what he obviously felt was a subpar performance. While the winner was being presented with a trophy and asked for comments, I made my way over to where Pronto was standing, surrounded by several other Alpha League teens who were apparently trying to cheer him up by praising his performance.

"Hey, Pronto," I said, getting his attention. "Good race."

He looked at me like he didn't know who I was. "Uh…thanks."

"Don't get too wrapped up in this," I continued. "Remember, you're just fifteen. You're going to get faster."

"Yeah…uh…yeah," he replied, brow furrowing like he was trying to think of something to say. "Uh…Jim?"

"Yeah?"

Relief seemed to wash over him. "Okay, so it *is* you."

Now I was the one looking confused. "Of course it's me! Who else—"

And then I remembered: I had shapeshifted, and didn't look like the Jim he knew. I glanced around to make sure no one else was watching (other than our Alpha League colleagues, that is), and then changed my visage so that he could see my real face for a second, then shifted back to my Kid Sensation persona.

"I'm sorry," Pronto said. "So many people are in costume here, and there are a couple of guys who could pass as your twin. Kid Sensation's twin, that is. I mean—"

"I know what you mean," I said, cutting him off. "Anyway, you did great. You'll be faster than these other guys in no time."

I made small talk with Pronto and the other Alpha League teens for a few minutes, then said my goodbyes and prepared to teleport to the next event. This time it was Electra who I was going to see in action.

She had originally been slated to be part of the live broadcast, but a last-minute schedule change had resulted in her being moved up. (Bearing that in mind, it's a good thing I decided to attend the prerecorded events.)

Electra was involved in a true exhibition — an open display of her electrical powers in a small gymnasium before an audience seated on wooden bleachers. The producers had originally planned to showcase her talents in a local stadium that had metal bleachers, but once they realized the nature of her powers and how well metal conducts electricity, they moved it to a more appropriate venue.

I had never been to the gymnasium in question before, so I popped up at a familiar spot a few blocks away and then zipped over at super speed. Dressed in an alternate (and more alluring) version of her Alpha League costume and sporting tinted goggles, Electra was just getting started when I arrived, and she put on an outstanding show. She made light bulbs shine simply by holding them in her hand; she powered up various electrical devices, from toasters to televisions. She ionized the air and made a young girl's hair stand on end. She even jumpstarted a car that had been brought inside with a dead battery. All in all, it was a very impressive display of her powers.

After she finished, she spent a little time signing autographs. While I was waiting for her to get done, someone tapped me on the shoulder. I turned around to find Pronto standing there.

"We meet again," he said with a grin.

"I'm sorry," I said. "If I'd known you were headed here, I'd have given you a lift."

"No big deal," he replied. He nodded in Electra's direction. "She's great, isn't she?"

I nodded, and at the same time picked up on a powerful emotion sweeping through Pronto, ringing out like a church bell at midnight: Pronto had a crush on Electra.

It shouldn't have surprised me. Electra was not only pretty, but also a very nice person. Truth be told, I was aware of the fact that lots of guys had feelings for her — part of the curse of being an empath — but I wasn't concerned because I also knew the depth and sincerity of her feelings for me. That being the case, I simply ignored what I was picking up from Pronto, which was par for the course in my case; I usually ignored the vast majority of the emotions I picked up from others, much as normal people tend to tune out conversations going on around them.

While we waited for the crowd around Electra to thin out, I saw Smokey and Sarah headed our way. It shouldn't have surprised me that they were here; Smokey wasn't participating in the exhibition, so it was only natural that they would show up to root Electra on.

When they got close enough, Smokey extended a hand for Pronto to shake and then introduced Sarah, at the same time eyeing me warily. Emotionally, I felt confusion and conflict coming from him, and it took me a second to realize why.

<It's me, you jerk,> I said to him mentally, and felt his bewilderment fade.

<Sorry,> he responded. <I thought as much, but I don't think I've actually seen you put on your Kid Sensation face before.>

I broke off the mental link without replying as Sarah suddenly extended her hand to me, saying, "And you are…?"

Smokey and I broke out laughing at that, and it took a few minutes for her to process the fact that I was not only the Jim she knew as Electra's boyfriend, but — as she put it — the "world-famous Kid Sensation."

"More like the world-*in*famous Kid Sensation," I said.

I don't think Sarah believed it until I did another back-and-forth shift between my real face and Kid Sensation. She had known I was a super, but she had never pried about my power set so there's no reason she should have known about me.

After that, the four of us waited around making casual conversation until Electra was done signing her name for the last time. She came over and greeted us warmly. Despite the fact that I didn't look like my actual self, Electra had no trouble recognizing me. Thanks to her power, she could identify people by their bioelectric fields, which were as distinctive to her as faces or fingerprints.

"Thanks for being here, guys," she said. "I really appreciate the support."

"No problem," Sarah said.

"That's what friends are for," Pronto added.

"Thanks," Electra said. "And I'm sorry I missed your race, Pronto. How did it go?"

Pronto seemed over the moon that Electra wanted to hear about his escapades and started nervously prattling almost non-stop about every detail of his run.

As he spoke, Electra leaned towards my ear and whispered, "I really glad *you* were able to make it."

I responded telepathically, opening a channel between us. <I'm just glad I found out about it being part of the prerecorded events.>

<Yeah,> she said. <Vestibule insisted on being part of the live broadcast so they bumped me in order to put her on. I barely got notice of the change myself.>

I nodded in understanding. Vestibule was a teen teleporter, who also had a career as a high-profile fashion model. She was a member (in name only, for the most part) of a superhero team, and also a bit of a prima donna who tended to attract media attention, so I could understand why the producers of the exhibition would want her has part of the show. It also didn't surprise me at all that she would want to be on during prime time. In fact, I was stunned that she didn't demand the slot reserved for me and Dynamo.

<Well, it's nice to know my absence here would have been noted,> I said, turning my thoughts back to the present.

<Of course,> Electra replied. <If you weren't here, I'd really have to hustle to make it in time to see the triathlon.>

<Now the truth comes out,> I said, raising an eyebrow. <Is that all I am to you — an efficient mode of transportation?>

<Of course not,> she said, giving me a peck on the cheek. <You're also a convenient sugar daddy when I need some money.>

I groaned audibly in mock frustration, which Pronto mistook as a cue for him to wrap up his story. He did so and then excused himself, taking off in a blur of motion.

"Dude," Smokey said, as Sarah gave me a particularly hard look. "That was so not cool."

"It's not what it looked like," I said, then proceeded to explain.

After everything was put into context for them, Sarah and Smokey seemed willing to retract their stamp of disapproval. I made a mental note to apologize to Pronto later, and then asked Smokey and Sarah about seeing the triathlon with us. Once they replied in the affirmative, I teleported the four of us to where the triathlon was being held.

Chapter 15

The triathlon was apparently amongst the day's most popular events. Upon arrival, my friends and I found ourselves swimming in a sea of bodies, most of them wearing costumes. It was like some kind of clambake for superhero fans.

The venue for the triathlon — at least the beginning of it — was a multi-purpose sports complex used by the city's professional baseball and football franchises. The portion that we were currently in was a seventy thousand seat arena with a retractable dome ceiling. The place wasn't filled to capacity, but there were certainly a lot of people present.

The triathlon itself consisted of three activities: weightlifting, running, and swimming. The competitors, of which there were fifty, were first required to lift a total of thirty tons. The items to be lifted included a car (weighing two tons), a truck (five tons), an armored personnel carrier (ten tons), and a tank (thirty tons). They could be lifted in any combination in order to achieve the obligatory thirty tons. For instance, a competitor could lift the car fifteen times, the personnel carrier three times, the tank one time, and so on; in each case they would have lifted a total of thirty tons, which was what was mandated for the first part of the competition.

The running portion of the triathlon consisted of two full marathons. The first would begin right after the weightlifting and was designed to start in the stadium and end at a nearby beach. At that juncture, competitors were required to swim twenty-five miles out from shore and back. After the swim, the second marathon would commence, ending back at the sports complex. With all that the competitors were required to do, it was easy to see why there was so much excitement about this event.

"Looking at the number of people here, they should've made this the main event instead of me and Dynamo," I remarked to Smokey as we found some seats that gave us a clear view of the action. Unfortunately, everyone around us was standing, so we had to stand as well in order to see anything.

"I heard it was a real toss-up," he said. "Ultimately, the producers felt that the public's fascination with Kid Sensation would be a larger draw."

"I'm flattered," I said, without any hint of emotion. "By the way, where's Dynamo? It seems like this type of thing would be right up his alley."

"Don't you know?" he asked. "He's saving up all his energy for his face-off with you."

I frowned, not liking that. It sounded like Dynamo was taking this whole competition thing far more seriously than I was — which was exactly what I didn't want.

A tap on my shoulder caused me to look around, and I saw Pronto standing next to me again.

"Hey," I said. "This is the second time you could have thumbed a ride, if I'd known we were headed in the same direction."

"I figured we'd bump into each other here," he said. "Truthfully though, I like running. It's what I'm built for."

I nodded, understanding what he meant completely. Before I forgot, however, I launched into an explanation of what had happened before, with me seeming to be annoyed with his telling of the speed competition. Thankfully, Pronto seemed to be a good sport about it.

"No need to apologize," he said. "There was something I needed to do anyway."

With that, the conversation ended and I probably would have put Pronto out of my mind completely, except for the fact that I felt a slight tingling in my shoulder where he had initially tapped me. It didn't really hurt; it just felt like maybe he'd put a little extra zing into it when he was getting my attention.

Maybe a little payback, after all, for my mistimed grunt?

I didn't have much time to dwell on the issue, though, because the competitors started getting into position for the triathlon. As with the earlier race between speedsters, I telescoped my vision in order to get a better look at them, most of whom were unfamiliar to me.

And that's when I saw her.

INFILTRATION

Chapter 16

She wore a costume consisting of a black bodice and a dark red cape. She was tall, probably on par with my own six-foot frame, with a caramel complexion, fetching brown eyes, and clear, flawless skin. Her dark hair was intricately braided and hung down just past her shoulders, and her features were so captivating that I could have stared at her all day.

All in all, she was undoubtedly the most beautiful girl I'd ever seen, with an allure that went beyond my ability to describe. (No offense to Electra.)

I was so fascinated by this girl that I didn't even take note when the triathlon began. One second I was watching her standing there, looking beautiful, and the next she was off to the races.

She went straight to the thirty-ton tank, as I somehow knew she would. She lifted it without any effort whatsoever, set it back down, and was gone again — dashing out of the arena to start the first marathon. She was incredible.

I felt something tugging on my arm, pulling it towards the ground. I looked down and was surprised to see Electra below me, yanking on my wrist.

"Where exactly are you going?" she asked, surprised and confused.

I suddenly realized I was actually floating in the air several feet off the ground. It dawned on me then that, although I had not consciously intended to do it, I had been about to follow the girl in the black-and-red costume out of the stadium.

What was wrong with me?!

I floated back down to the ground. Fortunately there was so much frenzied yelling and screaming around us that nobody had really taken note of my antics. Nobody other than Electra that is, and she did not seem particularly happy.

"What are you trying to do?" she asked in a perplexed voice.

I gave a noncommittal answer about being lost in thought and forgetting where I was, but I don't think she bought it. She eyed me suspiciously, but I did my best to pretend that I didn't notice, turning my attention instead to the giant screens around the stadium that stayed focused on the competitors.

Frankly speaking, it really wasn't a competition. The girl who had captured my attention essentially ran away with the whole thing. She was one of only seven females competing in the triathlon, but there was no other competitor — male or female — who could catch her. She ran like the wind, she cut through the water like a torpedo, and, of course, she lifted the tank like it was a feather. The only person who came close was a bare-chested fellow known as the Pelagic Prince, who claimed to be the heir to an underwater kingdom, and even he was a distant second.

As the triathlon ended, Electra thrust a paper napkin at me that she'd gotten from somewhere.

"Here," she said.

"What's this for?" I asked.

"To wipe the drool from your chin."

I didn't take the napkin but I conceded her point. I was acting like some stupid, love-struck idiot, but it hadn't been intentional. I simply had no explanation for why I found that girl to be so fascinating. Speaking of

126

her, my conversation with Electra had distracted me enough that I hadn't caught her name when they announced her as the winner.

Oh well... It was probably for the best that I didn't know anything more about her. My reactions thus far with respect to her had been far from typical or exemplary. Reflecting back on my conversation with Sylvia, I sincerely felt that a ten-second attention span would suit me just fine if it would help break whatever hold this girl had somehow gotten on me.

I wasn't quite that lucky.

INFILTRATION

Chapter 17

I practically sleepwalked through the other early events, barely registering who the participants were or what the competitions were about. For a while, it was an effort to even maintain awareness of the friends who were with me; my thoughts were fully occupied with images of the girl from the triathlon. Still, I do know that Pronto took off again after the triathlon ended, while Electra, Smokey, Sarah, and I stayed together.

Gradually, however, my obsession (you couldn't call it anything else) lessened, and by the time of the live broadcast I was somewhat back to normal. At that point, however, I had been so distant — mentally and emotionally — that Electra was barely speaking to me.

Long story short, I spent a good part of the live broadcast essentially groveling before my girlfriend, trying to believably express remorse for behavior that I honestly had no true rationale for. Thankfully, my transgressions had been few and of limited duration. Thus, although she was still not completely over her anger, I was able to get back into Electra's good graces before I had to get in front of the cameras.

Because I'd spent much of the live show breaking in a new pair of kneepads, I really only had time to pay attention to one of the prime time events: the competition featuring Vestibule squaring off against Actinic, the young super who was supposed to render the explosive inert in the bomb scenario I had bungled. Oddly enough, it turned out to be one of the more interesting match-ups.

Having the power of teleportation made Vestibule a formidable adversary for almost anyone. Thus, it had come as a bit of a surprise when it was revealed the previous week that her opponent for the exhibition would be Actinic. Even more surprising, Actinic had actually volunteered.

The competition between them was set up to take place in the same gym where Electra had showcased her talents and was rather simple to boot: Vestibule and Actinic would be placed in a large room created in the center of the gym through the raising of four glass walls. Sitting on opposite sides of the room were two metal containers, one for each of them, with circular holes in the top. When the competition started, a jillion plastic, colored balls were going to drop down into the middle of the room from the ceiling. The two competitors were to find as many gold balls as possible in a two-minute period and drop them into their respective containers.

Each ball was sprayed with a chemical compound that was to identify its color. Whenever a ball was deposited into one of the containers, a sensor would read its chemical signature and either grant a point (for gold balls) or subtract one (for any balls that weren't gold). The winner would be the person with the most points at the end, as noted on a large monitor just outside the room housing the competitors.

Vestibule was representing a West Coast team called the A-List Supers; she was nominally a teen member, although she spent most of her time on the red carpet rather than going toe-to-toe with bad guys. Actinic was, of course, a teen from the Alpha League, so he had our support (along with that of many other locals sitting in the bleachers). Still, it looked like a less-than-favorable match-up, to say the least.

"This is going to be a slaughter," Smokey said. "All Vestibule has to do is teleport to wherever she sees a gold ball then teleport to her container."

"Sounds like she should have been pitted against another teleporter," Sarah said.

"Or at least a speedster," Electra added, finally allowing me to hold her hand again after an hour or two of rebuffs.

A buzzer sounded before I could make a comment, and plastic balls rained down around the competitors in the room.

Vestibule went into action immediately, winking in and out of existence as she teleported around the room looking for gold balls. As soon as she had one, she popped up next to her container and dropped it in. After about fifteen seconds, she had a comfortable lead.

On his part, Actinic hunted around patiently until he found a gold ball. Then he smiled, in a way that not only said that "I have a secret," but I-have-a-super-duper-extra-special-classified-off-the-record-you'll-never-guess-it secret. Then he raced over to his container.

Once there, still holding the gold ball, he reached down with his free hand and grabbed a blue one. He closed his eyes, clearly concentrating deeply for a second as his lips pressed together firmly. Then he opened his eyes, and one corner of his mouth tilted up into a cocksure grin as he dropped the blue ball into the container.

All four of us — along with a great number of other people — groaned collectively as we assumed that Actinic had put the wrong ball into the container. What followed next was stunned silence as we saw Actinic's gold ball count go to "1" on the monitor.

He picked up another ball — a red one this time — frowned in concentration, and then dropped it into the container. His count went to "2." A thunderous roar of support sounded from the crowd.

"How's he doing that?" Sarah asked, caught up in the excitement as Actinic reached for a third ball.

"He has the power to change the chemical composition of things!" I shouted, trying to make myself heard over the crowd. "He's altering the chemical spray on each ball so that the sensor in the container reads them all as gold!"

"It's genius!" Smokey yelled.

Actinic's count began to zoom as he basically reached down to grab any ball, held it for a second, and then dropped it into his container. An infectious frenzy swept through the crowd as they saw what many had assumed would be a rout being dominated by the underdog.

Clearly frustrated at how her initial lead started diminishing, Vestibule stared at Actinic to see what he was doing. She obviously didn't understand what was happening because — apparently thinking the answer was merely volume — she scooped up an armful of balls of various colors and dumped them into her container. Her score immediately decreased by double digits. Vestibule looked like she wanted to cry.

When the buzzer finally went off, signaling the end of the competition, the score was a lopsided 89-to-13, in favor of Actinic. However, following the exit of the competitors from the glass room, there was a heated exchange between Vestibule, some of her handlers, and the competition judges.

Actinic, obviously perplexed, simply stood to the side, enjoying the massive cheers and adoration of the crowd while those in charge tried to sort out whatever issues had arisen. After several minutes of debate, one of the judges came over and had a conversation with him. Actinic didn't seem happy about what he was being told, but in the end he simply nodded, a little stone-faced, and shook the hand of the judge who had been talking to him. The crowd, overwhelmingly behind Actinic, could sense that something was wrong and started booing and making catcalls.

Shortly thereafter, the judges called for silence, but had to wait a few minutes for things to settle down. Then they announced that — although the rules stated that the highest point total would win — the spirit of the competition was that the highest number of actual gold balls should determine the winner. That being the case, Vestibule had prevailed.

Personally, I didn't need to hear any more. I thought Actinic had done fantastic; it was exactly the kind of thinking and ingenuity that made someone a super worthy of the name. Moreover, he was accepting the loss (actually, being stripped, in my opinion) with good grace.

Followed by my friends, I quickly stepped down to the gym floor and over to Actinic.

"Congrats!" I said. "That was great!"

"Yeah," Smokey added. "You're the *real* winner here."

Sarah and Electra added their congratulations to ours, and kissed him on the cheeks.

"Thanks, guys," Actinic said, blushing.

Unfortunately, he didn't get a chance to say more than that because much of the crowd, following in our footsteps, had left the bleachers and come over to congratulate Actinic as well. Smokey, Sarah, Electra, and I remained in a tight formation, but were collectively pushed away from him. Sensing that there was nothing more to say here (and noting that I had to get to my own event soon), I teleported the four of us away.

Chapter 18

We popped up at a local shipping port, the site of the competition between me and Dynamo. I had actually been here several times before to pick up some equipment with Braintrust, so I was fairly familiar with the place. In teleporting Electra and our friends here, I had simply assumed that they'd want to be present to support me. Now that we had arrived, it suddenly occurred to me that I should have queried them about it first.

"Are you kidding?" Sarah asked, pooh-poohing my concerns. "Of course we want to be here!"

"Yeah, man," Smokey added. "I mean, you and Dynamo? This is what everybody's been waiting for."

It wasn't exactly what *I* had been waiting for, but I didn't need to hash out my concerns with anyone again. Time to just get this thing over with.

I had made us appear near the port's main office. At the moment, most of the action was centered on an open area near one of the piers, where quite a number of cameras and lights were set up. In fact, with it being dark outside, almost the entire pier was lit up, like some deity was shining a celestial flashlight on it.

For all I knew, however, maybe it was like this all the time. This was, in fact, one of the largest and busiest ports in the country. Thousands of shipping containers — as much as forty feet in length and filled with all kinds of goods — were shipped in and out of here like clockwork twenty-four hours per day. In fact, there were thousands of them stacked atop each other all over the place — as high as small buildings in some places.

INFILTRATION

Looming overhead and spread out along the pier were at least half a dozen gigantic port cranes. I could also see lots of other equipment nearby: forklifts, toploaders, reach stackers, and more. There were also railroad tracks that led in and out of the area.

All in all, the place looked like it was far too busy to have time to host the kind of affair we were here for.

"We're going to head on over," Smokey said, pointing towards the area with the lights and cameras. I nodded, noting not only that there were numerous television technicians hanging around, but — as with some of the earlier events — hundreds (maybe even thousands) of spectators present. Moreover, I could make out Sylvia Gossett and Dynamo standing in the midst of the cameras, apparently waiting on me. I took a deep breath, then teleported to where they were.

Sylvia was going through some kind of sound check when I popped up, while Dynamo merely stood nearby, just idling. I hadn't spent a lot of time in his presence, but was definitely acquainted with him. Tall, muscular, and with a noble bearing, he fit the super-strong hero archetype to a *T*.

Glancing at the spectators, I noticed for the first time that there were actually pedestrian crowd control barriers in place to keep them back, along with armed security. Presumably the steel, gate-like barriers were there for the fans' own safety — something to keep them out of the field of play when this bout between Dynamo and me was underway. Nearby, as at events I'd seen earlier in the day, huge screens had been set up to allow those assembled to follow the action.

A second or so after I appeared, the crowd noise began to die down. Sylvia, noting the change in ambient

135

sound, looked around and finally spied me — just as the spectators broke out into a booming cheer...for *me*. They were actually cheering for *me*.

I couldn't help but grin slightly at that. I raised my hand and gave the crowd a friendly wave. The cheers sounded even louder.

If he was at all surprised that I didn't look like myself, Dynamo didn't show it. He wandered over to shake my hand, smiling. "About time you showed up."

I reached out empathically, trying to tell if Dynamo had been speaking jovially or in irritation, but he was a jumble of conflicting emotions: excitement, annoyance, hope, dread. He was like a groom on his wedding day. That being the case, I couldn't get a read in terms of which emotions were actually reserved for me as opposed to anything else that might be going on.

He didn't immediately release my hand, and I thought for a second he was going to try to give it an extra hard squeeze — something you occasionally experience with jerks who have above-average strength (and often self-esteem problems) and a compulsion to project their own superiority. But when that didn't happen, I quickly reassessed and — noting that he had his other hand raised and was looking at the crowd rather than me — realized that he was priming me for a photo op. (The thousand-watt flashbulbs that started going off were also a clue.)

"Smile," Dynamo said between clenched teeth as he waved. "You look like someone just made you drink out of a toilet."

I half-snickered at that, and then just mimicked him, smiling and waving as the light from numerous camera flashes washed over us.

INFILTRATION

After about twenty seconds, he released my hand and we took a step back from each other. At that moment, Sylvia stepped between us, grinning and holding a microphone.

"You took your time," she muttered in my direction. "Could you have gotten here any later?"

She didn't wait for the smart-aleck reply that she probably knew was coming. Instead, she flicked on the microphone and began talking.

"Thanks for staying with us, ladies and gentlemen, and thank you for your generous donations up to this point," she said. "We've now come to the final event of the evening..."

Sylvia then launched into a well-prepared, two-minute spiel about Dynamo and me being gifted individuals with fierce competitive spirits, humble natures, blah, blah, blah. I tuned most of it out, but thankfully remembered to wave when my name was mentioned as they called Dynamo and me forward to start the competition.

The contest between us wasn't particularly complicated. Hidden all around the port were twenty specially-minted silver coins — ten for Dynamo and ten for me. We were each given a tracker that would lead us to the first of our respective coins. After retrieving the first coin, we were to head over to the port's rail yard, where two modified train engines sat on parallel tracks.

At the back of each train engine was a coin slot at about eye level. We were then to deposit our coins in the slot of our designated train engine, which would cause the locomotive to start moving. Depositing the coin would also trigger the tracker to show the location of the second coin, which we would subject to the same procedure —

as well as the third, fourth, and so on until we had found all ten of our respective coins. And with each coin deposited, the train engines would move further and faster down their respective tracks. The first to deposit all ten coins would win.

Obviously, any edge in this competition would probably come from the ability to get from Point A to Point B in the shortest amount of time — a piece of cake for a teleporter. I was amused (and almost insulted) that they'd selected this as a "contest" for me. Then again, I'm sure Vestibule felt a little cocky before her event, and only a strict interpretation of the rules had saved her bacon. Maybe there was more here than met the eye.

Unfortunately, I didn't have any time to try to figure out what the angle might be, because a few seconds later, they handed us our trackers and then the start gun fired.

Dynamo and I flicked on our trackers. A digital map appeared, set up along the contours of a directional grid with *North*, *South*, *East* and *West* marked. A red dot appeared on the map, obviously indicating the location of the first coin.

Dynamo and I began moving out at almost the same time, although in different directions. Like a lot of supers with enhanced strength, he was far faster than a normal person. However, I'd never seen any indication that he was as fast as a true speedster, so I didn't really have a lot of worries.

I shifted into super speed and took off. As I began to move, the map grid shifted as well, like a compass. Following the direction indicated by the tracker, I soon found myself among the stacks of shipping containers.

INFILTRATION

As I had previously noted, almost the entire port was lit up, like someone had plugged in a two-billion watt bulb overhead. I soon found out at least part of the reason for this: the whole place was practically littered with cameras. Some were strung on lines overhead, others were affixed atop shipping containers, and still more were set up at ground level.

It made sense, of course. This match between me and Dynamo was taking place live. With that in mind, they obviously needed footage of what we were doing to keep everyone who was watching — whether they were couch potatoes following the action at home or part of the crowd viewing everything on nearby jumbo screens — engaged.

I put the cameras out of my mind and focused on the tracker, which led me to a narrow opening between two containers. It was only about six inches wide, and thus far too tight for me to even shimmy into sideways in my current state.

I phased the two containers, making them insubstantial, and simply walked down the narrow corridor (if it could be called such). When I reached the point where the tracker said the coin was, I looked down; there was nothing there.

I looked at the tracker again and confirmed that I was in the right spot.

Hmmm... Maybe they buried it?

The ground in this area was actually concrete and none of it looked fresh or new, but I squatted down anyway and closed my eyes, concentrating. I focused on making my hand insubstantial enough to pass through physical matter, but solid enough to feel anything it might encounter. When I felt my hand was properly phased, I swept it back and forth through the ground. I could feel rebar, bottle caps and a mishmash of other items, but no coin.

I stood up and looked at the tracker again. There was no doubt I was in the right spot, but maybe... I rubbed my chin in thought.

The tracker was only capable of showing location in two dimensions, like a sheet of paper that only has length and width. If you lay an object — say, a coin — directly on the paper, you can pinpoint its location just using length and width. (For example, it might be resting on the paper five inches from the top and two inches from the left side.)

However, if you place the coin beneath the paper, you'll need another dimension — depth — to figure out exactly where it is. Likewise, if the coin is above the paper, it might cast a shadow down, giving you a two-dimensional hint of where it's located, but you still need a third dimension (height) to figure out exactly where the coin itself is.

I looked up. There, stuck to the side of one of the containers with clear packing tape, was the first coin. Of course, I had phased it along with the rest of the container, but it took a nanosecond to make it solid again, and it dropped down into my open palm.

Grinning to myself, I got ready to teleport to the rail yard when I caught sight of one of the cameras focused on me. At that point, I recalled that millions of people were watching at home, and I remembered Mouse's advice about putting on a good show.

With that in mind, I changed tactics and went with super speed, zipping over to where the train engines were located. Dynamo was just leaving the area when I got there, presumably in search of his second coin. I watched his train engine starting to pull away for a second, and then placed my coin in the slot of my own locomotive. I watched to make sure it started moving, then dashed away to find coin number two.

This time, it was a bit easier. The tracker led me directly beneath the operator cabin of one of the port cranes. Again finding nothing on (or in) the ground, I assumed that the coin must be above me.

The crane itself was several hundred feet in height, and the cabin was located close to the top. I flew up and, after a quick inspection, found the second coin on the roof of the cabin. I flew back down to the ground and streaked over to the rail line. My train engine had moved about one hundred feet and was starting to slow down when I inserted the second coin. Reenergized, it started picking up speed again. (I couldn't help but notice that Dynamo's locomotive was already farther down the track, meaning that he had already deposited his second coin.)

I zoomed off in search of coin number three...

****

Although I hated to admit it, this little competition between me and Dynamo was actually turning out to be fun. Occasionally, as I ran back and forth looking for coins, I would catch snippets of commentary from Sylvia, who was expertly calling the action like a play-by-play announcer at a football game (and actually doing a fine job of making both Dynamo and myself look like heroes just for participating).

The best thing, however, was the crowd. They cheered exuberantly whenever one of us found a coin and whenever we put them in the locomotive slots, and it felt great to know that I had their support. I suddenly had a better understanding of what Mouse had meant about having the general public in your corner.

As our coins never seemed to be located in close proximity, Dynamo and I initially only saw each other in passing — usually as he was leaving the area with the rail tracks and I was coming in, but around the fifth coin I caught up to him; I passed him around the seventh. Nevertheless, at the ninth coin we were practically in a dead heat, with both of us putting our coins into the slots at the same time. That's when things got interesting.

As we had been told, depositing each successive coin into the slot on the train engines made them go farther and faster than before. Still, through the first eight coins, the locomotives had only traveled about three miles from the starting point. However, when Dynamo and I inserted our ninth coins — practically at the same time — the two engines let out twin shrieks that took both of us by surprise and then went flying down the tracks like they had rockets attached to them, sparks shooting from the wheels.

For a second, both of us just stared at the locomotives roaring down the rails, and I was absolutely certain that there was some kind of malfunction. Then it dawned on me that this was intentional.

I turned and took off, in search of the last elusive coin. My departure seemed to bring Dynamo back to himself, because a second later he was in motion...and right behind me. It seemed that this time, the last coin for each of us was located in the same place.

INFILTRATION

Our trackers led us right up to the end of an area marked as "Pier 3," a broad walkway that extended out over the waters of the bay. By that time, my speed had allowed me to pull away from Dynamo somewhat, so I stopped at the edge of the pier, noting that the tracker indicated that the last coin was below me.

My costume was waterproof, but I still hadn't planned on getting wet. Discretion being the better part of valor, I decided to check to make sure that coin number ten wasn't simply taped to the underside of the pier or something.

As I was squatting down and preparing to phase my hand through the pier, Dynamo showed up. He never hesitated, running straight at me like a crazed bull trying to gore a blind matador. I phased, thinking that perhaps — in single-minded pursuit of victory — he had somehow failed to see me. I needn't have bothered.

When he was about ten feet away, Dynamo suddenly leaped high into the air, jumping in an arc that I realized would take him over me and towards the water just off the edge of the pier. While airborne, he tucked his legs in and turned a flip directly overhead, and then straightened out as his body started its downward trajectory. He hit the water like an Olympic diver, barely creating a plop — despite still having the tracker in his hand. I couldn't help smiling, thinking that I had to give the guy props for showmanship.

A second later I realized that he'd had the right idea, as my search on the underside of the pier turned up nothing. The coin was undoubtedly submerged.

So much for not getting wet. I leaped off the pier and into the water, probably far less gracefully than Dynamo had.

Below the surface, it was disturbingly dark. I cycled my vision through the electromagnetic spectrum until I could see almost as well as in daylight, and then began swimming straight down towards the last coin, as indicated by the tracker.

Arms and legs moving at super speed, I cut through the water as if fired from a gun. Ahead of me, on the floor of the bay, I could see Dynamo holding some kind of steel chest about the size of a loaf of bread. He ripped it open like it was paper, reached inside, and pulled out a silver coin.

He dropped the remains of the case, the two halves slowly drifting down next to a similar case that was also on the bay floor — presumably mine.

Dynamo waved at me as I reached the bottom, and it occurred to me that he must have enhanced vision of some sort to be able to see through the murky water at that depth. He squatted and then quickly extended his legs, driving himself towards the surface. I phased the other case, swiped my hand through it, and retrieved my last coin before turning and heading back up myself.

I could see Dynamo up above me, making a beeline for the surface. Although my arms and legs moved so fast as to be nothing but blurs, each of Dynamo's strokes, while not as numerous as mine, were far more powerful and propelled him towards the surface like rocket. In short, while I was undoubtedly much faster on land, in the water we were more evenly matched.

That said, I did manage to gain on him, but not enough to keep him from breaking the surface first. I wasn't very far behind, though, and once I got out of the water, I was going to make him eat my dust. As my head broke the surface, though, I received quite the surprise: a sharp crack in the air that I immediately recognized. A sonic boom.

No...it couldn't be.

I flew up out of the water and landed on the pier, then took off like a bullet, running in the direction of the locomotives while simultaneously telescoping my vision.

The train engines were still moving away at top speed and were probably ten miles away from us. I scanned the area between myself and the locomotives, and saw what I was dreading: Dynamo. And he was running at Mach speed.

That faker! All this time, in addition to super strength, he also had super speed!

At the rate he was going, I didn't think I'd be able to catch him, not before he reached his locomotive. Still, I had to try.

I turned on the jets, running for all I was worth. I could hear the crowd cheering madly, but forced myself to ignore them. All that mattered was catching Dynamo.

Frankly speaking, I could have made better time if I went airborne and actually started flying. For some reason, though, it was important to me to win this the way I'd been playing all along — with my feet on the ground. It had, unexpectedly, been a lot of fun, and taking to the sky — like teleporting at this juncture — would have somehow cheapened the experience. I might lose, but that seemed like a very minor thing at the moment.

I was so wrapped up in my thoughts that I almost failed to realize that I was gaining on Dynamo. Not just gaining on him, but seriously cutting into his lead. Had he pulled up lame or something? Unlikely; Dynamo was one of the nigh-invulnerable set. There was very little that could really hurt him.

Still, as I caught up to him, I gave him a thorough look-see, and from what I could tell, he seemed fine. Even empathically, I didn't pick up on any sensation of pain, just iron will and determination. Then the truth hit me.

Dynamo *didn't* have super speed, not really. It wasn't truly part of his power set. He was actually more like a cheetah, with an adrenaline-fueled burst of speed that only lasted a short time. Thus, I was now passing him easily.

I made sure I put a little distance between us, then eased up off the gas a little. I didn't need to win by a country mile. In fact, at the moment, winning in and of itself seemed a lot less important than what the matchup between me and Dynamo represented. This was the kind of friendly competition that people enjoyed. This was the kind of contest that built camaraderie. This was the—

Something whizzed by my ear, so close that I shirked a little. To say I was surprised would be an absolute understatement. There's practically nothing that ever passes me when I'm moving at super speed, so I had been caught almost completely off-guard.

Looking closely, I saw the thing that had almost clipped me: a round object of shiny metal.

Unbelievable! It was Dynamo's coin. Still moving at super speed, I glanced back to where Dynamo himself was. He was no longer running, having stopped and apparently thrown his coin towards the slot on his locomotive.

I had to admire the guy's grit and tenacity. Like a baseball player with a hundred-mile-per-hour fastball,

Dynamo could throw much faster than he could actually run. In short, this was a race again.

I hit the gas and started gaining on Dynamo's coin, my competitive fire (and the desire to win) reignited by my opponent's throw. After a few moments, I had caught it and actually had the ability to pull ahead, but decided to keep it close. We were getting near the locomotives, but I had a few seconds to admire what Dynamo had done.

It was unquestionably the finest throw I had ever seen. The trajectory, the accuracy, the sheer power behind it... It all told me a lot and more about just how good Dynamo actually was. In terms of supers, he really was going to be one of the best.

Unfortunately, his best wasn't going to be good enough today — not simply because I was going to beat him, but because, as we got closer to the locomotives, I could see that the angle of his coin was slightly off. It was slowly tilting such that, while it would undoubtedly hit the slot, it would be so slanted that it wouldn't go in the hole as intended.

Too bad. The crowd would have gone nuts if something like that happened, even if he didn't win. It would be so over-the-top that people would probably donate like crazy. We might even set a new fundraising record.

Hmmm...why not? It's for a good cause.

Decision made, I telekinetically reached out for Dynamo's coin, stopping its angular digression without disturbing its forward momentum. Held steady, it was right on target as the distance between it and the slot closed.

INFILTRATION

Exercising some dramatic license, I extended my own arm, hand out, with my last coin gripped between my thumb and forefinger. The two coins were neck-and-neck; it was going to be a photo finish.

As we reached the locomotives, the other coin slid neatly into its hole a split second before I pushed my own into its slot, making Dynamo the undisputed winner of the competition.

INFILTRATION

Chapter 19

All of the participants (at least those who didn't fly immediately out of town) met at Jackman's after the exhibition. Now that the pressure of performing had passed, we could relax and enjoy each other's company.

The exhibition itself had actually wrapped up about two hours earlier. Following the end of the broadcast, most of us had retreated to our respective homes, hotel rooms, or what have you in order to freshen up and change.

Personally, using super speed always kicks my metabolism into high gear, so — in addition to changing both my attire and my appearance after teleporting home — I also wolfed down three ham-and-cheese sandwiches, a pack of cashews, three apples, and half a gallon of juice. That was enough to get my appetite under control and would keep me from ordering everything on the menu at Jackman's.

I also spent a little time with Mom and Gramps, talking about the exhibition. Most of their comments were centered, of course, on my competition with Dynamo. They thought that it had been an absolutely thrilling finish, so from that standpoint it was definitely a success.

After promising not to stay out too late, I had teleported to Jackman's, which is where I now found myself.

I popped up in the parking lot, which was surprisingly full of not only cars, but also people. I glanced towards the restaurant and it immediately became clear why. Through the large glass windows that formed the front of Jackman's, I could see that the interior was completely packed. It was standing room only — filled well beyond legal capacity — and the place was sure to get a citation if the fire warden happened by.

Scanning the inside, I recognized quite a few of those present. Vestibule sat at a booth near the front window, with a small entourage of what I assumed were other models. Despite being blatantly vapid and vain, she was being overtly courted by a handful of guys. On the table in front of her sat the trophy she had received for winning her competition with Actinic.

Not too far away, Actinic himself was sitting at a table with some friends, smiling and chatting animatedly. Apparently, losing the trophy hadn't disturbed him to any great degree, and with good reason. The judges were so impressed with what he'd done that — after stripping him of his victory — they'd made up a "Most Ingenious" award just for him, presenting him with a certificate at the end of the show.

Failing to see my own tight circle of friends inside, I turned my attention back to the parking lot, which contained a considerably larger population at the moment than the restaurant interior. Aside from brief forays inside to get food and drinks, these people seemed perfectly content to hang around outside. Thankfully, a couple of teens with weather-related powers had seen fit to exercise a little discretion, resulting in an Indian summer — at least for tonight. There also seemed to be a bit of spillover from the exhibition, as I saw more than a few instances of teen supers putting their powers on display: speedsters racing around the block, metal rods being bent with bare hands, and so on.

After a few minutes, I finally saw Sarah sitting on the hood of Smokey's car on the far side of the parking lot. Although I didn't immediately see Electra or Smokey, I assumed that they were close by and started making my way over.

I was about halfway there when I came across Dynamo. He was standing with a small group of other teens, including a few from the Alpha League, discussing the latest blockbuster action flick.

We hadn't really had a chance to speak after the competition, as the broadcast had been coming to a close. I'd only had the opportunity to speak a few congratulatory words to him on-camera, and I don't think either of us had hung around for long following that. Concerned that I might have sounded curt before, it seemed like a good time to let him know that my earlier congratulations were sincere.

I waited outside his circle of friends, standing in a conspicuous manner. After a few moments, he seemed to notice me; he excused himself from his group and came towards me.

I extended a hand to him, which he took. However, he cut me off before I got a single word out.

"That wasn't how it was supposed to go down," Dynamo said.

"Huh?" I muttered, confused.

"The competition," he said as he let go of my hand. "*You* were supposed to win."

I shook my head, perplexed. "I'm sorry. You lost me."

"Look, I've seen you in action, watched clips of you going through the training exercises. You're a guy who likes to win."

"I suppose," I said, not sure where he was going with this.

151

"And there's nothing wrong with that. We all like to win. But tonight was about charity, so I was willing to make a deal with you. I'd throw the competition if you'd agree to put on a good show."

"What do you mean, a 'good show'?"

"Just give the people their money's worth — make it last."

"In other words, no teleporting."

"Among other things, but yeah. Unfortunately, you showed up late so I didn't get a chance to see if you'd be on board. But it turns out that you were, even without having a conversation about it."

"And you figured that out just from the fact that I didn't teleport?"

"That, and your helping me to win."

I shook my head, feigning confusion. "I don't what you're talking about."

"Dude, please," he said, rolling his eyes in mock exasperation. "Don't blow that smoke in my direction. I can hit a pinhead with a grain of sand from two miles away. Throwing that coin into a slot is something I could do with my eyes closed. It was supposed to miss by a hair's breadth, but you made it go in."

I was silent for a moment, and then finally spoke. "Like you said, it was for charity. I wanted to give the people a good show."

Dynamo nodded in agreement, looking at me in a way that suggested he was seeing me in a new light — or maybe for the first time.

"You know," he said, clapping me on the shoulder, "maybe Kid Sensation isn't the arrogant, pompous, know-it-all that people say he is."

"And maybe," I said with a grin, "Dynamo isn't a smug, vainglorious snob who thinks he's superior to everyone else."

Dynamo laughed heartily at that.

"Later, man," he said as he shook my hand again and headed back towards his friends.

"Hey," I said, my voice making him spin back around towards me. "Where's your award?"

Like Vestibule and the other winners, Dynamo had received a trophy. As befitting the winner of the night's main event, it had been monstrously huge — about as tall as me.

"I left it at home," Dynamo said. "It just seemed like bad form to bring it here and rub it in your face, loser."

Now it was my turn to laugh. Despite all the talk about Dynamo and I being rivals of some sort, it seemed much more likely that we were going to be friends. Good friends, in fact.

Lost in thought about how the rumor mill had gotten something so wrong, I continued walking absentmindedly towards Smokey's car. I had barely gone three steps when someone behind me spoke.

"Excuse me," said a clearly feminine voice in a tone, manner, and direction that made it obvious that the speaker was addressing me.

I turned around to see who it was…and my heart skipped a beat.

It was the girl from the triathlon.

Chapter 20

I had rarely thought about her over the past few hours — had practically forgotten about her, in fact. But seeing her now, standing right there in front of me, brought on an unexpected surge of emotion. I felt a schoolboy giddiness coming over me as I looked at her, and I found myself amazed that I had thought about anything other than her recently. I felt a stupid, idiotic grin forming on my face but found it impossible to stop myself.

"You've changed," she said matter-of-factly.

I glanced down at my clothes. I was wearing a blue golf shirt and a pair of khakis.

"Yes," I finally acknowledged, still grinning, and then struggled to find something meaningful to add. "So have you."

It was true; she was no longer in her costume. Instead, she was wearing sandals, black palazzo pants, and a lacy, white, short-sleeved top that hung ever-so-loosely off her shoulders.

"No," she said with a shake of her head. "Your appearance." She swirled her hand around her face for emphasis.

Her voice had a magical quality to it, something hypnotic. And, although her English was perfect, I thought I could detect a slight accent, but I wasn't sure.

"Oh, that. Yeah, I did," I said. I frowned, as something suddenly occurred to me. "Wait a minute; how'd you know that?"

Basically, although I kept having weird feelings around this girl, I had never seen her before. Still, she somehow had connected my Kid Sensation countenance with my real face.

"Your aura," she said.

"My what?"

"Aura. There's an...atmosphere, you might say, that I can sense around people. It's reflective of their nature — their personality — and stays the same no matter what they do."

"So you can use it to recognize or identify people — even shapeshifters."

"Precisely."

"Interesting. So, what exactly does my aura look like?"

She stared at me for a second, seeming to look at me, through me, and around me all at once.

"It's a bright, pulsing light, shifting through a wild kaleidoscope of colors. I'm not sure I've ever seen another like it."

"I thought they were all different anyway, like fingerprints, and that's how you used them to identify people."

She gave me a patient, understanding smile that made me feel like I was a kid failing to grasp a basic concept in school.

"I probably didn't explain myself very well," she said. "Most auras only reflect one or two colors, and will shift through various shades of them, with the intensity of their light staying the same."

"But if they change shades, how are you still able to identify one as belonging to a particular person?"

"Some of the underlying features always stay the same, so I can still associate a certain aura with a specific person. It's similar to the way you might be able to identify a woman, even if she changes the color of her lipstick, eye shadow, or blush."

"I think I understand," I said. "But my aura is different, you say?"

"Yes. Yours, as I mentioned, oscillates with diverse coloration."

"Is that a good thing?"

"I don't know. It's something outside my experience, so it never even occurred to me that someone could have such an aura."

"So, I'm unique?" I asked, smirking.

"Apparently so. I guess that's why you're known as Kid Sensation."

Normally, I don't pay attention when people call me that. It wasn't a name I personally picked; it's a tag the media slapped on me because of my power set. When this girl said it, though, it was like I was hearing it for the first time — and I discovered that I really, *really* liked it.

"And what do they call you?" I asked.

She looked mildly surprised for a second, but then recovered. "I'm sorry. I never introduced myself, did I? They call me Atalanta."

I burst out laughing.

"Now that," I said, chuckling, "is a very fitting name."

"So, you know the story," she said.

"Of course. Legendary female warrior, unable to be bested by any man."

She smiled, seemingly pleased that I knew the origin of her namesake.

"After today's triathlon," I continued, "I don't think anyone would argue that it doesn't suit you."

"Thanks."

"What team are you with, by the way?"

"The Argonauts."

I raised an eyebrow at that. Argo was a small, isolated island nation that seldom dealt with the outside world. One of the few interactions that it had with other nations concerned petroleum production. Argo's territorial waters were apparently rich in oil and gas (not to mention a few other minerals), and the country — as a whole — was extremely wealthy.

When the extent of Argo's oil and gas reserves had first come to light three decades earlier, an aggressive world power had sent a fleet to essentially conquer the island. That's when everyone first learned that Argo had its own team of supers, and they were both powerful and formidable.

There were only three of them — two men and a woman — but they had no trouble beating back the aggressor, which lost a score of battleships, aircraft carriers, and other vessels. No one had dared try to invade Argo since.

"I didn't realize that the Argonauts cared for this kind of competition. The exhibition, that is."

She shrugged. "It's good for us to get out and see the world." She then gave me a very serious stare. "And for the world to see us."

I understood without her having to say anything else. Atalanta's presence and participation here was for more than just charity. Her dominance at the triathlon was meant to show the world that Argo was still protected by powerful supers, with more coming up through the ranks.

"So," I said, trying to keep the conversation going, "how many super teens do the Argonauts have?"

That one got me another blatantly hard stare, although Atalanta said nothing. I should have realized that that kind of information would be confidential. As an awkward silence started to build, I racked my brains trying to come up with something else the two of us could talk about.

"Well, is this how you normally meet guys?" I asked. "You come up to them and offer to tell them about their aura?"

"No. No, I—" She stopped unexpectedly, eyes going wide. "I'm sorry, I almost forgot."

"Forgot what?" I asked.

"Please," she said, looking around warily. "Can we speak privately?"

I shrugged. "Sure."

She didn't really reply, just rose straight up into the air. I watched her in surprise; I hadn't even known she could fly. Around us, a few people took note of her departure, and then went back to their respective conversations. (She wasn't the first person to take to the air tonight from the parking lot.)

I was on the verge of flying up after her, when I realized how conspicuous that would be. I looked over towards Smokey's car, and this time I spotted Electra. She was talking to Sarah and didn't seem to have spotted me yet — she probably didn't even know I was there — but the last thing I needed was for her to see me flying off with some chick she'd accused me of drooling over. I looked up at Atalanta, wrapped her in my power, and teleported us to my school.

We appeared in the school courtyard, near an aging, rusting lamppost. Suddenly in unfamiliar surroundings, Atalanta went into a fighting stance, eyes unexpectedly glowing with silver light.

"Whoa," I said, hands raised defensively, while thinking she looked impossibly beautiful. "We're all friends here. I just brought us some place where we could talk privately, like you asked."

My words didn't seem to register immediately with Atalanta, who stayed visibly tense and battle-ready for a few seconds, then slowly lowered her guard.

"I'm sorry," she said. "What you did was...unexpected."

"Then I'm the one who should apologize."

"No, it's okay." She appeared to reach into her back pocket and pulled out what looked like a folded piece of paper. "I believe this is for you."

I took the paper from her, which turned out to be a folded postcard. There was a picture of a gorgeous beach on the card, and an inscription:

Having a great time, mostly because you aren't here...

It was signed with the letter R.

I stared at it for a moment, flabbergasted, and then read it again, unsure of what to make of it. I gave Atalanta a confused frown, and she responded by shrugging in a beats-me manner. I read the postcard a third time, and then everything became amazingly clear. I couldn't help but laugh.

Rudi!

The card was from my friend Rudi, whom I'd previously rescued (along with her little brother, Josh) from a government installation! She was writing to let me know that she was okay, although that was pretty much a given.

After being rescued, Rudi and her brother had gone their own way, presumably to reunite with their parents. Although only ten years old, Rudi was a powerful precognitive who could see the future in clear detail. I'd had no doubt that she and Josh would find their parents, and that Rudi's power — which had been underdeveloped with she was first taken by the government — would keep them one step ahead of any pursuers. The postcard was a clear indication that Rudi and her clan were safe.

"Where did you get this?" I asked Atalanta, openly curious.

"It was very strange," she said. "I was flying on patrol" — she gave me an odd look, evidently feeling she'd let something slip, but went on with only a slight pause — "when I came across a balloon just floating in the air. That card was tied to it, along with a sticky note addressed to me. It asked me to give the postcard to Kid Sensation. I didn't know how important it was, so I thought it better to pass it along in private."

"Well, I can't thank you enough."

"Sure you can," she said. "You can thank me by telling me what it's about."

I debated for a second. There was no way I was telling her the whole story. I may have been getting inexplicably caught up in the grip of powerful emotions around her, but I hadn't gone crazy. Not *that* crazy. Not yet, anyway.

"It's just a postcard from a friend," I said, trying to sound dismissive. "Getting you to deliver it was a bit of a joke."

INFILTRATION

Atalanta didn't seem particularly satisfied with that answer, but it was all she was going to get. I made sure she was ready, and then teleported us back to Jackman's.

Chapter 21

We reappeared back in the parking lot, essentially in the same spot where we'd been speaking before. Ostensibly, she'd fulfilled her purpose in approaching me by giving me Rudi's postcard. However, still fascinated with her and not quite ready for us to go our separate ways, I tried making small talk — asking about her background, life on Argo, and so on — and got mostly canned responses. I was about to try a different tack when I saw Smokey approaching us.

"There you are," he said to me when he got close enough. "I've been looking all over for you."

"Sorry," I murmured. "I got caught up."

"So I see," Smokey said, eyeing Atalanta. There was an odd silence for a moment, and then I quickly made introductions.

"Of course," Smokey said, shaking Atalanta's hand. "You won the triathlon. You were great, by the way."

"Thank you," Atalanta responded, almost shyly.

"I don't mean to interrupt," Smokey said, "but I need to steal this guy away for a second. Do you mind?"

"No, not at all," Atlanta replied, at which I felt a little hurt. "I didn't mean to hold him up."

"Thanks," Smokey said as he threw an arm around my shoulder and began guiding me away. "He's got something he needs to do."

I glanced back towards Atalanta, but she had already turned away and started speaking to someone else.

"So what exactly is it that's so important?" I asked Smokey.

"Your girlfriend," Smokey answered. "She sent me to get you."

An abrupt tide of guilt and shame washed over me, and I found myself getting defensive.

"She could have come herself," I said. "We were only talking."

"She could have, but I think she was afraid she'd come off as being in crazy-jealous-girlfriend mode."

I chuckled at the thought. "Why would anyone think that?"

"Because she's in crazy-jealous-girlfriend mode!" Smokey said adamantly. "Why do you think?"

He stopped walking and turned, facing me.

"Let me ask you something," he said. "It's none of my business, of course, but do you still like Electra?"

"Of course," I said, frowning. It was a stupid question.

"Then you can't go around ignoring her and chatting up other girls."

"Hey! I wasn't chatting up anyone!"

"Look, man, I can't tell you what to do, but Electra's my friend. If you're going to break her heart, don't do it in public like this where she'll be completely humiliated."

He turned and continued walking towards his car. A moment later, I sheepishly followed.

****

I spent the next hour lavishing attention on Electra and trying to be Mr. Perfect, Mr. Right, and Mr. Wonderful all rolled into one. It's not that I felt that Smokey was right in what'd he said, but the fact that I felt guilty about even casual conversation with Atalanta meant that something was wrong. As before, though, being out of her presence seemed to make me come back to my senses.

I still had no explanation for Atalanta's effect on me. Was she a Siren of some sort? It was possible, but I didn't pick up the same sort of emotional vibe from her that Sirens usually give off. It was something I'd have to give serious thought to later.

On her part, Electra basically ignored me at first, acting as if she couldn't see or hear me. It was a little juvenile, but I could sense that she was angry, disappointed, and greatly hurt, among other things. Eventually, though, she came around, and by midnight I was mostly forgiven — again.

Yes, all was right in my world once more. At least for another five minutes, which is when my emergency beacon went off.

Chapter 22

It wasn't really a beacon; it was actually my cell phone, but it was simultaneously vibrating, sounding a siren, and — when I pulled it from my pocket — flashing an orange light. And to be fair, it wasn't just my phone; it was the same story with all of the teens with the Alpha League.

Basically, we'd all been given modified phones by the League. They generally operated no differently than ordinary phones, but did have a few perks, such as being able to send confidential communications, code and decode messages, and — of course — serve as an emergency signal. Right now, we were supposed to get back to Alpha League HQ as soon as possible.

There were about twenty of us at Jackman's, and in less than a minute we were all huddled together in the parking lot. We had all turned off our phones' emergency signals at that point, but the sound of the sirens was replaced with voices — some from those of us with the Alpha League, some from the other super teens, who had gathered around us. Of course, none of us knew anything at that point, but that didn't stop the questions from coming in rapid-fire fashion.

"Does anyone know what's going on?"

"How bad is it?"

"What have you heard?"

Electra, trying to get everyone's attention and failing, suddenly threw up her hands, shot a bolt of electricity into the air, and shouted, "Quiet!!!"

There was an immediate hush as everyone turned to look at her.

"No one knows anything yet," she said. "Our job at this point isn't to speculate, but to hustle back to HQ on the double."

Electra turned to look at me. "Jim, take us there."

I nodded, and then asked, "Is everyone ready?"

There were a few nods, but no votes in the negative. I saw Smokey give Sarah a quick kiss and hand her his car keys. Assuming that no one else had any pressing goodbyes, I teleported us to Alpha League HQ.

****

I popped us into the main break room, an area with lots of recreational activities and games — shuffleboard, table tennis, etc. — as well as a kitchen and fully stocked pantry. It was not only big enough to accommodate everyone comfortably, but was also complete and functional (not that anyone would be in here goofing off tonight). I then teleported myself to Mouse's lab, assuming that he was the one who'd signaled the emergency. He was waiting on me when I popped in.

"Right on time," Mouse said. "Where's everyone else?"

"Main break room," I said.

"Good. Take me there."

A second later, we were back in the break room. Mouse wasted no time.

"Listen up! I want to get this in one take," he said. "Forty-five minutes ago, the city came under attack. The Sycamore Building is gone."

"What do you mean 'gone'?" someone asked.

"I mean there's a gargantuan pile of rubble where — an hour ago — a sixty-story skyscraper stood," Mouse said.

"Was it a bomb?" another person asked.

"We don't know yet," Mouse said, giving me a knowing look. "What we do know is that about a quarter of an hour later, a whole block in the warehouse district got flattened. Finally, fifteen minutes ago, the West Shore Bridge got taken out. It's a twisted hunk of metal lying at the bottom of the bay now."

"How many...how many people?" someone asked.

"Too many," Mouse replied. "But you can't worry about that right now."

"What do you need us to do?" Smokey asked.

"We dispatched a team when the Sycamore Building went down," Mouse said. "Then another to the warehouse district. Now I'm going out with a third team to the bridge.

"Basically, these attacks have us stretched thin, and I need you guys to pick up the slack. I'm putting some of you on a tentative fourth response team, to go into action if and when necessary."

Mouse looked around, then started pointing and rattling off names. "Dynamo. Nightshift. Boomstick..."

I waited patiently for Mouse to call my name, confident that I'd be one of those chosen, but he never did. Instead, he identified about seven other teens, each of whom seemed to puff up a little with pride.

"You guys are the next group to go out," Mouse said. "But again, only if necessary. As to everyone else, commence maneuver Tango Foxtrot as soon as I leave."

There were a couple of nods, as everyone seemingly acknowledged Mouse's orders. Tango Foxtrot meant that HQ would go on high alert. In conjunction with that, everyone would commence certain pre-assigned duties: some would go on patrol, others would watch monitors, etc. Electra, as one of the current team leaders, would be in Command Central, where she would be plugged into everything that was going on.

Having finished his briefing, Mouse turned to me. "Get me up to the copter."

I nodded, and a moment later we were on a helipad, which sat under a retractable dome ceiling on the roof of Alpha League HQ. Two other supers, Feral and Esper (along with BT, surprisingly), were already inside the helicopter, the blades of which were just beginning to spin in anticipation of takeoff. The ceiling was already open, so obviously they had only been waiting on Mouse, who turned and prepared to head towards the helicopter.

"Hey," I said, grabbing his elbow, "these attacks. It's the same as what Alpha Prime and I came across last night."

"It seems like it," Mouse said.

"Then why didn't you put me on the fourth response team? I've seen this stuff before, dealt with it. I should probably be coming with you now."

"Look," Mouse said, raising his voice as the sound from the helicopter blades began to get louder, "we don't know what's going on here. The timing of these attacks, the number of them, the disparate locations…I need to know there's someone here at HQ that I can trust to keep their head — and keep everyone else from losing theirs — if something goes haywire. Someone experienced in dealing with crises. That's you."

The disappointment must have shown on my face, because he went on.

"Don't worry," he continued. "You'll have plenty of other opportunities to put yourself in harm's way down the road. Right now, though, I'm trusting you to help keep everything stable here at HQ."

He emphasized his vote of confidence with a slap on the back, and then ran over to the copter and got in. A few seconds later, it rose up into the sky, and then they were gone.

INFILTRATION

Chapter 23

My role, under Tango Foxtrot, was to conduct patrols. It wasn't a duty I was particularly keen on, but we all have to do our part. Fortunately, being a speedster, I could zip through all of my designated areas in practically no time. Moreover, since I only had to go through my assigned zones once an hour, I actually had a lot of free time, which I chose to spend in Command Central with Electra.

Practically speaking, Command Central was the control room for Alpha League HQ. Filled to capacity with computers, monitors, and all sorts of equipment, it was nominally the hub of all League information and activity. From here, automatic defenses could be turned on, you could access cameras to see various areas on the grounds, you could contact units in the field, etc. (Of course, Mouse could do the same and more from his lab, but that was apparently one of the perks of leadership.)

Electra and two others were on duty in the room, studiously watching the monitors and cameras while checking in with all the teens to make sure that nobody was slacking off. In between patrols, I leaned back in a computer chair not far from Electra, feet plopped up on a nearby desk. Outside the room, Dynamo and his team were on standby, simply waiting for the word to swing into action.

Electra gave me a slightly exasperated look, but didn't say anything. I suppose she could have ordered me out, but I hadn't really done anything and had been completely silent for the most part. (Plus, I think she wanted to show that she could lead without being distracted in any way by me.) In essence, it was looking like it would be a long, boring night.

All of that abruptly changed, however, about twenty minutes after Mouse's departure. That's when one of the others in Command Central — a girl called Audible Annie — noticed something on one of the monitors.

"Look at this," she said, pointing towards one of the monitors in front of her. "There's some kind of weird haze showing up."

Electra and the other person assigned to Command Central — a guy called Auger — stepped over to take a look.

"Maybe it's a camera malfunction," Auger said.

At this point I joined them, looking over Annie's shoulder. The picture displayed on the screen appeared to be that of a place undergoing construction. There was a large open area surrounded by high walls, with a non-working fountain in the center. I recognized it as a portion of HQ being contemplated as an interior courtyard. Ultimately, if those plans were approved, it would have benches, flowers, etc. — in essence, a small park.

I also saw something else that was familiar to me: a shimmering incandescence (apparently the "haze" Audible Annie had mentioned) that I had just encountered the night before with my father.

"Get everybody down there now!" I screamed. "We're about to be attacked!"

Chapter 24

In retrospect, calling it an attack was being generous — and paying a compliment — to our adversaries. After sounding the alarm, I had teleported myself, Auger, Electra, and the fourth response team to the courtyard where the shimmering had been spotted. We had barely arrived when the incandescence vanished and we found ourselves facing a group of invaders.

There were about twenty-five of them, all decked out in balaclavas and body armor, and carrying laser weapons. The two sides stared at each other for a moment, and then — almost in unison — everyone screamed and it was on.

Dynamo charged at the center of their ranks, immediately drawing their fire. If their lasers had any effect on him, I didn't see it, because he rammed through them without hesitation, knocking men aside like tenpins.

Electra fired an arc of electricity at one guy's weapon, making it explode in a shower of sparks. The force of the blast blew the man backwards, and he fell to the ground, unconscious.

On my part, I phased and then went through the enemy's lines, teleporting any weapons I saw into a basement storage area that the Alpha League maintained for firearms.

Likewise, all of the other super teens present put their powers to work taking out the bad guys. Surprisingly, our attackers seemed to have no supers of their own with them. Long story short, without their weapons and facing superior firepower, our assailants were seriously outclassed. We mopped the floor with them, and the whole thing was over in just a few minutes, with most of the bad guys unconscious and the remainder on their knees with their hands behind their heads, fingers interlocked.

All of us teens looked at one another, smiling and probably thinking the same thing: that we had seriously spanked the bad guys. Giddy with adrenaline, one or two teens even started to chuckle. A few others joined them. Then the chuckles turned into snickering. A few seconds later, all of us were laughing (although still keeping an eye on our prisoners).

In retrospect, I probably should have teleported the bad guys to holding cells, a number of which we actually have at League HQ. However, the other teens were absolutely euphoric about the win we'd just had, and it didn't seem completely inappropriate to let them have a little emotional release (okay, it was probably more like gloating) in front of the guys who had just attacked us.

It wasn't until a few seconds later, when I ceased laughing long enough to catch my breath, that I heard a high-pitched beeping. A multitude of beeps actually, although they were sounding off almost in sync.

I sobered instantly. It was the same sound I'd heard the previous night when the three supervillains—

"Everybody back!" I screamed, looking towards the guys we had just beaten to a pulp. Sure enough, each of them had one of the black bands around his wrist, with a crystal flashing crimson.

There was no laughter now from the other teens. Heeding my warning, they had backed away. A few seconds later, as I expected, the shimmering appeared and surrounded our assailants. And then they were gone. All of the other teens looked stunned.

"What just happened?" Auger asked with naked incredulity.

"They got away, obviously," Dynamo answered, somewhat angrily.

"How?" Auger asked.

"That's the sixty-four-dollar question, my friend," I said.

Having seen this scenario play out before, I hadn't been caught totally by surprise. Most of the others, however, just stared dumbly at the area where all the bad guys had been just a minute ago. Their escape wasn't due to anything that we had done wrong (in fact, there probably wasn't anything we could have done to prevent it, even if I *had* teleported them to a holding cell), but I could feel disappointment, a sense a failure, and similar emotions rising up in the others. I was on the verge of offering some words of encouragement — maybe let them know that even Alpha Prime hadn't been able to prevent the same thing from happening to him — when someone spoke from the doorway that led from the courtyard to the building.

I looked and saw a man whose appearance was a complete enigma. He was dressed as though he had leaped from a nineteenth century Victorian painting, wearing dark trousers, a jabot, and an ulster coat. His face was covered with bizarre designs: ancient symbols, weird hieroglyphs, obscure characters. (And, although only his face was exposed, I knew that those strange emblems covered him from head to foot.)

It was Rune, the erstwhile magician of the Alpha League. As I watched, a small glob of blood formed near his temple and then trickled down the side of his face.

INFILTRATION

"A little help here, please," he said. "I think I've been injured."

Chapter 25

One of the other teens offered to help Rune back to his room. His wound didn't appear serious, and he felt he could take care of it with his magic once he got back to his quarters. As he left, something odd occurred to me: I hadn't actually seen Rune while we were fighting the bad guys.

Of course, that didn't mean anything. He was a powerful magician; he could have been out there fighting invisibly and gotten hurt by friendly fire. He could have been hit by a ricochet of some sort. He could have been injured fighting somewhere else and come back here to convalesce. Or he might have just slipped in the shower. Who knows?

I teleported the rest of us back to Command Central. Once there, I found myself involuntarily stretching and yawning. It had been a long day; in fact, it was actually the *next* day.

Electra saw me yawning and put on her team leader hat, making a command decision: half of us were going to be allowed to sleep for two hours while the others stayed on duty. At the two-hour mark, we'd switch. Of course, she put me in the first group that was to get some rest.

Overall, it was a good decision on her part in that a lot of us were tired, but she didn't actually have to do it for me. I have the ability to consciously control almost all of my bodily processes and functions. With a few tweaks, I'd be wide awake and able to go for days without sleep. I'd have to pay for it later, of course, when my body went back to normal, but that seemed like a fair trade.

Electra, however, had made a decision as team leader, and — if I were going to start acting like a team player — I needed to obey it. Therefore, I simply nodded and told her I'd be in the break room, which is where I teleported to a moment later.

Once there, I went to the pantry, looking for something to eat. I eventually settled on three cans of pineapples (which I quickly devoured) and then stretched out on a nearby sofa. I was asleep within seconds.

****

I came to groggily, with rough hands shaking me.

"Hey, Sleeping Beauty. Wake up."

I opened my eyes and saw Mouse leaning over me.

"It's about time," he said. "I thought I was going to have to kiss you to get you awake."

He stepped back a little as I swung my feet to the floor and sat up.

"How long have I been asleep?"

"About four hours, according to what Electra told me."

"Four hours! I was supposed to switch—"

"Relax. The response teams started filing back in about an hour into your little power nap. That being the case, I told the other teens to stand down. I sent them all home."

"Oh? Does that mean I can go home, too?"

"Not exactly. Can you take us to my lab?"

I nodded, and a second later we were there. Braintrust was nearby, fiddling with some device on a worktable.

"Hey, Jim," she said.

I waved back, then turned to Mouse. "I'm going to use your bathroom to freshen up."

"Knock yourself out," he said. "There are extra toiletries under the counter."

I nodded and teleported. Five minutes later, I was back, feeling somewhat more presentable after a shower and having gone through my usual morning routine. I'd even popped back home for a change of clothes. (I suppose I could have actually showered in my own bathroom rather than Mouse's, but was afraid it might wake Mom and Gramps.)

"So, where are we?" I asked.

"About the same place we were yesterday," BT replied.

"Well, that's progress," I said sarcastically.

Mouse sighed. "We've been trying to reverse-engineer this thing — figure out what kind of weapon they're using by working backwards, starting at the scene."

"No luck?" I asked.

"None whatsoever," BT said. "It's the same story as what you and Alpha Prime experienced. There's no residue at any of the sites, no bomb remnants...nothing to give us a starting point. Usually there's *some*thing."

"Unfortunately," Mouse said, "I think we're up against a clock. I'm thinking that maybe there's some type of indicator present after these explosives — if we can call them that — go off, but it dissipates right away. That's where you come in."

I thought about it for a moment. "You want me to immediately teleport you to the site the next time these guys blow something up."

"Exactly," Mouse said. "Maybe then I can pick up a trace of something before it vanishes — assuming I'm right."

"Fine by me," I said. "But you'll have to deal with me hanging around all day."

"What? You hanging out in my lab?" Mouse asked, feigning shock. "That'll be a new experience."

"Anyway," I said, ignoring his attempt at humor, "do we have any clue yet what these people want? Why they're doing all this?"

"Negatory," Mouse said. "There was no threat before any of the stuff that happened last night, no demands, no nothing. I mean, just knowing what they were after would be a big help in trying to stop them. But I can't make sense of their actions."

"Like destroying the overpass," I said.

"Yeah," BT agreed. "It's not clear how that benefited them. All they did was show up and fight you and Alpha Prime afterwards."

Mouse's eyes suddenly lit up. "Maybe that was the whole point."

"What do you mean?" I asked. "They just wanted to fight us?"

"Not you, specifically," Mouse replied. "Your old man."

"Yeah, that's a career path with lots of potential — fighting the world's greatest superhero," I said. "My father's invulnerable."

"Well, yes and no," BT said.

I frowned. "What do you mean?"

"Supervillains are always trying to come up with new weapons to hurt AP," Mouse said. "You know that, right?"

"Yeah," I said. "And they always fail."

"Eh, somewhat," Mouse said. "The truth is, they don't fully understand that one of your father's strengths is that his body is always adapting. For instance, you said that when those guys showed up at the overpass, they shot AP with something like a laser."

I nodded. "It was something like a laser light, yeah. It came from their maces."

"And the first time they shot him, it seemed to hurt him," Mouse stated. "But the next time not so much, right?"

"Right," I answered. "Does that mean something?"

"Yeah," Mouse said. "After that first shot, your father's body adapted, became immune so to speak. That's why after that he wasn't particularly bothered by that same weapon."

"Think of it this way," BT said. "The first time you shoot him with a bullet, it goes into him and causes some damage. The next time you shoot him, maybe it causes a scratch. The third time you shoot him, the bullet doesn't even break the skin."

This was news to me. I had simply assumed that my father was invulnerable, plain and simple. I didn't know that getting hit with new weapons was like getting inoculated to him.

"So, if I understand you," I said, thinking, "that whole scene at the overpass may have been solely about testing a new weapon against my father?"

"Think about it," Mouse said. "If any villain threatens this city, this country, this planet — at some point they're going to have to face Alpha Prime. It would be nice to know ahead of time if you have a weapon that will hurt him."

"But what about last night, then?" I asked. "Alpha Prime wasn't part of every response team."

"No," Mouse said, "just the first, but they didn't come after him then. Or any of the response teams. Instead, they attacked this place."

"Which also didn't make any sense," BT said. "They sent in a very weak team — no supers, mind you — to do...what? And then they yank them all back after basically just a few minutes?"

"There's obviously something here that we're not seeing," Mouse said. "Whoever's behind this has a lot of power, but they seem to be using it wantonly, indiscriminately, without any sense of purpose."

A new thought occurred to me. "Those guys who attacked here last night. Did you investigate the courtyard where they appeared and disappeared?"

"Yeah," BT said. "It's the same story — no evidence of any type of technology we're familiar with. Apparently it's something outside of our experience — maybe something more advanced."

I guffawed. "Well, this is a good joke. You're two of the biggest brains on the planet, and you can't figure this out? You mean, there's someone out there smarter than you two combined?"

Apparently I hit Mouse below the belt with that one, because he smacked his fist on the worktable next to him.

"It's not that easy!" he exclaimed. "This isn't like any technology I've ever seen, alien or terrestrial. It's almost like it isn't science at all. In some ways, it's actually more like...more like..."

Mouse trailed off, staring into space, obviously thinking intensely. Brow furrowed, he began drumming his fingers on the worktable. After about a minute of this, I couldn't take it anymore.

"It's more like what?" I finally asked.

"More like…magic," Mouse muttered, as if he couldn't believe what he was saying.

Chapter 26

"Magic?" I repeated.

Instead of responding, Mouse suddenly began typing something on his computer tablet.

"Magic," said BT, nodding her head. "Of course."

"You say that like it's obvious," I said. "Before Mouse mentioned it, the thought had never occurred to you."

"It's not so much that it didn't occur to me — either of us, in truth — as it was the fact that it was automatically excluded," BT retorted. "You and Alpha Prime mentioned a bomb with respect to the destruction of the overpass. Ergo, we focused on explosives technology — the material rather than the mystical."

"Plus, magic typically doesn't operate like this," Mouse added, finally looking up from his tablet. "Don't get me wrong, there's magic strong enough to cause the kind of damage we've experienced, but you rarely ever see this level of destruction. The amount of power required is just too difficult to manipulate."

"I don't follow," I said.

"Think of it like this," BT said. "Imagine that magic is like a handgun. With proper training, almost anyone can safely handle it, agreed?"

"Sure," I said.

BT went on. "Now, if someone wants a weapon that's more powerful than a handgun — say, a mortar or grenade launcher — they'll need additional training."

"Gotcha," I said. "Using our analogy, a magician who wants more power probably needs to study and become even more conversant with magic."

"Correct," BT said, "but beyond a certain point, there will be magic that a magician can access but that he won't be able to control. Using it will be like setting off an atomic bomb — an uncontrolled nuclear chain reaction."

"So, a magician might be able to drop a magical version of an atomic bomb," I said, "but once it goes off, he can't stop it. He can't control how much damage it causes."

"In a nutshell," Mouse said. "But what we've seen — especially last night — is a high level of devastation that was held strictly in check geographically. You usually only see that in someone with enhanced abilities, which means they studied magic for a long time. That's why the most powerful wizards and such tend to be advanced in age."

"So what does that mean?" I asked. "We're looking for an octogenarian with a wand?"

"Not necessarily," BT said. "Just like prodigies in music and such, there are wunderkinds when it comes to mystical abilities. People who show mastery of the metaphysical at an early age."

"Even counting those, though, there can't be a lot of people capable of controlling the magical equivalent of a nuclear bomb," I said.

"There aren't," Mouse agreed. "There's maybe a handful on the entire planet. There's Rune, of course, but he's one of us. Gloriana Mano is another."

"Hand of Glory?" BT said quizzically. "She's still locked away somewhere in a medically induced coma. If it were her we'd know, because she'd be trying to destroy the world and wouldn't be shy about it."

"There are also a couple of guys on other superhero teams," Mouse said, "but I'm assuming they're beyond suspicion. After that, the drop-off is pretty steep in terms of ability, and we go to a mid-level tier. There are a bunch of villainous wannabes at that rank — like Mystic Kabbalah and Diabolist Mage, to name a few — but then we're back to this being more power than those dorks can control."

"Maybe not," BT interjected. "Increased magical power usually comes in one of two varieties: lifelong study, or objects of power."

"So what, you're thinking that maybe somebody found a charm or something that gives enhanced magical abilities?" I asked.

"It makes sense," Mouse said. "It wouldn't be the first time it happened. And these guys are always hunting for a mystical this or a magical that — some trinket or relic that'll make them the second coming of Merlin."

"So what if one of them did find something like that?" I asked. "Maybe not the magical equivalent of an atomic bomb, but something a little less powerful — say, an object on par with a mystical rail gun."

Mouse rubbed his chin for a moment, thinking. "I guess I'd argue that they still have to learn how to use it."

"Maybe that's what's been going on," I said.

Mouse frowned, thinking, then shot a look at BT that was so intense that you'd have thought there was some sort of mental communication between them.

"It makes sense," BT said a few seconds later. "Someone found a new toy and is figuring out how it works."

"That would explain a lot," Mouse said. "Maybe it wasn't just using the maces on Alpha Prime that was a test. Maybe it's been everything they've done up to now."

"It would also clarify why they haven't been making any demands," BT added. "They're still figuring out how all the pieces fit together."

"Okay," I said, "so they're not quite licensed to drive yet. What's our next step — before these guys get comfortable behind the wheel?"

"We don't have one," Mouse said. "We're on 'pause' at the moment."

I was a little befuddled. "You're kidding, right? We just figured this thing out!"

"Actually, we haven't figured anything out," Mouse replied. "All we've been doing is talking, and that's all it is: talk. Speculation, conjecture, and guesswork. We need an expert, which is why I sent a message to Rune."

I suddenly recalled Mouse typing on his tablet just a few minutes earlier. Apparently he'd sent for the arcane cavalry.

"Okay," I said. "Is he on his way?"

Mouse shrugged. "Rune's a bit of a paradox. He's not the kind of guy you can think of as being 'on call.' He kind of does his own thing, although he's usually there when we need him."

"In other words," BT said, "you don't know where he is."

"I have certain channels I can use to get a message to him," Mouse said defensively. "And that's what I've done. But no, I don't know exactly where he is. He went abroad to check out some hoodoo ritual a few weeks back and I haven't heard from him since."

"What do you mean?" I asked in surprise. "Rune's here."

Mouse's bug-eyed expression clearly showed that this was news to him. "You've seen him?"

"Yeah, right after we thumped the bad guys in the courtyard," I said. "Didn't anyone tell you?"

Mouse shook his head, and then started typing again on his tablet, speaking as his fingers flew furiously. "No, we didn't really ask for a head count, and since everyone was tired, we didn't try to get a full debrief. We got the condensed version from Electra and sent everybody home with milk and cookies."

"Well, there's not much more to tell," I said. "Rune apparently popped up while we were fighting, got bopped on the noggin, and asked for someone to help him back to his room."

Mouse stopped typing for a second and looked up. "Wait a minute. Rune got hurt?"

"Yeah," I said, "but from what I could see it didn't look too bad, although it was a head injury."

"That's one for the record books," Mouse said as he went back to typing. "I've never seen that guy get so much as a scratch."

"By the way, how is it that Rune already has a finished room here?" I asked.

"Rune doesn't require much more than four walls for living space," Mouse said. "Apparently his magic provides whatever other creature comforts he requires. I had to beg him to let me install drywall and flooring."

Mouse made a final tap on his tablet with a flourish. "Got him!"

He pointed to one of the large monitors situated nearby, where the screen had changed from displaying data to an image of a wide hallway. Walking down the corridor was Rune, still dressed as I had seen him the night before. In addition, he was carrying a brown satchel slung across his shoulder.

"How'd you find him?" I asked. "Biometric tracking?"

"No, that doesn't work when it comes to Rune," Mouse responded. "His magic usually blocks it, so I didn't even try. I just went with motion sensors."

Watching him on the screen, I saw Rune walking tentatively and looking around in an odd, scatterbrained manner.

"What's wrong with him?" I asked. "He looks like he's lost."

"You said he took a blow to the head," BT replied. "Maybe he's got a concussion."

I nodded, having received a concussion myself in the not-too-distant past. I could vouch for the fact that it could definitely turn your memory into a block of Swiss cheese.

Mouse sighed as Rune tried a door on one side of the hallway and timidly stuck his head inside when it opened. "It looks like he's on the third sub-basement level, and I don't think the PA system is working down there yet. We're going to have to go get him."

"Not a problem," I said, staring at the expanse of hallway on the screen. "I recognize that area; I've been down there before. I can pop down and bring him back."

"Thanks," Mouse said.

"Don't mention it," I said. "Besides, even if the PA system was working, he looks too confused to find his way here."

I teleported to the hallway where Rune was, appearing behind him. He still had his head in the doorway that I'd seen him peeking into on Mouse's monitor.

"Excuse me—" I said.

Rune yelped, turning around almost in fright and slamming the door shut. I felt apprehension and anxiety — almost outright panic — pounding through him like white water rapids.

"I'm sorry. I didn't mean to startle you," I said. "Mouse wants to see you."

I felt his nerves settling down a bit, but not much.

"Mouse?" he said, questioningly. Then a light bulb seemed to come on. "Oh, Mouse! Yes, of course!"

"Is it okay if we go right now?

"Absolutely," he said, taking a step towards me. "That's fi—"

"—ne," he finished, and staggered a little bit, off-balance. I had teleported us while he was speaking. (He had also been in the process of walking, which left his equilibrium a bit off when we appeared.)

Mouse came over, not wasting any time on small talk. "We've got a situation, and I need your opinion on whether magic's involved."

Mouse launched into an explanation of what was going on and our suspicions about magic playing a role in things. Rune seemed to be paying attention, but on an emotional level, he seemed to be a complete wreck. There was a mounting worry and dread in him that seemed to be growing by leaps and bounds. Moreover, it seemed to be taking a physical toll, because the unusual symbols that covered his body — and which were normally in motion — were completely still.

"Well," he said, when Mouse had finally finished, "it certainly sounds as though a level of mysticism is involved. I shall endeavor to consult the proper portents to see if divination of these events presages an ill omen for all affected."

As he spoke, Rune had casually but determinedly made his way to the door leading out of Mouse's lab.

"And now," he said, grabbing the handle and opening the door, "I go to commune with the esoteric. Good day."

He exited, emotions still gyrating wildly, leaving us staring at the door as it closed behind him.

"What the...?" I began, more than a little perplexed. "Was it just me, or was that completely weird?"

"You mean what he said?" Mouse asked. "It wasn't *completely* weird if you know Rune. I was more surprised to see him walk out of here. He uses the door less often than you do. Most times he just vanishes."

"Well, let's just hope he gets us an answer quickly," BT said.

"I'm not exactly sure he said he'd give us one at all, but I'll make sure he knows it's a rush job," I said.

I shifted into super speed and dashed out the door. Rune was walking down the hallway outside Mouse's lab, away from me. I shifted back into normal speed.

"Hey, Rune," I called out, jogging leisurely in his direction.

Rune glanced back at me, then turned face-forward again and walked around a corner, never breaking stride. I turned the corner, just a second or two behind him — and bumped into Dynamo. Rune was nowhere to be seen.

"Sorry," I began. "I was looking for—"

I abruptly stopped speaking as, empathically, I felt a familiar surge of emotions coming from Dynamo: anxiety, dread, and more that — just minutes earlier — I had felt coming from Rune. Moreover, now that I looked him over, Dynamo was wearing Rune's clothes.

The truth hit me like an uppercut from a heavyweight boxer: this wasn't Rune *or* Dynamo. It was a shapeshifter!

Chapter 27

The shapeshifter had pulled a neat trick. Once around the corner, he had immediately changed his appearance. Most people only look at the faces of those they encounter, so even though I was right behind him and his clothes had not changed, he had been counting on my being fooled by a new face. It was actually a good strategy, and one that I, as a fellow shapeshifter, had used myself on occasion.

What he hadn't banked on, however, was my ability as an empath — that I would see through his ruse because of his emotional broadcasts. He did, however, see the light of recognition in my eyes and instantly sensed that the jig was up.

The shapeshifter swung at my head. I phased, and the intended blow passed harmlessly through me, striking the wall with enough force to echo down the hallway. The shapeshifter screeched in pain, cradling the fist that had struck the wall with his good hand. Apparently, although he could mimic Dynamo's appearance, he didn't have his powers. Good to know.

I swung, putting a little extra zip into the blow and making my fist solid just before it connected with his chin. His head snapped to the side. I immediately teleported behind him, gripped his head in my hands, and smashed it into the wall hard enough to crack the plaster. Then I teleported back in front of him and planted a solid fist in his gut. All of the air came whooshing out of him, and I phased as he fell forward, passing through my insubstantial form and hitting the floor face-first. I was pretty sure he was unconscious, but I gave him a good kick in the ribs just to make sure, and then wrapped him in my power and teleported.

****

"So," Mouse said, looking at our prisoner, "we've been infiltrated."

"Apparently," I said.

Our shapeshifter was still unconscious, stretched out on a cot in a nullifier cell. A nullifier is a device that — as the name implies — nullifies super powers. Alpha League HQ had several cells equipped with them for those occasions when we had to hold supervillains. I had teleported the shapeshifter to one of them after coldcocking him in the hallway. I had then contacted Mouse, who had hustled over to join me, leaving BT in the lab.

The cell itself was essentially what you would expect, containing a cot, a sink, and a chair, along with floor-to-ceiling walls at the back and on both sides. However, whereas you would typically envisage bars at the front of an ordinary cell, ours contained a powerful force field.

Now that he was in a nullifier cell with his powers turned off, I could see what the shapeshifter actually looked like. He was a little shorter than me — maybe five-ten — and rather on the thin side. He was about fifty, with sparse, graying hair and an oversized nose. In short, he wasn't particularly impressive.

In addition to tossing him into the nullifier cell, I had also taken the liberty of stripping him of his clothes and all personal effects. (Actually, I had simply teleported it all off him.) Thus, all he wore at the moment was a sleeveless white T-shirt and a pair of boxers with cartoon characters on them.

"His name's Proteus, by the way," Mouse said. "He's a well-known shapeshifter, allegedly able to fool almost anybody."

"I've heard of him," I acknowledged. "And looking at the way he almost pulled a fast one on us, I'd say his reputation is well-deserved."

"Well, with his subterfuge revealed, we at least have a better idea of what last night was about," Mouse continued. "All of the destruction around town was probably to get as many supers as possible away from HQ. Then the attack on HQ itself was to distract anyone still here, allowing our friend here to sneak in."

"A double distraction," I said. "And apparently it worked — at least enough to get him in. We still don't know exactly what he was after."

"We may not *know*, but we do have some hints."

With that, Mouse turned once again to the items I had removed from the shapeshifter after capturing him, all of which were laid out on a nearby table. He had already gone through them twice before, but if anything had caught his attention, he'd kept it to himself.

There was nothing special about the clothes, but I had found one of the beeping crystal bands (which was silent at the moment) on one of his wrists, as well as a watch on the other. Other than that, there were just some interesting odds and ends in his satchel, things that a junk dealer might have an interest in.

Mouse picked up one of the items from the satchel, an interesting curio that looked like a miniature seashell painted a funky shade of purple. It fit snugly in the palm of his hand.

"What are you thinking?" I asked.

"First and foremost," he said, "why take on Rune's appearance?"

I shrugged. "He's the League member least likely to be present, maybe, decreasing the odds that you'll be discovered."

"I thought that, too, but there's got to be more to it than that, and I think this shell is it."

"What's so special about it?"

"Remember our discussion earlier, about how it's possible to get magical power from some objects?"

"Yeah."

"Well, whenever we recover one of those items from a villain with mystical powers, we generally hand it over to Rune."

"Of course. He's the League member with the most experience with arcane objects, so he's the best person to keep it safe."

"Exactly, and — as far as I know — Rune has always had a habit of keeping such things in his room. Like this seashell."

I was surprised. "That's from Rune's room?"

"I'm almost positive, unless there are two of them. But I'm sure I've seen this one before in his quarters. And it's a safe bet" — he fumbled through some of the other items from the satchel — "that a number of these others are from there as well."

"So our prisoner came here not just to infiltrate the place in general, but with a specific agenda that involved becoming Rune."

"Yes. And I guess he was aware of the building's layout since he knew where Rune's room was."

"Uh, maybe not," I said. "Remember? He said he was injured and asked for help getting to his quarters."

"So we basically showed him the way. Great."

Before I could respond, there was a slight groaning from the nullifier cell. We both turned to look and saw Proteus rising groggily to his feet.

He massaged his jaw where I'd hit him, then froze suddenly like he'd been turned to stone. He looked at me and Mouse, and I could feel anxiety welling up in him. (This guy seemed to constantly be on edge.)

"How…how long have I been out?" he asked fearfully.

"About a half hour," Mouse answered.

Proteus stared at him in shock, looking as though someone had just shoved him in front of a subway train. Without warning, he screamed and charged at the front of the nullifier cell.

"No! Wait!" Mouse exclaimed. "There's a—"

Proteus hit the force field at the front of the cell with more force than I thought he was capable of. The force field yielded for a moment, bowing inward, and then pushed back out, flinging Proteus back across the cell. I was certain he'd had the wind knocked out of him, but he was on his feet again in a second, practically screaming.

"Please!" he screeched. "You have to get me out of here! You have to get me out of here *now*!"

"Actually, we don't have to do anything," Mouse said. "But answer our questions and we can make sure that you're at least comfortable in there."

"You don't understand!" Proteus pleaded. "I can't stay in here!"

He looked around at the walls like they were sprouting teeth to devour him with. His emotions were frothing over as I felt all kinds of stress gushing out from him empathically.

"What's wrong with him?" I whispered to Mouse as Proteus continued muttering (to no one in particular) about needing to be released. I thought he'd been close to panic before, but his previous emotional state was the picture of calm compared to what he was going through now.

"I don't know," Mouse replied. "Maybe he's claustrophobic."

"Let me try something," I said to Mouse. I reached out telepathically and peeked into Proteus' brain. Then I asked my question.

"Why do you want to leave so badly?" I asked.

This was a trick my grandfather had taught me. Basically, when you ask someone a question that's within their realm of knowledge, the answer appears unbidden in their mind. Thus, a telepath rarely needs for a person to respond verbally to a query; the answer usually flashes through their brain.

Such was the case with Proteus. And the answer I saw almost stunned me completely.

"Oh, crap!" I exclaimed after a moment, and then teleported away without giving Mouse any type of explanation.

I appeared in the hallway on the third sub-basement level that I'd retrieved the fake Rune from earlier. I dashed over to the door he'd been looking in when I'd appeared and snatched it open. It was a small maintenance closet.

INFILTRATION

I scanned the floor and saw almost immediately what I was looking for: a thumb-sized piece of glittering green crystal. I reached down, grabbed it, and then teleported to the middle of the bay.

I popped up floating above the water. I did a quick survey and noted that the only ship in the vicinity was a nearby oil tanker. I flung the crystal down into the water and then turned myself and the tanker insubstantial. (Much later, it would dawn on me that this was the first time I'd phased an object so massive — the first time I'd even attempted to — but at the time I didn't give any thought to the challenge it represented.)

No more than five seconds later, there was a colossal smacking sound, as if an overweight giant had done a belly flop into the bay. It was a deafening crack that reverberated through the air, like the peal of a gong in a mountain temple.

At the same time, there was a gargantuan splash, like some monstrous but invisible force had hit the water, striking with such incredible force that there was no doubt in my mind that the oil tanker would have been flattened had I not phased it. Almost immediately, ripples surged radially outward from the area where I had thrown the crystal, then became massive, growing waves — an inland tsunami rushing towards the shore at impressive speed.

I was incredibly conflicted. I knew how catastrophic waves like this could be and felt an overwhelming desire to do something. At the same time, the Alpha League had just escaped a well-timed sneak attack by the skin of their teeth and were actually still in danger.

INFILTRATION

As they got closer to shore, the waves grew in height — getting up to about twenty feet — but their speed slowed tremendously. Seeing this, I made a calculated decision to go back to League HQ. The waves were definitely going to be detrimental (there would be some significant flooding, among other things, and the expected accompanying damage), but stopping these attacks was a higher priority.

I teleported back to the nullifier cell area and filled Mouse in on what had happened at the bay. While he spent a few minutes contacting authorities and mobilizing support, I turned my attention back to Proteus.

The guy was in complete meltdown. He had crumpled to his knees, tears streaming down his face, spouting what could — at best — be described as indecipherable gibberish in between wracking sobs.

Telepathically, I reached out, trying to ask questions that we needed answers to. This time, it was much harder getting rational responses or making sense of the answers. Proteus had undergone some type of near-complete mental collapse. By the time Mouse finished dealing with the situation at the bay, I felt I'd gotten as much out of him as possible.

"Okay," Mouse said. "Give it to me."

"First," I said, "let me say that I got as much as I could. It's a mess inside his head, and I can't do a deep dive under the best of circumstances."

"Yeah, he's having a nervous breakdown. He thinks HQ is about to be destroyed and him along with it."

"Well, I think we avoided that, although it was a close call. Basically, we were right about the dual distractions. Everything that happened last night was about getting him inside."

"Did you find out why?"

"Yes. He needed to get those things" — I pointed to the various knickknacks from his satchel — "from Rune's room. Of course, he didn't know where Rune's room was, which is why he faked the head injury and asked for help. We walked him right to it."

"But Rune's room is usually protected and full of magical booby traps when he's away. How'd Proteus get in and out of there safely?"

"He had some type of charm, a pendant, but it only had a one-time use so he just left it in Rune's room."

"Well, it couldn't have taken that long to scoop up whatever he wanted from Rune's quarters. Why was he still putzing around here hours later?"

"The green crystal. He needed to find a place to leave it, because it told them where to attack."

"So basically, the crystal acted like some sort of guidance system for their mystical weapon," Mouse said, rubbing his chin in thought. "I guess that explains why he was wandering around the sub-basement levels."

"Yeah. When I showed up to get him, he'd just dropped it into that maintenance closet. His orders were to plant it half an hour before the scheduled time for attack. That would give him thirty minutes to get away."

"But thirty minutes later, he found himself locked up in our cell, about to be pancaked along with the rest of us."

"That's the gist of what I was able to get," I said sheepishly, suddenly ashamed of my telepathic limitations.

INFILTRATION

"You did great," Mouse said, clapping me on the shoulder. "It's more than what we knew an hour ago. As for getting more out of him, I've sent for Esper. She'll be able to root out any other worthwhile info."

I nodded, acknowledging that bringing Esper in was the right call.

"Wait a second," Mouse said. "You mentioned something about Proteus having orders. Orders from who?"

I shook my head. "It's not clear. It's too murky in there." I tapped my temple for emphasis.

"What about the stuff he snatched from Rune's room? Any idea what it's for?"

"No, but I picked up on the fact that it's needed desperately. His mandate was essentially to come back with them or don't come back at all."

"Come back?" Mouse repeated quizzically.

As if on cue, the band with the crystal that I'd taken from Proteus — still lying on a table with the other things taken from him — began to beep. Someone was trying to yank our prisoner offstage.

An idea suddenly hit me, one that had been bouncing around in the back of my brain since the moment we'd found out about Proteus. I phased my body and undergarments, and my outer clothes fell to the ground. I immediately began putting on the clothes Proteus had worn when he'd pretended to be Rune.

"What do you think you're doing?" Mouse asked.

"What's good for the goose is good for the gander," I said as I pulled on the trousers. "They infiltrated us; we need to infiltrate them."

"What?! You?! Jim, I can't let you do it!"

201

I continued dressing. "Mouse, I'm the only one who *can* do it!"

"Then we'll come up with another plan!"

"Like what?"

"Wait for Rune! This is his forte! He'll get my message soon, put in an appearance, and help us rein in the other side's magic."

The beeping stepped up in volume and pace.

"Mouse, we don't have time to argue about this! You yourself said it earlier: we are up against a clock, but worse, it's one we can't even see. We are operating from a serious disadvantage here in the sense that we have almost no intel. This is our first, best, and probably *only* opportunity to get in front of this thing. Now you've got about twenty seconds to decide whether to say yea or nay to this."

Mouse stared at me, obviously weighing a million different factors, and then blurted out, "Do it."

As I finished getting dressed, Mouse stepped over to a nearby table covered with equipment. He grabbed something from there and started tinkering with it. I had just completed my fashion statement by putting on Proteus' shoes when he tossed me the item he'd been working on. It was a small, black, quarter-sized object that looked a little like a button ripped from someone's winter coat.

"Homing beacon," Mouse informed me, and I nodded, putting it in a pocket. I turned and took a good hard look at Proteus, and then shifted myself into a duplicate of him.

The beeping was now almost a continuous drone as I slapped the band with the crystal on my wrist, and then put on our prisoner's watch as well. I turned to

Mouse, who had just swept all of Proteus' loot back into the satchel, which he then tossed to me.

"No," I said, trying to hand the satchel back as I stepped into character and began speaking with Proteus' voice. "Whatever these people want with this stuff, we need to keep it from them."

"You said it yourself," Mouse countered. "It was come back with this or not at all. Who knows what they'll do to you if you show up without it?"

"But—"

"No 'buts'!" he said adamantly. "It's all for nothing if we lose you the second you get there!"

I didn't like it, but he had a point. I placed the strap of the satchel over my shoulder. Mouse and I looked at each other, but neither of us said anything. Finally, he gave me a knowing nod, which I returned. Then the shimmering formed around me, and everything vanished.

Chapter 28

A few months back, I made a bold decision to teleport to a place I'd never physically been before, only seen on a screen. It was the first and only time I'd ever done such a thing, and I had ended up walking into a trap. This felt very much like the same thing.

Unlike the instantaneous travel experienced with teleportation, my journey actually took a few seconds. However, I had traveled from one place to another on prior occasions using magic (which I assumed this was), so I was familiar with the slight disorientation and sensory deprivation it entailed. Then I felt something solid under my feet and the shimmering around me vanished.

I found myself in a large, windowless chamber. It was well-lit, but from some source I couldn't make out. Oddly enough, the place seemed to be completely devoid of furniture, which might explain why everyone in the room was standing.

Not just standing, though, but standing and looking at me. And these weren't simple, ordinary folk. From what I could see, the fifty or so individuals in the room were mostly — if not all — supervillains.

Off to one side, I saw Retread Fred. I recognized another criminal called Barnacle, and yet another known as Slim Solar. There were dozens of others that I recognized and many more that I did not, and all wearing the same dark bodysuits as the three who had attacked me and Alpha Prime at the overpass. In short, outside of a prison documentary, it was the largest gathering of infamous and immoral villainy that I'd ever seen. (You'd have thought they were having a convention or something.)

INFILTRATION

"Well?" said a voice in front of me. It seemed to have come from a man dressed in something like a dark druid robe. The hood of the robe was pulled over his head, but not enough to hide his features. He appeared to be in his early forties, with dark hair, brown eyes, a sharply pointed nose, and a mostly-black (but neatly trimmed) beard that was just beginning to show touches of gray. He also carried a long, wooden staff that seemed bedecked with odd ornaments on its upper end. I recognized him as a sorcerer called Diabolist Mage — one of the guys Mouse had referred to as a "dork."

"Well," he said again, "do you have it?"

I was unsure how to respond (and still a little surprised, to be honest), and stood there staring at him in silence. Diabolist Mage sighed in exasperation and nodded at someone to the side of me. The next second, a guy with scaled skin and large, claw-like hands came over and removed the satchel from my shoulder.

Diabolist Mage let go of his staff — which remained standing straight up on its own — as the satchel was handed to him. He scrambled to open it, as excited as a kid unwrapping a Christmas present. Lifting the flap, he peered inside.

"Yes!" he shouted excitedly, tilting his head towards the ceiling with a look of pure joy on his face. He walked over to where his staff still stood, and then reached into the satchel and removed something that looked like a bracelet. He slipped it over the head of the staff — at which point it began glowing with a soft blue light — and slid it down. He had only taken it about two inches down when the light from the bracelet seemed to pulse, and then the bracelet itself shrank in size until it fit tightly around the staff.

Next, Diabolist Mage removed a piece of glass that resembled nothing so much as a big, blatantly fake diamond about a knuckle-length in size. He placed it in an open spot on the head of the staff, where it sparkled brazenly for a moment like the real thing.

All in all, there were about a half-dozen items that Diabolist Mage removed from the satchel, placing them all on his staff while everyone else in the room stood and watched. The last item was the purple shell Mouse had previously held, which the Diabolist merely sat on top of the staff. Surprisingly, the shell seemed to extend itself, wrapping slowly down and around the head of the staff in a winding pattern until it covered all of the other items garnishing the staff's head. Then it began to glow with a steady purple light.

Gingerly, almost in awe, Diabolist Mage reached out and grabbed the staff. Then he lifted it up over his head, smiling broadly, in a gesture of triumph. The purple light flared like a star, casting a violet fluorescence on the entire assemblage, which broke out into cheers.

Diabolist Mage lowered the staff and the room went silent again. He looked at me.

"Good work, Proteus," he said. "You should go rest up now."

Not quite sure what to say, I simply nodded and looked around, hoping for some indication of which way I should go. There were actually double doors set in all four walls, but I had no idea which way to go. After a few moments, the situation started to get awkward.

"Proteus, what's wrong with you?" the guy with claw-hands asked.

"Disorientation from the transference, most likely," Diabolist Mage said.

"It didn't affect him before," Claw-hands said.

"The effects are cumulative for some people," Diabolist Mage said, "like drinking alcohol. Having one beer might not affect you, but after three, you start getting tipsy. After five, you can barely stand up."

Claw-hands nodded in understanding, and then reached over to take my arm. "Come on, let's get you to your bunk. Then you can get out of those crazy clothes."

****

Turns out that Claw-hands actually went by the name Monitor. He had guided me out of the chamber where Diabolist Mage had been holding court through a set of side doors, and we now found ourselves walking down a wide, expansive hallway, occasionally passing other people.

Monitor seemed to be more the quiet type, but I needed intel. That meant I needed to get him talking.

"So," I said, "anything interesting happen while I was gone?"

"Only if you count sitting around waiting on you to get back as interesting. It's a good thing you came back with the goods, too. Otherwise, the Diabolist was going to let Imo pop your head off like a cork."

Hmmm... Apparently there was some merit to Mouse's insistence that I bring the satchel with me. Of course, with my power set, I would never have been in any real danger, but it was nice to know that the bad guys were probably feeling relaxed and would maybe let their guard down.

"Then that means everything's ready?" I asked.

Monitor shrugged. "That depends on the big man."

"Yeah, the Diabolist."

"No," Monitor said, eyeing me suspiciously. "The *big* man."

"Oh, right. The boss."

"Yeah, the boss," Monitor said, still giving me a funny look.

"Sorry. I must still be disoriented from the transference."

That seemed to allay Monitor's concerns, but I was sweating bullets. I had almost stepped in it there; I'd need to be very careful in the future, but I had learned something extremely valuable: someone other than Diabolist Mage was in charge.

Presumably, the person running the show was somewhere on the premises. I still didn't know where I was, but I got the impression — based on the wide hallways and ten-foot-tall doors everywhere — that the building we were in was enormous. It also seemed ancient, with all of the floors and walls cut from harsh, gray stone. Occasionally, one of the walls would dare to sport some artwork — usually an aged portrait of some aristocratic noble in a timeworn frame. Overall, the place had an antediluvian feel to it.

As we walked — up stairs, across landings, down hallways — I quickly debated my options. Telepathic communication was on the first page of my playbook, so I mentally reached out, trying to contact Mouse, Electra, Gramps...anyone I knew. No luck. We were either in a remote location, or simply outside my telepathic range.

Of course, I still had the beacon on me, which hopefully meant that the Alpha League now knew the location of their adversaries. With any luck, they would be busting down the doors here in a few hours — I checked Proteus' watch, only to find that it had stopped working — depending on exactly where we were geographically.

Also, I could always teleport back to Alpha League HQ, and then come back here with the cavalry in tow. A slight chill seemed to pass through me as I considered that option, and it occurred to me that I probably didn't have enough intel yet. Exactly how many bad guys were there? What was this magical weapon that they had? Who was the 'big man'?

As I pondered these and other questions, Monitor guided me up a final stairwell, around a corner and to another long hallway. Unlike the previous passageways we'd traversed, however, this one had evenly-spaced doors on either side running down its entire length.

We marched about a third of the way down the hall and then stopped in front of a door on the left wall.

"Well, here you are," Monitor said, and then went back the way we'd come. Apparently we'd arrived at our destination.

I tried the doorknob and found it unlocked. Taking a deep breath, I opened the door and stepped inside.

The room I found myself in was nothing special. It was about fifteen-by-fifteen feet in size and contained three single beds — one against the rear wall, and one against each of the side walls. At the head of each bed was a small nightstand with two drawers. There was also a bathroom and a mid-sized closet with sliding doors. The interior of the closet was divided into three sections, each of which contained a distinct style of clothing, as well as several of the black bodysuits that almost everyone here seemed to favor.

Beyond that, the room was fairly nondescript — there wasn't even a window. Taking into account the division of closet space and the number of beds, it was also safe to assume that I had roommates. Needless to say, I wasn't keen on the idea of having to share living space with other people — even if it just turned out to be a couple of hours. (I was here as a spy, after all.) Despite the fact that it was a flagrant invasion of privacy, I rifled through the drawers on the three nightstands, looking for any usable info. Thanks to pictures, letters, and other personal items, I was eventually able to figure out which bed was mine (the one on the right) but not much more than that.

I was tempted to flop down on the bed and take a moment to catch my mental breath, but didn't feel like I had the time. I needed to do some recon, and it occurred to me that it might be better to do so as inconspicuously as possible. That being the case, I headed to the closet and took another look at the clothes hanging there. I took a wild guess as to which section belonged to Proteus, grabbed one of the black bodysuits from that area, and then changed clothes at super speed. A moment later, I was dressed like almost everyone else here. Then I turned invisible and phased through the wall.

Being unfamiliar with my surroundings, I flew around randomly at first, trying to see as much of my new home as possible. This was part of my typical routine, as it let me mentally register physical locations so I could teleport there later if necessary. Had Mouse been present, he probably would have chided me for having changed clothes since I was gathering intel while invisible. Long experience, however, had taught me that when in Rome, do as the Romans do. (A motto to abide by even if you're invisible.)

I flew through the place as fast as I could without arousing suspicion. (At super speed, someone would have eventually found it odd that there were gusts of wind blowing through a building that didn't appear to have any windows.) I was happy to find that my initial impression was proven correct: the structure was enormous — practically a castle. Moreover, in phasing through walls, ceilings, and floors in all directions, I slowly began developing a mental blueprint of my new home.

As I made my way through various rooms, I also tried to garner an estimate of exactly how many residents the castle had. My best guess was that there were several hundred, but — by eavesdropping on a number of conversations — I determined that most of them were ordinary human beings. Less than a hundred were actually supers of any sort.

There was only one odd thing of note that I encountered. As I was exploring, I noticed that if I went far enough in one direction, I eventually came to a wall that, for some reason, I couldn't phase through. I could phase *into* the wall, but I couldn't go *through* it to the other side. It was as if the wall was a swimming pool: phasing into the wall was like jumping into the water — easy enough to do. Phasing through to the wall's other side, however, was like being in the pool and trying to swim through its concrete bottom.

This was completely foreign to my experience; I had never run into anything that I couldn't phase through before. Even more, I came across this anomaly four times with walls in four different directions. (I also found the same phenomenon limiting my phasing ability when I flew up as high — and as low — as I could.) In short, there was some kind of barrier keeping me from phasing through what I assumed were the outermost confines of the castle.

Unfortunately, I didn't explore every nook and cranny of the castle — far from it — but after about forty minutes of snooping I had gathered a respectable amount of information. I teleported back to my quarters to reassess my intel and decide on my next move.

I made sure that I was invisible when I popped back into the room. As luck would have it, no one was there. After becoming visible, I sat down on my bed and mentally began to take stock of my situation.

The main issue, of course, was whether or not it was time to fly the coop. I had information regarding the enemy's numbers, their leadership, and their position. (Or rather, the beacon I was carrying should indicate their location.) On the flip side, I still didn't know who the main guy in charge was, I didn't know their plans, I didn't have any new information on the weapon they had been using, and I was sure that the items from the satchel had helped them in some as-yet-unknown way. I felt an odd frigidity, like an icy breeze, as I contemplated what to do, but promptly dismissed the feeling. Weighing everything in the balance, it seemed that the best course of action was to stay until I found out more.

I had just come to that conclusion when the door to the room flew open. I jumped into fighting stance as a young blond man rushed into the room. Like everyone else here, he was wearing a black bodysuit, along with a pocket belt.

"Easy there, killer," he said, smiling at my aggressive reaction to his entrance. "It's just me, Case — your roomie? One of them, anyway."

After he said his name — Case — I came to the sudden realization that I had heard of this fellow before. He was a cruel, vicious criminal wanted in a score of countries for kidnapping, murder, and a dozen other felonies. The fact that someone with his reputation was here said a lot about the company I now found myself keeping.

I was so focused on recalling everything I could about Case that I didn't really notice that he was saying something to me about calming down. At that juncture, I noticed that I was still in an aggressive stance — something that was making Case incredibly tense.

"Sorry," I said, sitting slowly back down on my bed. "Guess I'm a bit jumpy with everything going on."

"Yeah," Case replied, relaxing. "I heard you came back from your trip a little addled." He twirled a finger around near his temple. "Hopefully the same thing won't happen to me."

"To *you*?" I asked as he started going through his nightstand drawer. "Are you going somewhere?"

"My group is mobilizing. Now that you've come back with the goods, Diabolist Mage and the big man say that we're ready to kick this thing off. Why waste a second when it's time to take over the world?"

As I pondered what he'd said, Case pulled a small, misshapen piece of metal from his nightstand. He kissed it, and then went to put it into a pocket on his belt.

"Good luck charm," he explained. "Ran all the way back here to get it. It never feels right when I shoot people without it."

INFILTRATION

"Shoot people?" I repeated, somewhat surprised.

"Only if we're lucky," Case mentioned with a wink, and empathically I felt a perverted, sadistic streak in him, a desire to inflict pain not just on others, but on others weaker than himself. "Well, I'm off."

He turned and left the room, closing the door behind him. A second later, I turned invisible and phased through the door, following him.

INFILTRATION

Chapter 29

Case ultimately ended up in the same chamber where I had initially made my appearance here. Still invisible and staying right on his tail, I phased my way inside. Standing at the doorway when Case entered was Gorgon Son, who handed him body armor, as well as a weapon from a gun case — a laser gun identical to those used by the guys who had attacked Alpha League HQ.

Case was one of the last guys to enter. His group consisted of about twenty people in all, and just looking at them gave me the unmistakable feeling of déjà vu. In essence, I got the distinct impression that some — if not all — of those gearing up had definitely comprised the band that had attacked us. (In fact, I also noted that they all had the same type of wristbands with crystals that the attackers had worn.)

Also in the room was Diabolist Mage. Staff in hand, he seemed to be waiting patiently as Case's group finished adjusting their armor and checking their weapons.

When I had been in this room previously, there hand been a lot of bodies present and I hadn't been able to take a good look around. Now, with fewer people blocking the view, I was able to notice something I had missed before — specifically, a mass of complicated-looking machinery that sat against one wall, emitting a low humming noise.

To a certain extent, the machinery resembled some of the complex computer equipment I had seen in Mouse's lab, with various lights, dials, and buttons. At the same time, however, it had bizarre symbols carved into the metal in some places, and sparkling crystals attached to it in others. Several peculiar, opaque tubes ran from the machinery into the floor and the wall. Finally, one portion of the machinery extended forward about five feet, resembling something like the barrel of an oversized weapon (and pointed directly at Case's group). Frankly speaking, I had no idea what to make of it.

Next to the equipment stood what I had at first presumed was a headless mannequin in a lab coat; I was stunned when I saw it move, touching a few dials on the equipment. Intrigued, I took another look and saw that the "mannequin" actually had a head after all, albeit one no bigger than the palm of my hand. At that juncture, I recognized the guy in the lab coat: an evil (but brilliant) scientist known as Grain Brain.

For a second, I wondered if he could be the person in charge, but decided against it. Grain Brain was typically the type to sell his services rather than initiate something on his own. He was more likely an employee here rather than the proprietor.

My attention, however, was drawn away from him as Diabolist Mage — finally satisfied that the group before him was ready — began to speak.

"Everyone knows the plan," he said. "Failure will be dealt with harshly, both by myself, and by *him*."

There were a few audible gulps at the last word, but the Diabolist didn't seem to notice. He turned and pointed his staff towards the equipment against the wall, and a purple ray of light shot from it, engulfing the machinery. A moment later, the symbols on the equipment began to glow with a yellow illumination as the opaque tubes seemed to pulse with life, like the exposed veins of a colossus, and an audible droning filled the air.

INFILTRATION

In a flash, I knew what was going to happen. Case's group was getting ready to attack someone or something else. The equipment in this room was the transfer mechanism, some kind of weird amalgam of science and magic.

As was becoming the norm for me, I mentally sifted through potential courses of action, noting once more a cool, brisk sensation as I did so. I could follow through with my thought from the previous night and transfer Case and his group — everyone in this room, in fact — to a holding cell at HQ. However, half the magicians out there are escape artists, and I didn't know if the Alpha League was prepared to hold someone like the Diabolist on short notice. Plus, even if the League was in a position to put everyone in this room on lockdown the second I teleported them, that would still leave their mystical weapon — which I hadn't seen yet — here in the hands of whatever big boss was actually running the show. Moreover, he would know that we were on to him, and right now my infiltration of their organization was probably our greatest strength.

At the same time, though, I couldn't just stand idly by and let our enemies launch another surprise attack. There had to be a way to clip their wings without tipping our hand. Then it came to me: Mouse's beacon.

I still had it with me, so I pulled it out. I floated down to where Case was standing, and then — using my phasing power — I slipped it into one of the pockets on his belt. I flew up above everyone's heads just as the barrel of the machinery that Grain Brain was fooling with fired in the direction of Case's group.

Diabolist Mage still had his staff pointed towards the machinery. Eyes closed, he seemed to be fiercely concentrating on something as he muttered what I assumed was an incantation under his breath. The shimmering I was now accustomed to seeing formed around Case's group, preparing to transport them…where?

As before, I was still hurting for good intel, and had few places to turn with respect to where to get it. Thus, I decided to take a bold step.

Reaching out telepathically, I lightly touched the mind of the Diabolist. With any luck, he'd be so focused on transferring Case's group that he wouldn't notice anything. Plus, I'm actually highly skilled, and can usually skim the surface thoughts of the average person without them ever knowing I'm there. Ideally, I wanted to peek inside the Diabolist's head and get an overview of what these guys were planning in the long run.

Unfortunately, we don't live in an ideal world or I did a less-than-ideal job of getting inside his head (or both), because the next second, the Diabolist's eyes snapped open. He growled almost like an animal, gritting his teeth hard enough to snap a dinosaur bone. He'd obviously felt something, and he glanced around the room trying to find whoever had invaded his privacy, radiating malice the entire time.

The light from his staff suddenly changed, dimming, resulting in an alteration to the shimmering around Case's group. There was a freaky shift in the position of the group, like an optical illusion that made it appear that Case and his fellows had all quickly jumped three feet to the right and then back again.

"Diabolist!" Grain Brain shouted, in a voice deeper than one would expect. Obviously, any distraction on the part of the Diabolist had an effect on what they were trying to do. I made a mental note of the fact.

Clearly still fuming, Diabolist Mage turned his attention back to the transfer. His staff once again started glowing as before, and a few moments later, Case and his group were gone. His primary task completed, the Diabolist raised his staff and it began shining a purple beam like a flashlight, which he began sweeping randomly around the room, across people and objects alike. I was pretty sure he wouldn't be able to see me, but — knowing almost nothing about magic and exactly what it can do — I took that as my cue to leave and did so.

Chapter 30

I was back in my room when a warning siren of some sort went off some time later. I had returned there after watching Case's team depart, and had found my other roommate inside when I arrived.

His name was Piler, and he was a grizzled, middle-aged merc starting to get past his prime. He was a bit of a talker, and I was just getting him going when the sirens started blasting.

"What the heck is that?" I asked.

"The all-assemble," Piler said, looking at me strangely.

"Of course," I said. "Guess I just forgot. Getting old, you know."

"Understood," Piler said. "I'm reaching the age where I can barely remember things myself."

He left the room and I followed — an excellent idea since I had no clue where I was going. Of course, as it was an all-assemble, I could have followed anyone because everyone I saw was on the move in the same direction.

After traversing a number of staircases and hallways, we came to a monstrous chamber bigger than a football field. It was a room I had passed through earlier while exploring, and it had struck me as the kind of place where a bunch of Vikings would sit around drinking and singing after raiding some village. Thus, I had mentally dubbed it the "Great Hall."

At the moment, it was standing room only as the entire population of the castle filed into the chamber. A few of those present, exerting super powers, either climbed up the walls for a better view or merely floated in

220

mid-air. (Frankly speaking, as I looked around and recognized some of those present, I was a little surprised at how peaceably they had assembled. Half these guys hated one another as much as they did superheroes.)

Towards the far end of the room, I could see the Diabolist standing on some sort of stone dais. It appeared that the action was likely to take place there, so I began working my way through the crowd in that direction, hoping to get a front-row seat for whatever was about to happen.

As I got closer, I saw that there was a group of people assembled in front of the dais, all in a straight line facing Diabolist Mage. They looked a little worse for wear, as if they'd just had sand kicked in their face at the beach, only the sand had been moving at one hundred miles per hour. It took me a second, but then I realized that this was Case's group that had left just a little while earlier.

Although I could only get a partial view of him from the side, Case himself looked like a boxer who had taken one too many punches to the head. His blond hair was unkempt, there was a distinct bruise on his cheek, and he held a hand against his side in a way that gave the impression that he was in pain.

Next to Case's group stood Gorgon Son, staring at them in menacing disapproval. In his hand he held a mace, which I assumed to be the same one he'd tried to bash me with.

Those assembled gave a wide berth to Case and his compatriots — as if they had some infectious disease — with the individuals at the front of the crowd getting no closer to them than twenty feet or so. It was already quiet in the room, but the few remaining whispers ceased abruptly as Diabolist Mage began talking.

"Well?" he said, staring at Case and his fellows but speaking to no one in particular. "I'm waiting for an explanation."

A deafening silence filled the chamber. It was clear that something had gone wrong, and Case's group was on trial for their lives. After a few moments, during which the Diabolist grew noticeably impatient, one of the group stepped forward.

"It was the Alpha League," the man said. "They were— "

"The Alpha League?!" shouted the Diabolist. "The Alpha League was destroyed!"

I could have smacked myself on the head. Proteus had actually been dispatched on a two-fold mission, one of which involved getting Alpha League HQ hammered by these guys' secret weapon. By coming back here as Proteus, I had apparently given Diabolist Mage the impression that their plan had worked. I inconspicuously attempted to worm my way back into the crowd a little bit, trying to avoid being seen by the Diabolist.

"Destroyed?" the man repeated. "No, they were on us before we could even get properly in position."

I fought to keep a smile off my face. The fact that the Alpha League had shown up meant that the beacon had done its job.

"What do you mean?" asked the Diabolist. "You shouldn't have had to get into the proper position. You should have *appeared* at the proper position."

The man, a brown-haired fellow with a five o'clock shadow who looked to be in his mid-thirties, looked nervous, unsure of what to say. He gulped, and then went on.

"We didn't appear at the designated location," the brown-haired man said. "We were about a mile east of the target zone. It took us about an hour to get there, and by that time the Alpha League had shown up. We were outmatched and requested recall."

This news did not sit well with Diabolist Mage, whose look had continually darkened with every word he'd heard. He gave an angry nod to Gorgon Son, who pointed his mace at the brown-haired man. A beam of light shot out from the mace and struck the man, who screamed and dropped to the floor, writhing in agony. Gorgon Son stepped over and hauled the man to his feet with one hand.

"Can you please explain to me why it took you an hour to cover one mile?" Diabolist Mage asked the man, who only appeared half-conscious while held in Gorgon Son's grip.

"Only... moved...cover," the man said groggily. "Maintain...surprise... League...knew...coming..."

The man seemed to pass out. Diabolist Mage made a subtle gesture to Gorgon Son, who slapped the man so viciously I thought his head would come off. Then again. He was preparing to do so a third time when a voice like thunder sounded.

"*Enough*," someone said in a commanding tone, with an inflection that reverberated off the walls.

Suddenly standing next to Diabolist Mage was another man. He was tall, muscular, completely hairless, and extraordinarily pale. He wore only a pair of trousers, and on his bare chest was an elaborate tattoo of a dragon. Somehow, despite his unique appearance and commanding presence, he had gained the stage next to the Diabolist without anyone even noticing him.

However, the minute he spoke, all eyes turned to him, and suddenly I sensed overwhelming feelings of fear, admiration, and respect coming from those around me. Even Gorgon Son, who seemed to be Diabolist Mage's right-hand man, inclined his head, acknowledging the newcomer's authority. Gorgon Son released his grip, and the brown-haired man flopped to the ground, unconscious.

There was now no doubt who was in charge. Who was running the show. Who the 'big man' was. It was this fellow, a fact that sent my mind racing because I recognized him.

It was the White Wyrm.

Chapter 31

The White Wyrm was one of the most noted and feared supervillains on the planet. Claiming descent from a dragon, he purportedly had a wide variety of powers — everything from super strength to telepathy, if you believed the rumors. (It was also said that he actually hated his "White Wyrm" moniker, which may be why everyone here constantly made reference to him by some other sobriquet.)

Regardless of what rumors were true about him, his involvement here meant that the stakes were even higher than anyone had imagined. Now I desperately needed to find out everything I could, because if there was anyone worth stopping with respect to anything they were doing, it was the White Wyrm.

"Don't kill the messenger who brings bad news," the White Wyrm said, speaking to the entire assembly. "Kill the messenger who fails to bring bad news when it's his duty to do so."

He turned his attention to the rest of Case's team. There was a cold fury in his gaze that was unnerving, and I was absolutely sure that those receiving the brunt of it would start to wilt.

"If the Alpha League was waiting for you," the White Wyrm said after a moment, staring at the men in front of him, "then someone told them you were coming."

At that, Diabolist Mage pointed his staff at the men on Case's team, and it gave off the same purple spotlight effect I had seen before. One by one, he shined it on the men in front of him until he came to Case. The light seemed to settle on him, and then intensify to such an extent that Case held up a hand to protect his eyes.

The light then narrowed until its point was a small dot — like a laser pointer — on Case's forehead. Then it began to move, swirling at first, around the area of Case's face. Next, it began zigzagging, running back and forth across his body in wild random patterns before eventually slowing down and then settling on a pocket on his belt. The very pocket I had placed the beacon in.

"Him," Diabolist Mage said a moment later.

"No!" Case screeched, backing away and looking terrified. "Not me! I didn't do anything! I—"

He stopped speaking as Gorgon Son caught him in a chokehold and dragged him up on the dais. Diabolist Mage came over to him, oozing malice, and popped open the indicated pocket on Case's belt. He reached in and pulled out the beacon. He stared at the little button-like object for a moment, then dropped it on the floor. He raised his staff and brought it down on the beacon. There was a short but intense flash, and when the staff was moved away the beacon was gone; no part of it remained — no ash, no broken circuit or wiring, nothing.

Diabolist Mage looked Case in the eye.

"You would have done better to shoot yourself than betray us," he said loud enough for everyone to hear. "Take him away."

Case made a whimpering sound as he was dragged from the room.

Diabolist Mage raised his staff, and again it blazed like a comet, casting an indigo hue upon everyone in the Great Hall.

"Let this be a message to all of you," he said to the crowd. "Disloyalty will be dealt with severely —

226

without exception, without mercy, and without remorse. Go."

No one needed to be told twice. There were low whispers and murmurs as everyone hustled out of the Great Hall, eager to put distance between themselves and the scene we had just witnessed.

Having been near the front when Case's team was being interrogated, I now found myself at the rear of those departing the chamber, the purple light from the Diabolist's staff still shining on our backs. I idled, walking at a slower and slower pace until I was the absolute last person to leave.

As I exited the room, the doors of the Great Hall slammed shut behind me of their own accord. There was a small clicking sound, and I knew that they were locked as well. I checked to make sure that no one was watching me, then turned invisible, phased, and went back inside.

The place seemed even larger now that the crowd had departed; the only people still in the room were Diabolist Mage and the White Wyrm. I floated up into the air and flew to the dais, which they were still on.

As I got close, I saw the White Wyrm turn to face the rear of the dais. He took about three steps, and then seemed to tap his foot on the floor. Almost immediately, blocks of stone in the floor started descending in a spiral pattern, creating a narrow, winding staircase leading down into darkness. This was quite likely how the White Wyrm had suddenly seemed to appear out of nowhere.

The White Wyrm began walking down the stairs, followed by Diabolist Mage (who, in turn, was followed by me). Neither spoke as they descended, and after a few moments, I heard a great weight shifting above me as the stones of the dais moved back into place. Simultaneously, what little light that had been entering the stairwell from the Great Hall vanished.

This presented no problem for me, as I was already viewing things in the infrared. An expanding purple glow below me indicated that Diabolist Mage was using his staff for light. I didn't know if the White Wyrm required any visual aid to see in the dark.

After a few minutes of traveling in this manner, we reached the bottom of the stairs, which terminated at a large room that appeared to serve as an office of some sort. I noticed an antique desk with a matching chair, several large tables covered with archaic parchments and scrolls, and some bookcases filled with dusty, ancient tomes. Light was provided by a number of well-placed torches.

I was most surprised, however, to see that the room had a window. It was situated on the wall behind the antique desk, and it was the only one I'd seen thus far. The view outside the window was pitch black, apparently showing a starless, moonless night.

The White Wyrm stepped behind the desk and looked out the window. Diabolist Mage stayed on the other side of the desk, waiting. On my part, I floated into one of the upper corners of the room.

"So, Diabolist," he said. "I believe an explanation is in order."

"Apparently we were compromised," Diabolist Mage said. "One of our men had a homing beacon that led the Alpha League straight to us."

"Not that. I'm not talking about that. I'm curious as to why that assault group ended up a mile away from the target. According to Grain Brain, you lost control."

INFILTRATION

Diabolist Mage coughed uncomfortably before speaking. "Your little shrunken-head pet is wrong. Why do we need him anyway? My magic can do everything his technology can, and more."

"First of all, we need Grain Brain because the blend of the mystical and mechanical serves our purposes by confusing the enemy. Those with roots in science will seek a technological answer, while those versed in the arcane will look for a magical solution. Both will be wrong in the aggregate.

"Next, Grain Brain's inventions enhance your magic, making it easier for you to accomplish things. Without them, your ability to control the power you've received is unreliable. Moreover, using them also helps reduce the risk that you'll inadvertently drain our secret weapon.

"Finally, don't forget that all of this newfound power you currently wield and boastfully speak of comes from a relic that *I* gave you. Without it, you would be just another street-corner magician doing card tricks on the subway for tips. So I'll ask you again for an explanation."

Diabolist Mage gritted his teeth in fury but kept a civil tongue in his head. "I didn't lose control. I was assaulted — a mind probe."

The White Wyrm glanced over his shoulder for a second, seemingly concerned. "Did they learn anything?"

"Of course not! I was aware the moment they set foot inside my brain. However, it was enough to break my concentration, and apparently make me lose the intended locus of the transfer."

"So," said the White Wyrm, turning all the way around to face Diabolist Mage, "you transferred them to the wrong location, which gave the Alpha League a chance to get involved, and ultimately caused a setback of our plans."

"You seem to forget that — despite any mistakes on my part — success would still have been possible if not for a traitor on the assault team."

"No, I didn't forget that. Nor did I forget that you decided to torture someone who was giving you valuable information on the subject."

"I've seen you do worse."

"*You* are wantonly cruel," the White Wyrm said, as if explaining something to a child. "*I*, on the other hand, am only cruel when it's warranted."

"We needed to send a message, about both failure and betrayal."

"Then, by your own standards, you should be punished for failing to destroy the Alpha League."

"That's not my fault! Proteus is to blame for that. He's the one who should be punished. I'll see to it—"

"You'll see to nothing."

"But Proteus is probably a traitor as well, since he didn't even mention that our weapon failed to take out the Alpha League."

"Didn't you say he was disoriented when he came back? He probably wasn't even thinking about it, especially if no one asked him a direct question on the subject. Also, if he betrayed us, why even come back? Why bring you relics that increased your power, that might make you capable of creating weapons that could defeat Alpha Prime? It seems far more likely that the traitor we uncovered today also gave the Alpha League a warning about our prior attack."

"Regardless, Proteus should still be disciplined, or it might send the wrong message."

INFILTRATION

"So now you wish to kill the courier who brings *good* news? In case you don't realize it, you've already sent a message. You let whoever tried to read your mind know that you can be easily distracted."

"The situation is more complex than you're making it sound."

"Oh? I seem to recall things being rather simple. You promised that you would be able to master the power you were given, but I see little evidence of it."

"I've mastered plenty!"

"Yes, if you only count the ability to destroy things — buildings, bridges, and the like. That's nothing — the equivalent of letting a child push the plunger on some TNT. Anyone can destroy. What's needed is mastery of the finer nuances of this power you've been granted."

"Such as?"

"The loyalty spell, for starters. You were supposed to cast a spell to ensure complete loyalty to me and my plans, as there is no honor among thieves. If it were done properly, we wouldn't have had a traitor on our team today and maybe your brain wouldn't have received a telepathic flyby."

"The spell is still in place. When I shined my staff on the assembly minutes ago, I screened everyone present, and they were all still under the influence of magic."

My ears perked up. I had been in that room when Diabolist Mage had shined his light on everyone. Did that mean that I was supposedly under a spell now? A *loyalty* spell? To *these* people?

"If the loyalty spell is still active and in place, then how do you explain our traitor?" the White Wyrm asked.

231

"I can't," Diabolist Mage said, shaking his head.

The White Wyrm seemed to take this in stride. He turned and began staring out the window once more. He stood there like that for several minutes, so still that he barely seemed alive.

Finally, Diabolist Mage pointed his staff and the window and said, "Perhaps I should—"

"Don't," said the White Wyrm firmly, raising his hand in a forbidding gesture while still looking outside. "I'm well aware of the dangers of looking out of the window — of staring into the void. I know that it supposedly drives men mad, which is why I had you remove all the other windows in the castle. But a healthy mind has nothing to fear; only the weak-minded need to worry about what is, or rather isn't, out there."

The last part of their conversation seemed odd to me, and I really didn't follow it. I had no idea what was so special about a window, but I didn't think it worth wasting a lot of time to find out.

Finally, the White Wyrm looked over his shoulder and spoke. "You should go, Diabolist. Work on mastering the powers you now possess."

Diabolist Mage didn't say anything, but I could tell from his emotions that he really didn't like being told what to do or being casually dismissed.

I thought the Diabolist was about to exit via the stairs and I prepared to follow him. Instead, however, he tapped his staff on the ground and simply disappeared.

Rather than stay there and watch the White Wyrm stare into space, I disappeared myself, teleporting back to my room.

INFILTRATION

Chapter 32

My sole remaining roommate wasn't present when I popped into our room, so I became visible and stretched out on my bed. I closed my eyes, trying to process everything I'd recently learned and plot my next move.

I knew who the major players were.

I knew that they had a powerful source of magic.

I knew that they had an army of bad guys who'd fight for them.

I knew that the destruction that had recently occurred was the result of Diabolist Mage manipulating his new power.

I knew that creating weapons strong enough to defeat Alpha Prime was on their agenda.

About the only thing I still didn't know was the source of the Diabolist's magic, although it was clear that the items I'd brought in the satchel had benefited him in some way.

Bearing all those facts in mind, maybe it was time for me to get back home and hand the reins to the Alpha League. Any intel I could provide would probably help — especially if Mouse, Esper, and the others had to come back here and face an armed militia.

Or maybe they didn't have to…

Something cool and ethereal seemed to touch my mind, and I jumped to my feet as inspiration swept through me, the seeds of a plan starting to sprout in my mind. It might not work, but it was worth a shot.

****

INFILTRATION

I had noticed that almost no one here carried any weapons, which probably wasn't a bad idea considering that the number of supervillains present made for a volatile mix of personalities. (Or maybe the loyalty spell the Diabolist had mentioned played a role in that, fostering camaraderie.) However, Case's group had gotten equipped with weapons and armor just before they departed. That told me that there was probably an armory somewhere on the premises. The only question was how to find it.

The easiest method would seem to be my little mindreading trick: ask someone where the armory was, pluck the answer from their thoughts, and be on my merry way. However, after my fiasco with trying to peek into the Diabolist's mind, I was actually a little gun-shy about skimming anyone else's thoughts. Still, in the end, I didn't have much choice unless I simply wanted to wander around invisibly from room to room until I came across what I was looking for.

However, rather than just trying to read the thoughts of random individuals, I adopted a different strategy. First, I tried to feel potential candidates out empathically. Those who are often the easiest to pluck thoughts from telepathically also tend to exhibit certain characteristics emotionally. For example, people who are somewhat insecure or extremely uptight are so burdened by their personal issues that getting in and out of their brain is usually a piece of cake.

Using this technique, I quickly learned that there were actually three armories, not one. I briefly pondered whether than meant that the bad guys had so much offensive weaponry that they had to store it in more than one place, or whether this was simply an attempt to avoid putting all their eggs in one basket. Mentally I shrugged, as it ultimately didn't matter; I was certain I could take out three weapons depots just as easily as one.

The first armory was located in close proximity to our quarters — basically, at the opposite end of (and around the corner from) the hallway that Monitor and I had entered when he had shown me to the door of my room. Oddly enough, the entrance was guarded by my old buddy Imo, who had clashed with me and Alpha Prime at the overpass. Hanging from his hip was the mace he had used in that earlier attack.

As might be expected, I had approached the area invisibly, flying near the ceiling. I phased through the wall above Imo's head and found myself inside what was probably a forty-by-forty foot room. I gave a low whistle, impressed with what I was seeing.

Every inch of every wall was lined with gun racks and weapons lockers. The gun racks themselves held a wild assortment of weapons, from assault rifles to submachine guns and more. The weapons lockers contained similar items, as well as several advanced weapons I couldn't even name.

The middle of the room was filled with several rows of shelving, and contained everything from ammo to gun cases to explosives like grenades.

All in all, it was a formidable amount of firepower. Although the Alpha League went up against armed foes all the time, I suddenly felt a lot better about my decision to destroy all this stuff before I skedaddled.

Usually when it came to weapons in the hands of bad guys, my *modus operandi* was to simply teleport the offending item to a secure location. In this instance, however, I didn't just want to disarm the White Wyrm and his ilk; I wanted to sow confusion — get them disorganized if I could — and few things were as good at creating chaos as explosions. Thus, my plan was to actually blow up each armory.

That being the case, I went to work at super speed, dumping all of the weapons into a couple of piles on the floor as quickly and quietly as I could. The only exception to this was a grenade belt that I, on a whim, picked up and slung over my shoulder after stocking it with both traditional grenades and those of the smoke bomb variety.

I was just about finished when the door to the armory was flung open and Imo stepped in. I thought I'd been as quiet as a mouse, but whether he'd heard something or been guided by simple intuition, Imo came into the room in battle mode — mace in hand and looking for a dance partner.

Still at super speed, I pulled a pin from a grenade and flung it in his direction. It struck him in the mid-section, but at that velocity, it was like being hit with a cruise missile. Imo was lifted off his feet, dropping his mace in the process, and carried down the hallway by the grenade, which was still buried deep in his gut like a fist.

I zipped over and picked up the mace. It was lighter than I had anticipated, but still felt solid enough to do an impressive amount of damage. I slammed the door to the armory just as Imo hit the floor of the hallway. A second later, the building shook with the sounds of an explosion as the grenade went off, and several of the weapons slid off the piles that I had stacked them in.

A moment later, I had pulled the pins on about forty grenades, tossed them into the various weapons piles, and then dashed out of the room and down the hallway. Along the way I passed Imo, who was still lying on the hallway floor. He was unconscious and his clothing was in tatters, but beyond that he didn't appear to be injured too seriously — despite the fact that the grenade blast had splintered the walls nearby and caused part of the ceiling to collapse on top of him.

The sound of voices and the distinct rhythmic patter of running feet made me realize that people were coming. I glanced back at the armory, where the grenades should be going off any second, and then took off running for the second armory, not caring anymore if anyone realized a speedster was present. A moment later, I was rewarded with a series of deep, rumbling explosions that sent tremors throughout the building.

INFILTRATION

Chapter 33

Initially, I had almost no trouble with the second armory, which was designed almost exactly like the first. Although it, too, had a hulking guard manning the entrance, I simply phased inside while invisible. Within a few seconds, I had all the weapons piled on the floor as before. I had just pulled the pins on a bunch of hand grenades when the door flew open and a whirlwind blew in, followed by the fellow who had been standing guard outside. A strong wind whipped around the room, and a moment later all of the pins were back in the grenades.

I didn't realize what had happened at first, but then it hit me: a speedster had come into the room and put all of the grenade pins back in place. I glanced around the room, and saw him — a young guy, barely out of his teens, and so hyper that he couldn't stand still (as evidenced by the fact that he kept zipping from side to side).

I teleported him, along with the guard who had come into the room with him, to the Great Hall (which, for some reason, was the first place I thought of). Then I went into super speed again and once more removed all the pins from the grenades. I was about to take off when the speedster I had just banished dashed back into the room and once again put all the pins back into the grenades.

Of course — he was a speedster. Teleporting him to another part of the castle had only delayed him slightly as it took him practically no time at all to return to the second armory. (Obviously it would take the door guard longer, since he apparently didn't possess the same speed.)

INFILTRATION

Disgusted, I removed all the grenade pins a third time and flung them towards the door. Lightning quick, the other speedster dashed over and nimbly plucked them out of the air one by one, and then put them back into the grenades once more.

I had to admit that he was good, but I was getting a little tired of him wrecking my plans. On his part, the speedster just looked at me, waiting. He gave me a cocksure grin, letting me know that this was fun for him. Other than that, though, he didn't make any type of aggressive move. What was he waiting on? Why wasn't he trying to go on the offensive?

Then it hit me: he was stalling. He was just keeping me occupied until reinforcements could arrive. Thus, I couldn't waste any more time on this guy. I needed a plan, and needed it quick. There had to be a way to turn the tables on this speedster.

The solution came to me a moment later. I smiled as I zipped around pulling out grenade pins again, hopefully for the last time (at least in *this* room). Like clockwork, the other speedster followed up almost as soon as I was done. However, as soon as he picked up a pin and tried to put it back into a grenade, I turned the latter invisible.

He froze momentarily, clearly unsure of what was happening. Obviously, he could feel the grenade in his hand, but he couldn't see it. More precisely, he couldn't see the hole that the pin was supposed to go in. He struggled mightily for a few moments, wasting valuable time, trying to locate the hole by feel. Then he dropped the grenade and reached for another. I made that one invisible as well.

INFILTRATION

When he couldn't find the pinhole on the second grenade, I saw panic start to set in. In real time it had only been a few seconds, but it was long enough for the other speedster to realize that this was a lost cause. He turned and dashed from the room, and I left hot on his heels.

A moment later, the armory exploded behind us. The other speedster decided to glance over his shoulder to get a peek at the devastation. As he did so, I tossed Imo's mace, which I was still carrying, at his ankles. It tripped him up nicely; he fell forward, his head hitting the floor with an audible smack, and then went tumbling down the hallway like a rodeo clown tossed by a steer.

I scooped up the mace, and then stopped to stare at the other speedster after he stopped skidding. He'd definitely had his ticket punched. Not only was he knocked out, but the ankle that the mace had hit seemed to be bent at an odd angle. Looking at that ankle and the discoloration that was starting to form around it, I had an odd feeling that, even if he had been conscious, this guy wouldn't be giving me any more trouble today.

INFILTRATION

Chapter 34

They were waiting for me at the last armory, which had the same layout as its predecessors. I should have known something unusual was going on; there was no guard posted outside. Invisible, I phased through the door, and found the room on the other side not just full of weapons, but also containing Diabolist Mage, the White Wyrm, Retread Fred, and Gorgon Son. The four of them were standing together on the far side of the room, in a corner near a weapons locker.

"—ic!" Diabolist Mage was saying. "I've got the power now!"

"You've got the power," the White Wyrm retorted, "but no control. Heeding your advice would lead to ruin."

"But—" the Diabolist began.

"Silence!" the White Wyrm exclaimed. "We will speak of this later. Right now, we have an uninvited guest to deal with." The White Wyrm looked knowingly around the room. "In fact, you're here now, aren't you?"

I had to admit to being surprised. It was pretty obvious that he couldn't sense me by any normal means, but the White Wyrm obviously had either some other power that let him detect my presence, or a well-developed sense of intuition.

"Come, come," he continued. "There's no need to be shy. We're all friends here."

I floated up to one corner near the ceiling and said, "With" — I teleported to another corner — "friends" — I teleported to a third corner — "like" — I teleported to the last corner of the room — "these…"

Speaking in an unbroken string as I popped around the room had made it seem as though my voice was coming from all around them, and the eyes of all four had darted around, trying to pinpoint my location. When I finished, the White Wyrm laughed.

"Ah, a teleporter," he said, eyes roaming around the ceiling. "My envy on having such a unique skill."

Again, I marveled at how he had discerned that I was a teleporter without being able to see me. If this was merely intuition on his part, it bordered on psychic ability.

"By now, you know something of our plans," he said. "And you know that no one can stop us."

"Really?" I said sarcastically, popping around the room again as I spoke. "I've been able to gum up the works without even trying too hard. I can only imagine what will happen when someone like the Alpha League decides to swat you flies."

"So you're with the Alpha League," the White Wyrm said. "Good to know."

My mouth almost fell open. I needed to shut up. Every time I spoke, the White Wyrm deduced some fact that I hadn't intended to divulge. I wanted to scream, but with my luck, the White Wyrm would glean something from that, too.

"Ha!" I exclaimed, trying to cover. "The Alpha League wouldn't get out of bed for this mad tea party you've got going on. They only deal with *real* threats."

"But would I be correct in assuming that it was you who planted that bug that led them to our assault team?"

I didn't say anything, but my silence was practically confirmation in itself.

"Be that as it may," the White Wyrm continued, "it occurs to me that we might be able to make a deal. I'd like to extend an offer to you."

"What kind of offer?" I asked. Whatever it was, the answer was going to be "No," but I was curious as to what he had to say.

"Please," the White Wyrm said, "I prefer to have these kinds of dealings face-to-face. Right now I feel as though I'm conversing with the ether."

It was undoubtedly a trick, but I was confident that I could handle anything that was thrown at me. I floated down to the floor in a corner that was adjacent to where my four adversaries were standing and became visible. Four pairs of eyes swiveled in my direction.

Diabolist Mage looked at me in unadulterated surprise. "Proteus?"

I winked at the Diabolist and smiled, but didn't verbally respond. I had effectively been viewed as Proteus since coming here, but that ruse was now over. Openly angry at having been duped, the Diabolist hissed at me and Gorgon Son made as if to move in my direction, but the White Wyrm stepped to the fore and held his hands out to his side.

"No," he said firmly over his shoulder, effectively guaranteeing my safety — for the moment.

"I'm listening," I said.

"You," the White Wyrm began, "have come here uninvited, infiltrated our group, sown dissension in our ranks, made us abort parts of our plan, destroyed our armories, and — in the process — caused untold damage to my ancestral home. In short, you have caused us no end of grief since your arrival."

I shrugged. "What can I say? It's a gift."

"Still," the White Wyrm went on, "I think we could use your unique talents, and I'd like to make a place for you in our upper echelons."

"And why would you want to do that?"

"No leader, no matter how great, can do everything himself. He needs lieutenants to help him. To carry some of the load. To address the minutiae so he can concentrate on the things that matter."

"And in your opinion, I fit the bill?"

"Why not? You're extremely gifted, resourceful, intelligent, and bold. I can make use of those talents."

"That sounds like a windfall for you, Your Majesty, but what's in it for me?"

"For you? Why… No!"

In focusing on my conversation with the White Wyrm, I had made the mistake of ignoring Diabolist Mage to a certain extent, and he had been slowly tilting his staff until it was pointed almost directly at me. Warned by the White Wyrm's shout, I phased as a beam of light shot out from the head of the staff. It passed harmlessly through me, but burned a hole through a gun rack that had been behind me, as well as the assault weapons that it held and the wall it was affixed to. I turned invisible and teleported to an upper corner of the room.

The White Wyrm turned and smacked Diabolist Mage with a vicious backhand that sent the magician sprawling.

"I specifically forbade any attack!" the White Wyrm shouted. "You would do well to obey your master!"

There was bloodlust in the Diabolist's eyes as he jumped to his feet, shouting, "And you would do well to remember who has the power here now — who holds the reins of your secret weapon!"

As he spoke, a purple glow — apparently emanating from his staff — surrounded him. The White Wyrm growled low in his throat; Gorgon Son and Retread Fred stepped back as it looked like their two leaders were about to come to blows.

While I watched these events unfold, my mind was racing, focusing on what the Diabolist had just said. He had mentioned their secret weapon — the one I had yet to find, the source of the power he now wielded. I suddenly had my own spark of intuition with respect to finding it.

"Thanks for the job offer," I said, popping around the room again as I spoke, distracting the White Worm and Diabolist Mage before they engaged each other. "Since it's for a management position, I'm sure you'd like to review my bona fides. Here's a copy of my résumé."

I pulled a grenade from the belt that I still carried over my shoulder. I yanked the pin out, made the grenade visible, and then dropped it on the floor between the White Wyrm and Diabolist Mage. Their reactions were immediate.

The Diabolist cracked the end of his staff on the floor, and a purple bubble formed around him. Gorgon Son spun around, gripped a weapons locker that was behind him, then lifted it bodily and slammed it on the ground between him and the grenade. In a similar vein, the White Wyrm stepped behind Retread Fred, obviously intending to use the rubberized villain as a shield. A moment later, the grenade went off.

INFILTRATION

The blast in the enclosed space was deafening and blew both shelving and various items to the other side of the room. Shrapnel flew in all directions; none, however, seemed to penetrate the bubble around the Diabolist. Likewise, the weapons locker seemed to protect Gorgon Son, although the force of the blast pushed both him and the locker back into the wall. Both Retread Fred and the White Wyrm were lifted off their feet, with the former eventually landing on top of the latter. That said, neither seemed to have suffered any real harm.

The White Wyrm shoved Retread Fred off him and was just getting to his feet when I dropped a smoke grenade. There was an audible hiss as white smoke gushed forth, filling the room. Watching them in infrared, I assumed from the way my four adversaries were waving their arms in an effort to clear the smoke that none of them could see anything. (And from the way they were coughing, they could probably barely breathe.) Now was the time for the bold part of my plan.

"Now I'll just drop a few more grenades to destroy the weapons here," I said, floating above the smoke, "then I'm off to take your secret weapon offline."

I dropped another smoke grenade — just to be sure no one but me could see anything — then teleported Retread Fred to the Great Hall. Following that, I dropped to the floor, simultaneously becoming substantial again and shapeshifting into a twin of Retread Fred. The bodysuit I was wearing suddenly became excessively tight and constrictive compared to a few seconds earlier, but I could deal with it. A moment later, smoke filled my lungs and I was coughing along with the rest of them.

"Diabolist!" I said, genuinely wheezing, "you have to get us to the weapon before *he* gets there!"

INFILTRATION

Diabolist Mage nodded, acknowledging the truth of what I'd said, although he surely had no idea who had spoken. He waved his staff in a circle and the smoke pushed out away from us, as if blown by a stiff breeze. We could all now see one another (not to mention breathe again). The Diabolist eyed each of us for a moment, then tapped his staff on the ground.

We vanished.

Chapter 35

We reappeared, seemingly moments later, in a spacious workroom that reminded me greatly of Mouse's lab. There was lots of complex machinery around, as well as numerous worktables covered with an assortment of papers, gadgets, and gizmos. The place even had its own mad scientist in the form of Grain Brain, who was diligently studying the readout from some piece of equipment.

"Grain Brain," the White Wyrm said, getting the scientist's attention, "we're about to have company."

Grain Brain nodded, and the White Wyrm approached him, apparently giving him the details of the presumably impending attack.

I looked around, desperately seeking the secret weapon, the source of the Diabolist's power. After a cursory glance, nothing immediately stood out to me. I took a deep breath and slowly looked around again, taking a few steps around the room as I did so. This time, something caught my eye.

Almost dead center in the middle of the room was a gilded, coffin-like metal box. It rose up to a height of about four feet, and was covered with intricate designs and adorned with numerous precious and semi-precious stones. Jutting out from the box on both sides were several of the same opaque tubes I had seen connected to the matter transfer equipment.

That had to be it — the magical object that these guys were using. I had only missed seeing it at first because it had been obscured by one of the worktables. The next moment, I received confirmation as Diabolist

Mage — accompanied by Gorgon Son — approached the box and pointed his staff at it.

A glowing strand, like a wire alive with electricity, seemed to reach out from the box and latch onto the staff. In fact, that's almost exactly what it was, as the wire appeared to transfer some kind of essence along its length from the box into the staff — and ultimately into Diabolist Mage. Even as I watched, the magician seemed to grow in stature, the power he was receiving becoming almost a presence on its own.

Empathically, I sensed the Diabolist feeling flush with power, invincible. Hegemony was taking hold in his mind as an inherent right that he possessed, and he exuded a wicked desire to establish dominion over the whole world — and crush anyone who stood in his way. In essence, the power he now wielded was driving him mad.

I checked my inventory, noting that I still had Imo's mace and the grenade belt looped over my shoulder. It might have seemed odd that no one had taken note of it, but — as I mentioned before — most people only look at the face when trying to identify someone.

I sidled closer, trying to casually narrow the gap between myself and the ornate box, as if I wanted a better view of it. As I closed the distance, I nonchalantly pulled a grenade from the belt. I gripped it in my palm, and then let my hand fall to my side in a natural manner. Whatever this thing was giving the Diabolist power, we were about to find out if it could survive being at the blast epicenter of an exploding grenade.

I took another step towards the box, at which point I noticed that it actually had a glass top, meaning that whatever was inside could actually be seen. Before I could get any closer, however, Gorgon Son turned in my direction. He held up his hand and shook his head in a do-not-approach gesture as Diabolist Mage continued gaining power. A second later, the weird strand withdrew from the staff and returned to the box. Gorgon Son rushed to the Diabolist, who appeared on the verge of collapse, and helped steady him.

With everyone evidently ignoring me, I took advantage of the opportunity and quickly stepped over to the box. I casually drew the pin out of the grenade, preparing to leave it on the glass top when I glanced inside and caught my breath. There was a man in there.

Looking at the man lying in the box, I suddenly realized that we were in far greater danger than we knew. Mouse had basically been banking on Rune bailing us out since this was a situation involving the mystical. However, it was clear to me now that we couldn't call on Rune to defeat these particular enemies.

Rune couldn't defeat their magic. Rune *was* their magic.

The man in the box was Rune.

Chapter 36

I stared at Rune, practically in shock for a few seconds, thinking that it couldn't be. It was definitely him, though; every square inch of uncovered skin sported weird symbols and designs. Moreover, the symbols moved — something that generally gave people the creeps and made Rune one of the less-popular supers (not that he cared about that kind of thing).

He was clearly the source of power that the bad guys had been referring to. Somehow, Diabolist Mage had found a way to siphon off Rune's magic and use it as his own.

As to Rune himself, I had trouble concluding that he was actually alive; dressed in nothing but a loincloth, he didn't even appear to be breathing. However, as I'd already noted, the graphics on his skin still moved, leading me to believe that there was life in there somewhere. Even if there wasn't, I didn't think there was any way I could blow up the box now.

Speaking of blowing things up, I found that I was still holding the grenade. Thankfully, I hadn't released the safety handle yet, but I didn't fancy the idea of teleporting it back home with me and Rune, which had suddenly become the new plan.

Now it was my turn to try to put a pin back in a grenade. I had dropped it while walking over to the box, so it had to be—

"Hey!" Diabolist Mage shouted in my direction. "Just what do you think you're doing?"

"Well, uh, I, uh," I began. Before I could get anything else out, Gorgon Son's eyes seemed to go wide. His line of sight went from the grenade to the belt around my shoulders, back to the grenade again, and then finally to my face. (I blatantly avoided looking him in the eyes this time.)

"That's not Fred!" Gorgon Son shouted, pointing at me.

The White Wyrm and Grain Brain suddenly looked in my direction. Gorgon Son looked like he was about to charge, and I saw the Diabolist leaning his staff towards me.

I threw the grenade towards the White Wyrm and Grain Brain; they both dove for cover, scrambling to get behind some computer equipment. I phased myself and the box containing Rune as Gorgon Son dove at me. He passed through without making contact with anything and smacked his head on a worktable that was behind me.

The Diabolist shot a beam of purple light at me, but it passed right through me again. This time, however, I felt something — like the beam had tickled me a little. It occurred to me then that maybe Diabolist Mage had gotten enough power to somehow affect me in my insubstantial form. It was not a prospect I relished.

At that moment, the grenade went off, blasting a hole in the floor and sending shrapnel and shards of stone flying everywhere. Something grazed the Diabolist just beneath the eye, making him jerk his head to the side in pain. When he looked my way again, I saw a jagged red line near his cheekbone that was already starting to weep blood.

The Diabolist gingerly put a finger to his cheek, flinching when he touched the wound. He looked at me with murder in his eyes. Near the computer equipment they had hidden behind, the White Wyrm and Grain Brain were just getting to their feet, as was Gorgon Son.

They, too, all looked as though they'd like to bite my eyeballs out. Obviously, I had overstayed my welcome.

No longer needing to pretend to be someone else, I shapeshifted back to my own face and body.

"Toodles," I said, holding up a hand and giving a little finger wave.

I wrapped Rune, box and all, in my power and tried to teleport us to Mouse's lab.

Nothing happened.

INFILTRATION

Chapter 37

Once, when I was very young and had just developed my teleportation power, I tried to teleport into a picture I saw in a book. It was one of those impossibly happy scenes, with cherubic kids running around and having loads of fun at a state fair or something like that. Of course, it didn't work because that place didn't actually exist. Every time I tried to go there, it was as though there was a blank spot in my mind where I should have pictured a destination.

The same thing happened when I tried to teleport myself and Rune. I felt a nothingness in mind, a sort of null-and-void insinuation with respect to where I tried to take us. First it was Mouse's lab. Then anywhere at Alpha League HQ. Then anywhere other than this castle. It was as if none of those places were there any more — like someone had hit some sort of universal "Delete" button with respect to them.

"Trouble, teleporter?" Diabolist Mage asked with an evil leer. "I think you'll find that there's nowhere to go. My power warps reality, changes it to suit my whims. At the moment, we're outside of all space and time. Nothing exists outside these castle walls. In fact" — his eyes started to glow with purple light as he performed some new deviltry — "as far as we're concerned, nothing else exists beyond this room."

It was a little difficult for me to process what he was saying, but I didn't doubt the truth of his words. Nothing else really made sense, and my own failure to teleport confirmed it. Moreover, I suddenly had a sort of clarity with respect to my previous inability to phase beyond the castle's outer walls. I couldn't phase all the way through those walls because there was no place on the other side of them to phase *to*. (I also had a sudden suspicion as to why no one outside the castle was in range of my telepathy.)

Furthermore, if the Diabolist were to be believed, my universe had literally shrunk even further and was now nothing more than this room.

It was a lot to wrap my head around, but I didn't really have time to dwell on it. I was trapped in here with an unconscious (possibly comatose or nearly-dead) ally, and four vicious supervillains. Figuring out all of the minor details would have to wait.

Laser light lanced through me a moment later. Grain Brain had pulled a laser gun from somewhere and was blasting for all he was worth.

"Stop!" screamed Diabolist Mage. "You'll hit the receptacle!"

Fortunately, Rune and I were still phased so we hadn't been injured, but it was worthwhile to note that Rune still held some value for these guys. Grain Brain eased up on the trigger, at which point the Diabolist seemed to breathe a little easier.

I was still trying to figure out what to do next when Gorgon Son leaped through me again, this time from behind. In my phased form, threats can practically be ignored, and I had dismissed him to a certain extent as I tried to figure out what to do. It was a very poor decision on my part.

As he leaped through my insubstantial body, Gorgon Son turned around so that when he landed he was facing me. Looking me in the eye, actually. And just like before, his eyes began to glow, his hair became a live, wriggling mass, and I suddenly found that I couldn't move.

For a few seconds, it was a repeat of the scene at the overpass, with Gorgon Son swinging at me and being unable to connect with anything while I strained to move.

"It's him — that kid from the other night," Gorgon said after a few moments of futile action with his mace, making an impressive deduction. "I have him, but I can't touch him."

While he had been swinging at me, the White Wyrm and Diabolist Mage had walked over, and now stood just to the rear of Gorgon Son.

"It appears that we have a Mexican standoff," the White Wyrm said.

"Maybe not," the Diabolist countered as his eyes started glowing again. "I believe my magic can circumvent his power. Give me a few moments, and I can make him solid again."

"And then?" Gorgon Son asked.

"Obliterate him," the Diabolist responded.

The White Wyrm chuckled, seemingly satisfied with what he'd heard from his comrades. He looked at me and cocked his head slightly to the side, as if contemplating something.

"Viewing your time here as a probationary period," he said after a few seconds, "I've come to the conclusion that you don't fit in with our corporate culture, and must therefore retract my offer of permanent employment. Best of luck in your future endeavors."

He turned and walked back towards Grain Brain as Gorgon Son started swinging at me again.

Based on what he'd done with reality, I didn't doubt that Diabolist Mage could probably make me substantial again. In fact, the mace that Gorgon Son was using was glowing with the same purple light as the Diabolist's eyes.

"Enjoy your last few moments of life," the Diabolist said. "With my enhanced abilities, I'll make the maces even more powerful than when we tested them on Alpha Prime. Thanks for being our guinea pig."

The Diabolist was as good as his word; I was starting to feel something from the mace as Gorgon Son continued trying to strike me. Like the beam of light before, it had started off gently, along the lines of being tickled with a feather — but was beginning to feel a bit firmer. In just a few minutes, the mace would start to connect with flesh and bone.

Mentally, I scrambled, trying to gain some kind of edge. A chill went through me as I remembered what Mouse and BT had said. I couldn't move physically, but I was still phased, so maybe my other powers still worked. If I could use them to break Gorgon Son's concentration...

I reached out telekinetically and poked him in the eyes. Hard. Gorgon Son screeched in pain, hands going to his face, and I felt myself free of his control.

I became solid, then stepped forward and walloped Gorgon Son on the forehead with Imo's mace. He staggered backwards, disoriented, stumbling into Diabolist Mage. Being jostled seemed to break the Diabolist's concentration, because the glow left his eyes, leaving me to assume that whatever magic he was employing to affect my phasing power had been halted.

Off to the side, Grain Brain opened up with the laser gun again (although now that I looked closely, it seemed more like a laser rifle). I phased, thankful that the shots passed harmlessly through me.

"Stop!" Diabolist Mage yelled, shoving Gorgon Son away from him. "Stop shooting!"

Either Grain Brain didn't hear the Diabolist, didn't react fast enough, or simply didn't care, because the shots kept coming. Overtly furious at being ignored, Diabolist Mage fired a purple spark from his staff at the wee-headed scientist. It struck Grain Brain in the thigh, blasting his leg off, and he dropped to the ground, wailing in unimaginable pain and clutching the stump where his leg had been. The White Wyrm, who had been standing next to Grain Brain, was blown to the ground, dazed.

I peeked into the box to check on Rune. He seemed no worse than before, the diagrams on his face moving almost with purposeful intent.

I teleported in front of Gorgon Son, who was still rubbing his eyes in effort to soothe the pain. I gave him an uppercut on the chin with Imo's mace. He went over backwards, hit the floor, and didn't move.

The Diabolist turned towards me, and I flung the mace at him. He batted it aside with his staff, but I used the distraction to teleport, popping up next to him. I grabbed the staff, intending to yank it away from him, and then found myself screaming as it felt like someone had smeared napalm on my hands.

I let go of the staff and staggered back a step, staring at my hands in agony. It looked like I'd had an accident while trying to juggle an electrified chain saw that was also on fire. My hands were raw and blistered — even charred in some places. I tried moving my fingers and almost collapsed from the pain.

The Diabolist laughed. "You overreach, my friend. My staff has the power of the Kroten Yoso Va! It rejects your tainted touch."

He pointed the staff at me, but before he could do anything, I teleported to a corner of the room, invisible. Being a speedster, I had a high metabolism, and I knew my hands would heal quickly, but not fast enough to deal with the threats in this room.

I concentrated for a moment, taking conscious control of my body — specifically, the nervous system. Over the next few seconds, I clamped down on the nerve endings in my hands, shutting off the impulses sending out the sensation of pain. The relief was almost immediate, and I found that I could once again move my hands without feeling like I was going to start blubbering.

Glancing around, the scene was still much as I'd left it. Diabolist Mage was desperately scanning the room in an effort to find me, head jerking around every few seconds in helter-skelter fashion. The White Wyrm was slowly getting to his feet, while Gorgon Son was still unconscious.

I teleported over by Grain Brain, picking up the laser rifle he had dropped when he lost his leg. The scientist had stopped screaming, but was making a weird mewling sound, apparently in shock. I ignored him and teleported behind the White Wyrm and stuck the barrel of the rifle in his back.

The White Wyrm, apparently no stranger to having the muzzle of a gun against his spine, slowly raised his hands in the air. I let out a heads-up whistle, causing the Diabolist to look in my direction.

"Release Rune and drop the staff," I said, keeping my prisoner between us, "or the big man gets it."

The Diabolist laughed. "Go ahead. It'll save me the trouble of doing it later."

"Honor among thieves," I said in a low voice, to which the White Wyrm merely replied, "Indeed."

Diabolist Mage pointed his staff at us and fired.

The White Wyrm dived aside and I phased and then teleported, this time popping up near the box holding Rune. Now that I thought about it, being next to Rune's box was probably the safest place to be, since the Diabolist didn't seem willing to risk harming him. And why should he? Rune was the goose laying the golden eggs.

Still, as long as the Diabolist was holding that staff, it seemed that nothing could touch him. That staff was the key... A little shudder went through me as a possible plan formed.

Diabolist Mage was looking around wildly again, now trying to keep an eye on the White Wyrm as well as look for me. I phased his staff, and it literally slipped through his fingers. The Diabolist's hands flailed madly trying to catch it, like a drunk trying to grab a falling bottle of wine before it smashes on the sidewalk.

Before it hit the floor, I teleported the staff; the Diabolist screamed in frustration as it vanished. The staff appeared next to me in solid form as I held it up telekinetically — no way was I touching it again, even with numbed nerve endings.

The Diabolist looked in my direction, teeth bared, and I felt a murderous fury build in him that I would dare take his staff from him. He growled, a low animal sound, and then charged at me, eyes glowing. He'd taken maybe three steps when a powerful shoulder rammed into him, knocking him off his feet. It was the White Wyrm.

INFILTRATION

Apparently the Diabolist's plan to eventually off him did not sit well with his former boss. The White Wyrm stepped over to where the Diabolist was still lying on the floor. He picked the magician up with one hand, holding him aloft, and then viciously slapped him with the other. (It was almost an encore performance of what had happened to Case.)

"You would eliminate *me*???!!! A dragon-born???!!!" the White Wyrm screamed, and then slammed the Diabolist face-first into the ground, hard enough to crack the stone floor. His sense of outrage was so great that he practically forgot about me...for a moment.

Breathing hard (and perhaps not having fully sated his aggressive tendencies), he looked around until he spied me. His eyes sparkled as he noticed the staff floating beside me, and he began walking in my direction.

"This is the problem with the criminal mindset," the White Wyrm said, seemingly talking to himself. "From petty crooks to mafia dons to supervillains, none of these worms seems to know their place."

"So it would seem...*worm*," said the Diabolist, rising to his feet and enunciating the last word so clearly that there was no mistaking his meaning.

The White Wyrm stopped, and then turned about. He and the Diabolist said nothing, and I felt black hate — vile and unfiltered — pouring off each of them with regards to the other. Then, without preamble, they charged each other, screaming.

When they closed, the White Wyrm wrapped his hands around the Diabolist's throat, squeezing mightily. At the same time, he pulled Diabolist Mage close until they were face-to-face. The White Wyrm's mouth opened wide, far wider than should have been possible — almost as if it had unhinged. Then he bellowed.

It was a sound no human being should be able to make, a monstrous roar that shook the walls around us. At the same time, the dragon tattoo on the White Wyrm's chest took on an eerie red glow, as if it were alive.

The Diabolist looked as though he couldn't breathe, as he desperately tried to loosen the White Wyrm's grip on his throat. His eyes were about to pop out of his skull, and his mouth was open as he desperately tried to get air into his lungs. Abruptly, his hands began to shine with a purple light, and he slowly began pulling his opponent's hands away from his throat. As he did so, smoke curled up from where he touched the White Wyrm's hands, and the air began to fill with the smell of burning flesh.

The White Wyrm screamed, and I knew that he was feeling the same burning sensation I had earlier. He headbutted the Diabolist, making him lose his grip and stagger backwards. The White Wyrm leaped at him.

As I watched, it seemed to me that their clash bore all the hallmarks of a battle to the death, and I wasn't sure who I wanted to win. If the White Wyrm proved victorious, I had no idea what the fading effects of the Diabolist's magic would be (assuming it did actually fade); we might be stranded — outside space and time — forever. If Diabolist Mage won, I'd be dealing with a half-mad magician with the power to warp reality.

Neither outcome was particularly appealing, and I found myself wishing that Rune would wake up so I'd have more options. Looking into the box, he appeared to be in the same state as before. The symbols covering him, however, seemed quite agitated — mixing, swirling, and looping in odd ways, as if they were trying to—

A blast of heat like the inside of a furnace wrenched my attention away from Rune and back towards the battle. Amazingly, the White Wyrm was now breathing fire, like his namesake, smothering Diabolist Mage in searing flames.

Oddly enough, the Diabolist — surrounded by a purple glow — was not harmed by the conflagration. He pointed a finger, and the White Wyrm was suddenly lifted off the ground. Diabolist Mage wagged the finger from side to side, which resulted in his adversary being repeatedly smashed into first one wall and then the other with bone-crushing force. After a few moments he stopped, and a beaten, bloodied White Wyrm dropped bonelessly to the ground.

Breathing heavily, Diabolist Mage turned towards me, the last man standing.

Chapter 38

Diabolist Mage drew back his hand, like a pitcher getting ready to throw, then launched a fireball at me. I teleported to a corner of the room, taking the staff along for the ride after making both it and me invisible. Furious, the Diabolist threw a few more fireballs randomly around the room, obviously hoping to get lucky. He never even got close.

Setting the staff down, I dashed towards the Diabolist at super speed and kicked his legs out from under him. He landed on his back with a whump that knocked the breath from him. He got slowly to his feet, and as soon as he managed to stand up straight, I did the same thing to him again.

I was getting ready to try it a third time, but instead of getting up normally, Diabolist Mage simply rose up into the air, floating in the center of the room. Around him was a bubble made of purple light — the same kind that had protected him from the grenade in the armory. There was no laying a finger on him while that was in place.

"Give me the staff!" he screamed in blatant frustration.

"And if I do, you'll let me go, right?" I responded — as if there were any chance of that happening.

"You can't hide forever," he said, filling the air with more fireballs.

"Actually, I can," I said, teleporting around the room as I'd done in the armory to keep him from getting a fix on my location. "This room may be all there is of the universe as far as we're concerned, but it's big enough for me to be able to keep away from you, whether I'm phased, invisible, or just teleporting around the place."

For show, I became visible for a moment, and then teleported, appearing first next to the box containing Rune, then popping up next to a worktable (where I swiped my arm across the tabletop, intentionally knocking a bunch of stuff to the floor), and finally popping up just an arm's length away from the Diabolist and sticking my tongue out at him before teleporting away.

"I could do this all day," I said.

"Very well," the Diabolist said. "You've forced my hand."

He looked towards the box that held Rune, and then made a come-hither gesture. Rune's unconscious body rose up forcefully, puncturing the box's glass top as if thrown through it, sending shards of glass flying. Held loosely upright, the body floated over next to Diabolist Mage.

"Now, give me the staff," he said, "or I kill your friend."

There was a moment of stunned silence while I gathered my thoughts. "You wouldn't," I finally blurted out. "He's the source of your power. You've been siphoning off his magic to use as your own."

"True," he said, "but I need the staff to continue doing so. It's been imbued with the Kroten Yoso Va, and is now more powerful than you can imagine. Without it, the power I currently have will eventually fade, and I'd rather die than go back to being the pathetic excuse for a magician that I was before. So yes, I'll kill your friend if I don't get it. You have until the count of ten to decide. One..."

The Diabolist began counting, but I paid him little attention. While he'd been speaking, I had reached out empathically, trying to determine if he was serious. Every emotion that I got from him rang with sincerity. He would indeed kill Rune if I didn't give him the staff.

I looked at Rune, trying to figure out the right course of action. I couldn't give this madman the staff; he'd be far too powerful. But if I didn't, he'd kill Rune, and it would be my fault.

As I looked, the symbols on Rune's body continued swirling — changing shape, size, position. A chill passed through me as realization dawned, and I knew what I had to do.

"...Ten. Time's up," the Diabolist said.

"Okay!" I shouted. "You can have it!"

I teleported to a position off to the side that put the Diabolist directly between me and Rune, and then became visible. The staff, visible now as well, floated next to me.

Diabolist Mage must have noticed my appearance via his peripheral vision, because the moment I became visible, he turned in my direction. He smiled when he saw the staff floating next to me, and the downcast expression on my face.

"Don't feel bad about losing this battle," Diabolist Mage said. "It was the only possible outcome. Even taking the staff couldn't change things, because it only yields up its power to a master of the mystic."

I smiled. "Thanks, I kind of figured that out."

The Diabolist frowned, plainly confused by my meaning, but I didn't give him time to dwell on it. Telekinetically, I threw the staff at him. It flew at the Diabolist in a straight line, like a javelin.

266

INFILTRATION

The bubble around Diabolist Mage vanished and he held out his hand, preparing to catch the staff in mid-air. I would have paid a million bucks to have a picture of his face as it literally passed through him and then struck Rune in the side, like a lance.

INFILTRATION

Chapter 39

From the reactions of Diabolist Mage, you would have thought someone had speared *him* rather than Rune. At first he appeared shocked, as if he'd just turned into a fish and was having trouble breathing on land. Then he became angry, furiously trying to get a grip on the staff that was sticking out of Rune but having his hand pass through it every time. Finally, raw fear and panic set in as he realized that he wasn't going to get the staff after all.

All of this took place over the course of about ten seconds.

Of course, after throwing the staff, I had phased the Diabolist, making him insubstantial just before it reached him. The point, needless to say, was to get the staff to Rune. It had taken me awhile, but I had finally paid attention to the changing patterns on Rune's body and understood that they were forming words, trying to give me a message — one that I didn't really see until almost the very end.

For a moment after the staff struck Rune, I thought I'd made a grave error. After all, having what was essentially a six-foot-long stake driven into your body isn't really on the Surgeon General's list of healthy activities. Moreover, Rune's body didn't initially react to the impact, although I did note that the entry wound didn't bleed. A few seconds passed by — during which time I was treated to the Diabolist's antics in trying to remove the staff — and then Rune's body jerked spasmodically. Then again. And a third time.

A strong, steady amber light began to shine from him, and Rune's body floated higher, chest thrust upwards and arms dangling. The light grew brighter, and

Diabolist Mage, who had dropped to the floor in terror, held up a hand to shield his eyes. On my part, I switched my vision over to another wavelength, one where the light was less bothersome.

The designs on Rune's body went completely bananas — madly swirling, spinning, and shooting back and forth. His body itself expanded, grew monstrously huge. It didn't stop until he was the size of a giant — at least twice my own height.

Suddenly, Rune's eyes snapped open, glowing crimson, and his body jolted upright — still with the staff sticking out. His eyes swept the room, a look of insane fury on his face, until they came to rest on Diabolist Mage.

"YOU!" he said in a booming voice, even more sonorous than the White Wyrm's bellow. "YOU HAVE MUCH TO ANSWER FOR!"

"No, please!" the Diabolist said, almost whimpering and cowering on the floor. "Mercy, I beg of you!"

"THERE WILL BE NO MERCY! NOT HERE! NOT FROM ME!"

As he spoke, Rune held up a tightened fist in front of him. At the same time, the Diabolist rose up off the floor and into the air. He kicked wildly, clawing at his neck as he was lifted by invisible hands around his throat. In just a few seconds, his tongue was lolling out and his face was turning blue.

"NOT YET, DIABOLIST!" Rune said, dropping him to the floor, unconscious. "DEATH WOULD BE TOO GOOD FOR YOU AT THE MOMENT! MAYBE AFTER A CENTURY AS MY 'SPECIAL GUEST,' BUT NOT NOW!"

Rune angled his head in my direction, and then started floating towards me.

"AND AS FOR YOU, 'KID SENSATION'!" he said, pronouncing my sobriquet with a sneer. "IMPERTINENT TEEN! ARROGANT SUPER!"

I reached out empathically in desperation, trying — and failing — to get a read on him. I didn't know if his ordeal had pushed him over the edge, destabilized him somehow so that he didn't know his allies any more. Regardless, I didn't want to hurt him — didn't know if I could — but I wasn't keen on letting him hurt me either.

As the gap between us shrank, I prepared to teleport to another part of the room, run around much like I had done a short time earlier with Diabolist Mage.

"LANCER OF THE DEFENSELESS!" he said, continuing to call me names. "TO YOU I SAY ONLY THIS—"

The giant Rune vanished, replaced by Rune in his original form, who gestured at the staff still sticking out of his body.

"Really, dude?" he asked. "A hole in my side? This was the best you could do?"

INFILTRATION

Chapter 40

Mouse had been right in saying that Rune was the guy to come to with any problems of a mystical nature. After yanking the staff out of his side himself (leaving a gaping hole that, to my surprise, promptly began to heal), he had immediately commenced cleaning house. This involved making the chamber where he'd been held part of the castle once again, then floating through the place room by room — with me in his wake — promptly dispatching any bad guys that we came across (which was basically anybody who wasn't him and wasn't me). The methodology for doing this was rather simple: Rune would just point the staff at someone, and they vanished.

Initially, I had thought that maybe in taking out the bad guys he was actually *taking out* the bad guys, Italian mafia style. It turns out, however, that the castle actually had an oubliette, which is a type of dungeon that only has one entry and exit point: a trapdoor in the ceiling. In short, an oubliette was used when you wanted to lock someone up for good, with no possibility of parole, and that was where Rune was transferring everyone. (The fact that the White Wyrm had one as opposed to a regular type of dungeon said a lot about his manner of dealing with adversaries.)

For the most part, I kept quiet and stayed out of the way, hoping for an opportunity to quiz Rune later about everything that had happened. However, at one point, after we had come across maybe half of the castle's inhabitants, I mentioned to Rune that the oubliette had to be getting crowded. His response was nonverbal: a facial expression of the do-you-think-I-care? variety. I stopped being an advocate of prisoners' rights at the point.

INFILTRATION

A short time later, all the bad guys had been rounded up, and we had most of the castle to ourselves. I took a deep relaxing breath; it was the first time I'd really felt safe since arriving here. Oddly enough, we had ended up in the chamber where I had first appeared in the castle.

Rune snapped his fingers, and the next second he was dressed in the clothes (or very similar attire) that I had worn when I arrived here. "Much better," he said to himself (and I had to admit it was an improvement over the loincloth).

"Now, you must have a million questions," Rune said, turning to me. "With all threats currently removed, it's the perfect time to lay them out."

He was right, of course; I actually had more like a *billion* questions, and had been waiting for a chance to ask them. I tried to sort them out in my brain, but simply didn't know what to ask first. Finally, I just opened my mouth and let fly.

"What are you?" I asked.

Rune laughed, a deep and hearty sound. "I'm a man, of course, like anybody else."

"Come on. You're about as much of an ordinary guy as Alpha Prime."

"Alright," he said, still chuckling. "After everything you've been through, you deserve a better answer than that. I'm an Incarnate."

"What's that?"

"The physical embodiment of certain...powers, for lack of a better term."

"And you can really warp reality?"

"I'm not sure 'warp' describes it properly, but yes, I can do that and more."

"Like what?"

Rune laughed again. "It would be a lot easier to list the things that I *can't* do than all those I *can*."

From anyone else, it would have sounded like bragging, but from Rune it merely denoted simple fact — like saying that two plus two equals four.

"So we really are outside of space and time?" I asked.

"At the moment, but it's not unprecedented," he replied. "For instance, you've probably heard stories of people who maybe got lost in the woods, met up with some strangers or spent the night in a strange place, and when they returned home found that something like a hundred years had passed."

I nodded. "Rip Van Winkle."

"Exactly," he said. "Although Rip was supposedly gone for only twenty years and actually grew older, which — being outside of time — you actually wouldn't expect."

"So if you don't age, you could stay in a place like this forever?"

"Yes. Time doesn't progress for you in here. Haven't you noticed that since you arrived you haven't been hungry, thirsty, or anything like that? Aside from something catastrophic happening to you physically — like being speared in the side with a staff — you could live in here indefinitely."

"Wait a minute!" I said in sudden alarm, remembering that Proteus' watch had stopped working (and now understanding why). "How long have I been here — compared to the people back home?"

Rune seemed to take a second to do some mental calculations before responding. "About four days."

"Four days! I didn't think it had even been twenty-four hours!"

"Not a big deal. When we go back, I can actually return you to any point in time after you left to come here, although I'd recommend insertion at the proper juncture."

That shocked me a little, and it must have shown on my face, because he went on.

"Look," Rune said, "don't spend a lot of time thinking about all this stuff. Being beyond space, outside of time, and so on — people have literally gone crazy trying to figure it all out."

His words brought to mind the conversation between Diabolist Mage and the White Wyrm, when the latter was staring out of a window into the "void," as he put it — and risking madness by doing so.

Recalling that scene, it seemed to me that Rune really was well-versed with this mystical subject matter. Maybe he really was power incarnate, but that raised another question.

"If you're so powerful, how'd you end up stuck in a box with the Diabolist sucking off your power like a leech?" I asked.

Rune sighed. "There are a number of arcane relics — objects of great power — that have been lost over the years, and for the most part I'm happy to let them stay that way. Every now and then, though, one gets found, and at that point I have to investigate."

"And that's what happened here?"

"In essence. The White Wyrm found an artifact that could siphon power from one object and transfer it to another."

"The Kroten Yoso Va," I said.

"Yes. However, it only works for those well-versed in mysticism, so he had to find a magician to wield it for him — preferably one he could control."

"Yeah, that worked out well for him. The Diabolist ended up giving him a beatdown in his own home."

"At first blush, though, Diabolist Mage would have seemed ideal. He had the requisite knowledge but limited ability, and was not particularly strong-willed."

"Well, that changed in a hurry."

"Power corrupts, as they say. Anyway, the short version of what happened is that I walked into a trap. Somehow, the White Wyrm knew that I was an Incarnate, and was aware that I would investigate the discovery of the Kroten Yoso Va. Once I showed up, the Diabolist used it to overpower me. Then they tossed me in that box, kept me comatose, and used my power to get the party started. Fortunately, Diabolist Mage was only able to get a portion of my power at any point in time, and the little bit he got, he had trouble controlling."

"But if you're as powerful as you say, I don't see how they ever got the jump on you."

"You don't understand," he said, shaking his head. "The Kroten Yoso Va was specifically created to keep Incarnates in check. It's a failsafe in case we ever get out of control, abuse the power entrusted to us. We have no defense against it."

Of course. Power corrupts, and absolute power corrupts absolutely. I guess if an Incarnate ever decided he'd look good wearing a King-of-the Universe crown, it would be nice to have a way to knock him down to size. Of course, that beget an entirely new line of questions concerning, among other things, who gave the Incarnates *their* power, but that could wait for another day. Instead, something Rune had casually mentioned earlier sprang to the forefront of my brain.

"Hey," I said, "you said something before about me deserving an answer after everything I've been through. How do you know what I've been through?"

"That's easy," he answered. "The same way I know everything that's been going on around here. I saw it."

INFILTRATION

Chapter 41

Apparently, in addition to numerous other abilities, Rune also has the power of astral projection. In short, his spirit (or soul, or essence, or whatever you want to call it) was able to leave his body and travel elsewhere on its own. Thus, while he was physically lying comatose in a box, his astral body had been free to move about the castle at will. In that way, he had become privy to the bad guys' entire plan.

I was a little skeptical at first, but then he gave me a detailed list of almost everything I'd done since arriving.

"But if you could see everything that was going on," I said after finally being convinced, "why didn't you try to get a message to me?"

Rune shook his head. "It doesn't work like that. It's not like you when you phase; other people can't see or hear me in my astral form."

"So you can't communicate at all?"

He held up a hand and waffled it from side to side. "Yes and no. I can't communicate directly, but if I focus I can, among other things, suggest ideas — nudge thoughts in a certain direction."

"Is that what you did with me?"

"Yes. The plan regarding the armory, when you were paralyzed by Gorgon Son, and a few other things."

I thought back to those times mentioned, remembering that I'd felt a little chill on each occasion when an idea occurred to me. I also recalled that same feeling with respect to several other instances.

"Wait a second," I said. "Were you also doing that those times when I was trying to decide whether it was time to report back to HQ?"

"Yes. I focused on trying to get you to stay here. You didn't know it then, but you couldn't have teleported back anyway."

"Yeah, I figured it out at the end, but what was the point of keeping me here prior to that?"

Rune let out a deep breath. "I didn't know if you could handle it. Not being able to teleport, that is."

I shook my head in confusion. "You lost me."

"As a super, you know that your powers are an integral part of your being, a basic element of who you are."

I nodded, knowing exactly what he was talking about. For a super, your powers are as much a part of you as your arms and legs; losing them is like being maimed.

"Bearing that in mind," Rune continued, "I thought that if you discovered the severe limitations to your teleportation power, it might damage you in some way — cripple your psyche or maybe send you into emotional shock — and I needed you sound and in your right mind. You were the only thing standing between the bad guys and total chaos.

"In short, I put a lot of effort into directing your mind away from certain thoughts about teleportation — especially teleporting anything anywhere outside these castle walls."

Listening to him, I suddenly remembered several recent occasions (like my skirmishes at the armories) when some degree of teleportation might have been the obvious solution to a problem, but it never really occurred to me. Apparently that was Rune's doing.

I frowned as a new question popped into my brain. "I just remembered that I came here as Proteus and stuck to that persona most of the time I was here. How'd you even know that *I* was *me*?"

"Oddly enough," he said, "on the astral plane, I see you as you — your *real* self."

I opened my mouth to ask another question and Rune gave a frustrated groan, rubbing his eyes with two fingertips.

"Dude," he said, "when I said that you must have a million questions, I didn't literally think that you had a million questions."

Undeterred by Rune's growing impatience, I continued trying to get information about things that had been bothering me.

"If I hadn't freed you," I said, "do you think we'd have been able to stop the White Wyrm and Diabolist Mage?"

Rune seemed to dwell on the subject for a moment before responding. "I don't know. Those maces that they attacked you guys with at the overpass were supposed to be strong enough to take out Alpha Prime. When they failed, Proteus was sent in to get relics from my quarters that would increase the power of the Diabolist and — ultimately — their weapons."

I lowered my head shamefully as I remembered who had actually come back and hand-delivered those relics to the Diabolist.

"Likewise," Rune continued, "with that group that Diabolist Mage transferred to the wrong spot. They were intending to attack a museum that had several mystical items on display that would have enhanced their abilities even more. Considering all that, I guess the short answer to your question is that if they had gotten all those items and subsequently increased the power of their weapons, they may have been in a position to defeat Alpha Prime and the rest of the League."

That was a disturbing thought, to say the least. It seemed that we'd been lucky rather than good with respect to stopping our foes.

"Last question — for now," I said, holding up my still-burned hands. "Do you think you can heal this?"

"Child's play," Rune said.

He leaned the head of the staff — which had caused the injuries in question — towards my hands. Knowing what the staff had done before, I was tempted to tell him to forget it, but decided to hold fast. The next second, the staff touched my hands, and the damage was undone. My hands were whole again.

"There you go," Rune said. "Good as new. And I also removed that love spell from you."

Love spell???

INFILTRATION

Chapter 42

The wrap-up of our little adventure was surprisingly uneventful from my perspective, as Rune did all of the heavy lifting. He brought the White Wyrm's castle back into what I had designated the "normal" universe. He magically transported the prisoners to appropriate holding facilities: supers to nullifier cells and non-powered individuals to ordinary lockup. Even the Diabolist — despite Rune's insinuation that he would torture the man for a century — was going to get a fair trial.

It would have been a fairy-tale ending of sorts, if not for one disturbing revelation: the White Wyrm had escaped. Like everyone else, he had been banished by Rune to the castle's oubliette, but when the time came to haul the prisoners out, he was gone.

"That guy is slicker than greased glass on an icy mountaintop," Rune had commented upon making the discovery. Of course, his escape probably shouldn't have come as a surprise. It was his own dungeon he'd been in after all, so he'd probably known of a secret exit.

I was contemplating all this as I sat on a stool in Mouse's lab, telling him everything that had happened. BT wasn't there so it was just the two of us, but I could fill her in later.

As Rune had said, four days had elapsed since I'd left pretending to be Proteus. I suppose since it was a school day I should have been in class, but no one had seen fit to press me about it. (I think there was an assumption that I needed a break after the experience I'd just had.)

"Well," Mouse said as I finished speaking, "I'm glad you made it back safely. All the while you were gone I had two sets of supers breathing down my neck."

"Two?" I repeated, surprised.

"Yes. First, I had to let your mother and grandfather know what happened to you. They seemed to take it in stride, but your grandfather looked like he wanted to lobotomize me with a rusty nail."

"That sounds like Gramps."

"Your old man was hardly any better. Called me an irresponsible egghead and flew off completely ticked. I think he finally got it all out of his system by smashing an asteroid or something."

I laughed. "What about Electra? She wasn't worried?"

"I think she was more upset that you left without saying goodbye, so I'm in the clear on that one. You'll have to smooth things over with her yourself."

Hmmm... That was a bridge I'd cross when I came to it. However, the thought of my girlfriend did bring to mind the fact that I was supposed to talk to Mouse about Vixen's issues. Unfortunately, it didn't seem like the appropriate time to bring it up, and there were other things I needed to discuss at the moment.

"What happened to Proteus?" I asked. "Did you guys ever get anything useful from him?"

"Esper rooted around in his head and was finally able to calm him down enough to extract some info. It's basically the same thing you told us with respect to why he was here — Rune's relics, the weapons they were trying to enhance, etc."

"Guess it's a good thing you gave me that beacon," I said.

INFILTRATION

"True," Mouse said with a nod. "It helped us keep that assault team from getting anything useful from the museum. Of course, when they popped up, we didn't know exactly where they were headed, but after awhile we could extrapolate it based on their movements. Even then, we kind of held back because we thought you were with them. Then Esper scanned them and said you weren't there, which I figured meant you'd used the beacon to give us a heads-up."

"Well, I'm just happy that it's all over." I got up, stretched, and prepared to leave.

"Hey, Jim," Mouse said. "You did great, as always. Keep it up."

I thanked him, and then teleported home. Mouse had already told Mom and Gramps (everyone, in fact) that I was back, so they'd been anxiously expecting me.

Mom, as expected, gave me a hug the minute she saw me. Gramps just stood there looking rather stoic, but empathically I could feel his excitement and relief. Oddly enough, I felt the same; I hadn't realized how much comfort I got just from being around my family.

I extracted myself from my mom's embrace, then telepathically brought them up to speed on what had happened. My mom mentally gasped once or twice, but otherwise made no comment.

Afterwards, I suddenly felt exhausted and headed upstairs to take a nap, uncharacteristically taking the stairs instead of teleporting.

Once in my room, I kicked off my shoes, lay down on the bed, and found myself asleep within minutes.

****

I woke up a few hours later feeling famished. Despite my absence for the past few days, Mom had continued cooking dinner for three each evening, so there were a fair amount of leftovers in the refrigerator. Switching into super speed, I devoured them in less than a minute and then drank half a gallon of water.

It was early evening at that point, so I decided, uncharacteristically, to call Alpha Prime. He was my father, after all, and he'd apparently been worried about me. Needless to say, he was overjoyed to hear from me, mostly because the phone conversation seemed to mark a change in our relationship: it was the first time I'd ever made an unsolicited call to him. On every other occasion that I had dialed his number, it had been because I was returning a phone call *from* him. Never before had I initiated such a call. Thankfully, he didn't dwell on the subject for long; he just told me that I'd done well and he was proud of me (which inexplicably made me happy, since I'd decided long ago that I didn't care about having his approval). We agreed to talk more later and hung up.

Next, I called Electra. Based on what Mouse had said, I wasn't quite sure what to expect, but he had apparently exaggerated her irritation with me.

"Mouse said I was upset with you?" she asked, laughing. "And you believed him?"

It turned out she was more worried than agitated by my absence. I asked if I could come see her but was rebuffed.

"Just stay home and get some rest," she said. "We'll catch up tomorrow after school at Jackman's."

And with that (and a quick kissing sound), she hung up. In all honesty, I was a little disappointed that

284

she wasn't a little more flustered with me (or demanding that I come see her), but it did give me an opportunity to address some other issues.

Now that I'd had some time to unwind and relax, a few other questions had occurred to me, and at the moment, there was really only one place to get the necessary answers. Ergo, I teleported to Alpha League HQ, right outside Rune's room.

The door was open when I arrived.

"Come on in," I heard Rune say from inside. "I've been expecting you."

I hesitated a moment, remembering Mouse's warning that Rune's room was protected by magic, but then accepted the invitation and entered. (I was only slightly surprised when the door closed behind me of its own accord.)

The first thing that struck me was how clean and orderly everything was. For some reason, I had garnered the impression that Rune's quarters were going to look like a hurricane had struck, with trinkets, baubles, and whatnot everywhere. Instead, although there were a few shelves containing curios, the place was exceptionally neat. In a corner I saw the Diabolist's staff, which Rune had obviously confiscated and added to his collection.

Rune himself was seated in an easy chair, reading a book. He motioned for me to sit on a couch across from him.

"I guess you've come up with a few more questions," Rune said.

"A few," I agreed. "Your powers, for instance."

"What about them?"

"They go way beyond what's needed for your role here as a member of the Alpha League."

Rune's eyes narrowed as he seemed to consider my statement.

"You're more perceptive than I gave you credit for," he finally said. "In truth, I have responsibilities that go well beyond anything you've ever imagined. The importance of the Alpha League — this entire planet, in fact — is minute, infinitesimal, compared to the duties I'm tasked with. My powers — and I say this with respect — are intended for purposes and obligations beyond your ken."

"So why are you even here then?"

Rune exhaled softly before responding. "I find this world...relaxing. Something about being here soothes me, removes the pressure that goes with being an Incarnate. I like the rich diversity of culture, the food, the arts..."

"Basically, you've gone native."

He laughed at that. "That's close, but it's probably preferable to say that I feel invested in what goes on here."

"In that case, why not use your power to make things better, like getting rid of all these supervillains who come up with doomsday weapons every other week? Or maybe end war, disease, or poverty?"

Rune was silent for a moment, and then asked, "How old are you, Jim?"

"Sixteen."

"So tell me, at your age, how would you like it if your mother still felt the need to feed you? Bathe you? Diaper and change you? Walk you to school?"

I frowned in distaste at the imagery his questions brought to mind, saying, "I wouldn't like it at all. To the extent that it's necessary, I prefer to do all that stuff myself."

"Exactly. The same is true of the world at large. I could fix all the problems you mentioned, but it's far better if the people of the world find ways to address those issues themselves."

I didn't want to admit it, but he actually had a very valid point. If world peace, for instance, were going to be meaningful and lasting, it needed to be something that people achieved themselves, as opposed to having it thrust upon them.

"Alright," I said after a few seconds. "I can accept that. However, there was another issue I wanted to address: the love spell."

Rune nodded. After he had mentioned it earlier, I was sure he'd made a mistake. The Diabolist had mentioned a *loyalty* spell in the castle, so I had been convinced that Rune had simply made a Freudian slip. That being the case, I hadn't questioned it when we had returned to HQ initially. However, having slept on it, so to speak, I was convinced there was more to the story.

"Are you sure it wasn't a *loyalty* spell?"

"No, it was a love spell. No doubt about it."

"But I recall the Diabolist saying that he checked everyone in the castle and we were all under a loyalty spell."

Rune guffawed. "Diabolist Mage was an idiot and a hack, even when he had my power. He didn't really look to see if you were under his spell; he only checked to see if you were under the influence of magic."

"I'm not sure I understand," I said.

"Basically, he only probed to see if there was a spell on you. When he saw that there was, he moved on without checking what the spell was specifically meant to do. Plus, even if he had delved a little deeper, I doubt that he was discriminating enough to have noted the difference. A love spell and a loyalty spell look a lot alike. They both engender similar emotions in the person under the spell: admiration, devotion, adoration, and so on."

"So, who put the spell on me?"

Rune shrugged. "Who knows? Could be anybody. But whoever it was did you a favor, because again, when the Diabolist looked, he saw that you were under a spell. I'm not saying they saved your life, but being under that spell probably kept you from blowing your cover."

"But I didn't feel like I was under a love spell. Wouldn't I have known?"

"Not in most instances. To a bewitched person, their own actions and compulsions always seem normal. However, the spell on you was somewhat asymmetrical — not exactly top-of-the-line. Being a little rough around the edges, it probably worked best with constant reinforcement."

"You mean someone put the spell on me more than once?"

"No. I mean that the enchantment was probably most effective when you were around the object of your newfound affection. You might be your normal self at any other time, but the minute you set eyes on them, the spell would kick back into high gear. Do you recall acting oddly or out-of-character around anyone recently?"

As a matter of fact, I did recollect several instances of inexplicable behavior on my part. And along with that thought came a certain insight as to who had put the spell on me.

INFILTRATION

Chapter 43

I found him on his way to school the next morning. Actually, I knew which school he attended and simply waited for him along what was the most direct route from his house. I wasn't exactly hiding, but he was so wrapped up in his own little world that he didn't notice me until we were only about twenty feet apart. When he saw me, he came to a dead halt, looking almost fearful.

"Pronto," I said.

Something in my eyes must have indicated that I was annoyed with him, because the next second I was looking at a dust trail. I took off after him, choosing to fly rather than hoof it on the ground. This gave me an advantage, as he had to follow the contours of the ground, as well as deal with the principle of friction.

Still, it was a merry chase (and under other circumstances would probably have been a lot of fun), with him showing not only impressive reflexes and cutting ability as he turned corners and zipped around objects, but also phenomenal swiftness — even for a speedster. In fact, it occurred to me that, had he stepped on the gas like this during the exhibition, he would have won the thing hands down. (Of course, he also had a powerful motivator at the moment: the thought of what I might do to him if I caught him.)

On my part, there were a couple of ways to end this quickly: I could simply teleport him. I could also telekinetically lift him off the ground or trip him up. Or do a couple of other things to end this pursuit. Instead, I chose to let it play out on Pronto's terms, and stuck to simply trying to catch him.

It didn't end the way you might have expected, with me gradually closing the distance and then bringing him down. Instead, we had made it outside of the city limits and were dashing down a dirt road in a lightly forested area when Pronto unexpectedly threw in the towel.

Breathing heavily, he just started pulling up, like a runner who had just crossed the finish line of a race. He walked over to a nearby tree stump and sat down on it as I landed nimbly nearby and walked over to him.

He was silent for a moment, and then asked, "When did you figure it out?"

"Yesterday," I answered, "with a little help from a friend."

"I'm sorry," he said, lowering his eyes. I felt intense shame in him, as well as remorse. "I guess you want to know why."

"I already know why: you have a crush on Electra."

He nodded, providing confirmation. In retrospect, however, it hadn't been too hard to deduce. When Rune had asked if there was anyone I'd been acting weird around lately, the obvious answer had been Atalanta. Then I remembered — just before I saw Atalanta for the first time — Pronto had tapped me on the shoulder, resulting in an odd sensation. Once I had an idea of who placed the spell on me, the "why" of it was elementary.

"But wouldn't it have made more sense to put a spell on Electra?" I asked. "Make *her* fall in love with *you?*"

"Love spells are too fickle," he said. "They'll make you fall in love with the next person you see, or the next person you kiss, or the next person who wrings a chicken's neck. Basically, there would have been a chance that she'd fall in love with somebody else if I wasn't in the right place at the right time and so on."

"So you cast the spell on me instead."

"Yeah. It was supposed to make you fall head-over-heels for the next compatible female you saw — other than Electra, that is."

"'Compatible'? What does that mean?"

"The next female you saw who was your type." When I continued shaking my head in confusion, he went on. "You know how they say that, if a person hypnotizes you, they can't make you do anything you wouldn't normally do?"

"Yes," I said, nodding. "They can't make you smoke, go cliff diving, or eat worms if those aren't things you'd do when *not* hypnotized."

"Well, love spells operate a little bit the same way. They work best when they focus on making you fall for someone you'd probably date anyway. Someone compatible. If you try to go against a person's natural inclinations — like make the head cheerleader date the biggest nerd in school — the spell's effectiveness is compromised."

"How do you know all this stuff?" I asked.

"My father's an enchanter, and love spells are his specialty. He's going to be furious if he finds out about this; I'm not supposed to mess with his spells."

I took a moment to digest that fact before continuing. "So your plan was to have me fall in love with someone else and then break up with Electra."

"Or have her get so angry that she'd break up with you."

"And then you'd be there as her rebound guy."

He shrugged and looked at the ground, not saying anything.

I stood there for a moment, debating what to do. I had been upset with him, of course, but hadn't planned to beat him up or anything — just let him know that I knew what he'd done and didn't like it.

I could also rat him out to the Alpha League, make sure Mouse and the others knew what he'd done. But what would that accomplish? He was just a stupid kid who made a stupid mistake. From what I could sense of his emotions, he'd learned his lesson and — hopefully — wouldn't do it again.

"We should be getting back," I finally said. "School's going to be starting soon. I'll teleport us."

INFILTRATION

Chapter 44

Electra was far more understanding than I thought she'd be regarding the love spell.

"Awww," she said, like someone admiring a cute puppy. "That is so sweet."

School had been out for a couple of hours, and we were sitting next to each other in a booth at Jackman's (which was fast becoming our regular hangout), sharing a sundae. I'd brought her up to speed on everything that had happened — especially Pronto's efforts to become her beau.

"That's what I thought, too," I said, "when I first learned about it and thought maybe you had cast it on me."

"Oh, please," she said in mock arrogance. "Do I look like I need a magic spell to get someone to fall for me?"

"Well, you wouldn't be saying it was sweet if his plan had worked and we'd actually broken up."

"That wouldn't happen," she said, scooping up another spoonful of ice cream.

"And why not?"

She seemed to contemplate this for a moment before answering. "Because you love me."

"I do?"

"Yes. You're wild about me, but it wouldn't be kosher for you to admit it because I might start taking you for granted, like girls are known to do. I might start thinking that I don't have to keep working hard for your affection."

I laughed. Empathically, I could sense her emotions, so I knew what she was doing. I decided to play along.

"No, babe," I said with a grin. "You'd never take me for granted. You worship me."

"Hardly," she said, smiling back at me. "If I really worshipped you, I'd buy you flowers more often. Maybe some candy every now and then as well."

"And if I worshipped you, I'd stop dragging you to chick flicks every time we go out."

"I deny it every time anyone asks, but those movies are actually growing on me," she said, almost in a confidential whisper. "But we're getting sidetracked. The point is that, even though I may test your patience a lot with my cockiness, hotdogging, and grandstanding — especially during training scenarios—"

"Hold on," I said, stepping out of the roles we were playing. "I do *not* grandstand—"

"Quiet!" she insisted, putting a finger to my lips. "Let me finish clarifying how you feel about me."

She removed her finger and gave me a light kiss on the lips before going on.

"As I was saying, you love me, and — assuming I don't cross certain lines — I don't foresee you breaking up with me any time soon."

"You're right. I couldn't bear the thought of breaking up with you. My life since we met has been a whirlwind romance and has made me a much better person. Before you, I was antisocial, standoffish, and well on my way to being a shut-in. Thank you for saving me from that."

Her eyes sparkled a little, and she leaned in to give me a kiss.

INFILTRATION

"Wait a minute!" she said, drawing back just before our lips touched and giving me a severe, withering look. "You'd better have been speaking as *you* and not *me* with that last comment!"

I laughed, invoked my Fifth Amendment right against self-incrimination, and then gave her a kiss.

THE END

Thank you for purchasing this book! If you enjoyed it, please feel free to leave a review on the site from which it was purchased.

Also, if you would like to be notified when I release new books, please subscribe to my mailing list via the following link: http://eepurl.com/C5a45

Finally, for those who may be interested, I have included my blog and Twitter info:

Blog: http://kevinhardman.blogspot.com/

Twitter: @kevindhardman

Made in the USA
Lexington, KY
30 August 2014